What Reviewers _____ _ ___ ____
Hallow Mass:

This story, the first in a trilogy, takes place in the Lovecraftian universe of hideous, unnatural beings and ultimate cosmic indifference. In Dunwich, Massachusetts, only a small, beleaguered band in the Antiquities Section at Miskatonic University is keeping back trans-dimensional horrors from wiping all human life from earth in preparation for the return of the Great Old Ones. . . .

 Into this simmering conflict steps Mercy O'Connor, an aimless party girl grad student in the Antiquities Section who has yet to find herself or her place in life. She's about to be thrust to the front lines of the age-old battle against ultimate evil, and her only ally is her department's security guard, a descendent of Zulu warriors who loves country music and Jesus with his whole heart. Against them are arrayed all of the unimaginatively powerful dark forces of evil from time immemorial.

So how could they possibly lose?

—Oregon Muse, book reviewer for the *Ace of Spades Headquarters* online magazine

HALLOW MASS

By JP Mac

Published by Cornerstone Media
La Cañada, California

ISBN-10:
1-532909349

ISBN-13:

978-1-532909344

10 9 8 7 6 5 3 2 1

HALLOW MASS

by
JP Mac

Hi Paul!
— JP Mac

CORNER
STONE MEDIA

Cornerstone Media
La Cañada, California

Also by JP Mac

Jury Doody
(ebook)

The Little Book of Big Enlightenment
(ebook)

Fifty Shades of Zane Grey
(ebook and softcover)

TABLE OF CONTENTS

"I love the idea that magic and witchcraft and battles between supernatural creatures could be raging all around us but just out of our sight."

—Anthony Horowitz

PROLOGUE

"Just because we find it morally repugnant for Dunwich warlocks to summon forth hideous beings who will strip our world of human life and drag Earth into another dimension, does not mean we have the right to label such behavior 'wrong.' Let's celebrate our differences."

— *Professor Audrey Klumm-Weebner, from her book:*

Old Ones, New Values—Fresh Insights on the Population of North-Central Massachusetts

From an article in the travel magazine Dumps of New England:

> Should you be looking for the interstate in North-Central Massachusetts and find yourself arguing with your wife, while simultaneously trying to silence two bawling children in the back seat, then you might accidentally drive through Dean's Corners, take a wrong turn past the Old Yankee Coffee Shop, and come upon a forlorn and despised country.
>
> A two-lane blacktop road ascends into a wooded region, past thick forests and a field filled with abandoned trailers, smothered in briars like jungle ruins. A very large faded wooden sign faces the road, splattered with bird droppings and graffiti. It reads: 'Bay

State Trailer Court. Live a Double-Wide Life!'

Since the court's sudden abandonment in 1980, when all 22 residents disappeared overnight, teenage boys from local towns such as Dean's Corners and Athol have clashed with teenage boys from the immediate area. Cryptic juvenile scrawls—taunt and counter-taunt—cover the termite-riddled wood. Over the decades, these spray-painted messages have built up like mildew in a neglected bathtub.

'Obed Whately is a fruit!'

'Lick my hairy <u>Athol</u>!'

'The Old Ones <u>Blow</u>!'

'Yog-Sothoth will make ye his bitch, bitch!'

Past the trailer court, stone walls line the road as if to funnel you upward into the hills. In the surrounding fields are ruined farmhouses that appear to have been abandoned shortly after the Revolutionary War. In front of one such derelict dwelling sits the remains of a very old ice cream truck—tires flat, windshield cracked, a rack of bells above the driver's seat rusted dark brown. Unusual. But in this region, the merely unusual is the closest you'll find to normal.

In adjacent lots, mingled among the weeds and brambles, lie newer homes with asphalt driveways and garages, built during the early 21st century housing bubble. They are officially unoccupied—though the homeless, drug addicts and fleeing criminals will squat for short periods. With their 'Bank Short Sale!' notices, these newer homes scurry to catch up with their older neighbors in decrepitude.

Your vehicle's navigation system won't work. That also applies to your family's smart phones, tablets, and other electronic devices. There's no logical reason why cell phone service, internet connections, and GPS would abruptly terminate; over the years, studies by various corporations, as well as state and federal agencies, have failed to pinpoint a satisfactory answer. Locals sometimes whisper that this region 'overlaps' other more frightening dimensions that operate according to laws quite alien from our own. But that's just colorful farm talk.

Occasionally, one passes a planted field and a seedy house, surrounded by rusted truck frames, abandoned refrigerators, and crudely painted, homemade advertisements for 'Fresh Eggs' or 'Powder of Ibn Ghazi. Cheap.'

You might be uneasy now. You might even attempt to ask directions. But the unkempt children who watch you like coyotes from trash-littered yards, and the furtive adults who quietly drift off at your approach, convey a sense that information is not freely dispensed around these parts. A simple question might come attached to an answer that'll leave you wishing you were a mute.

As you rise above tangled forests and lonely fields, the mountains appear. They are not a comforting sight. On occasion, odd hissing noises issue forth loudly from the slopes as if large cornered rats were about to spring. Summits are too circular, too symmetrical. How do you get mountaintops that round? Strange stone pillars ring the summits, mingled with the remains of cell phone towers melted into steel lumps, as featureless and inert as modern art. Impossibly thick lightning bolts periodically shimmy down from sable clouds, scoring the summits and leaving them marinated in ozone. But this has been attributed to global warming, or a unique micro-clime. After a time, you keep your eyes fixed upon the road ahead and avoid staring up. You can't shake the feeling of driving through an unsettled, dangerous landscape where you are vulnerable, isolated, beyond help.

Suspension bridges—the newest seventy years old—span gorges and brush-choked ravines where vegetation conceals depth. Your hands tighten on the wheel of your GMC Yukon and you hope the rickety wooden planks hold up until you're past. Now and again, the blacktop road descends into stretches of rank, unpleasant marshland that smell like a colossal plugged-up drain. In spring and summer, fireflies flash like advertisements for small lost souls. Come dusk, whippoorwills erupt in their eerie piping cry. Locals despise whippoorwills, calling them psychopomps, or soul catchers, and sometimes kill them with baseball bats.

Vast numbers of bullfrogs add an annoying bass to the persistent disquieting whippoorwill serenade. So loud is the racket that it can override even the most powerful stereo system. All your iPod music sounds as if it were recorded in a primeval swamp.

For long stretches, the blacktop road parallels the upper reaches of the Miskatonic River, winding like a pit viper along the base of the rounded hills. As the steep wooded hillsides crowd in on the blacktop, you might grow claustrophobic, anxious for the sight of a porch light or even the flashing bar of a cop pulling you over—anything to shake the feeling of being engulfed by the mountains. In this unsettling stretch there is only a single turn-off, a paved road leading to the ruins of an ill-fated Pocumtuck Indian gambling establishment. The Big Luck Casino was partially destroyed, then abandoned after the 1991 outbreak.

An 'outbreak' is what area residents call an incident, or series of incidents, set in motion by mysterious, outré ceremonies tied to a local devil cult, fond of human sacrifice. This cult is said to be worldwide, malicious, dangerous, and patient. What the cult's black magic ceremonies produce—'unleash' is a word often used—is a matter of conjecture. But rumors suggest some form of monstrous otherworldly entity or entities that thrive on property destruction, livestock mutilations, gruesome deaths, and disappearances. The most fevered rumors point toward the initiation of a ceremony that will lead to the destruction of life on earth. On at least three occasions in the last hundred years, these outbreaks have resulted in interventions by the Antiquity Section of Miskatonic University, located a ninety-minute drive to the east. What possible good are college professors in cases involving mayhem and carnage? Another odd quirk in a deviant land. Even more aberrant is the fact that local authorities have known of these university interventions and tacitly supported them.

Incidentally, these outbreaks have another colorful name.

They are called 'horrors.'

As the landscape gradually widens, you pass over a timber-truss bridge with a roof and siding that haven't seen paint since the presidency of Gerald Ford. To your surprise, you discover a small community, crouched between a bend in the Miskatonic River and spreading along the base of Round Mountain, rising above the landscape in a vertical wall. The village is a hodge-podge of architectural styles. There are ancient homes from the late 17th and early 18th centuries with steep gables, deep porches and triple-casement windows. Nearby might be a boxy, multi-windowed home in the 19th century Federalist style. Cheap bungalows have sprouted up everywhere like weeds. Paved streets are marred by potholes, some quite considerable and covered over with boards. There is a single stop sign. The ruins of a Waffle House slumber next to a gas station heavily fortified with burglar bars. You spy a hardware shop next to Osborn's Grocery and Drug Store ('EBT Accepted Here'). Consider Osborn's the unofficial civic center of Dunwich, where locals sit and stare at you like crows on a telephone line. Osborn's squats at a crossroads. Turn right and you will eventually return to the world of traffic signals and malls and functioning police departments. Turn left and you will descend into the black bowels of this haunted region, passing the turn-off to Cold Springs Glen and soon arriving at Sentinel Hill, where traditionally more people ascend than descend.

Beyond the crumbling ruins of a church lies a small motel, Ye Great Olde Inn. Who stays at Ye Great Olde Inn ('We Now Have

Ice!')? More importantly, why would anyone wish to stay there? Conjecture abounds. Clever people believe the inn can't possibly turn a profit and must somehow be propped up by organized crime or a federal grant. Yet it's been reported that a steady flow of guests arrive and depart, sometimes hailing from far corners of the earth. Many carry, or inquire after, certain ancient texts. A Boston columnist once speculated that the visitors were members of an international nudist colony since many run naked up Sentinel Hill, especially on April 30 and October 31— which the locals quaintly call Hallow Mass. The columnist speculated that perhaps these were important nudist dates and should be respected.

In and around the village, even with your windows up, you'll notice a feculent odor, pungent and powerful, as if the village sewer line were periodically refreshed with pig droppings. You'll remember the stunning foulness long after. You'll use it as a benchmark for comparing other stinks. No other noxious odor will ever quite measure up, and that includes diapers.

Suddenly, to your relief and olfactory delight, you've passed by the stinky little community. Winding around the base of a few more hills, the road gradually descends to level ground, finally hooking up with the old Aylesbury Pike—now County Road 29— where you'll find that your navigation and cell phone function again. Stay on 29 into North Aylesbury, where there are street lights and cars and regular people and dollar discount stores and cops parked in the Denny's lot and a modern bridge across the

Miskatonic into the pawn shops, liquor stores, and Section Eight housing of South Aylesbury. Once past the Patrick Henry Mall, you'll spot an onramp where you may finally merge with I-91 north to Brattleboro, or south to Springfield, take your pick.

In time, you'll laugh and tell people about your detour and your thoughts and fears and how silly and childish they all seemed. Maybe over beers with your softball buddies you'll say, 'This is how scary it was: my wife actually shut up.' That'll get a laugh. But you won't tell them about the nights when you can't sleep and the house settles and makes furtive sinister sounds, and you lie awake remembering the round hills and how they reminded you of a locked door holding back something vicious and hungry that pressed against the wooden panels, bending them out toward you with a soft incessant creak.

In the morning, you'll once more be a tired—but rational—man. There was nothing, is nothing, so there's nothing to sweat. Months and years will pass. One day, your son will steal your car for a joyride and rear-end a trial attorney. And you'll wind up acquiring a second job to pay for your daughter's basketball camp because her coach says she could win a scholarship to a Division Two college. Bone weary fatigue will become your default state.

And one morning over coffee, you'll read online about a murder back in that little stinky Massachusetts community—a crime so brutal and shocking it will be the top story on Yahoo News. It won't be the first time your eyes have locked onto sick informational nuggets from that disturbed region. After all, two months earlier you held off going to lunch, pausing to read a few paragraphs about the state seizing children from a family that had clearly degenerated to the point of reversing evolution, or, at least, selecting a new direction: abnormally large chinless children with furry black legs and odd rounded feet like those on a circus elephant; piebald reptilian skin on the chest and back, yellow and black squamous like the tail of a coral snake. You skim a section hinting at even more substantial deformities which authorities blamed on poverty, tainted drinking water, and carnal familiarity between first cousins.

In a heartbeat, decades have passed. Your kids have graduated college with crushing debts, including the daughter who never got the basketball scholarship. They've moved back home and they can't find jobs, but eat a lot. Despite holding down two jobs, you can't retire because the economy now sucks as a matter of course. Your wife's body sags in places you never thought possible. (Not that you're any bargain.)

At work, you've got a report to finish for the snotty 27-year old regional sales director. But instead you surf the Web, maybe check out your 401(k) after the market tanks again. And, more often than not, you'll see that CNN links a video report from the *Arkham Advertiser* about teens racing from Dean's Corners to North Aylesbury along the same roads and bridges you drove across. A Trans Am was found crashed in a gorge with the top peeled back like a banana. Four teenage boys from Athol were listed as missing. You recall the malodorous stench and remember the eerie round hills and how you gripped the wheel of your SUV like a mouse cringing beneath the talons of a barn owl.

Maybe you'll duck into the break room, unable to focus on the report, unable to forget. And for the first time in a long time, you'll mutter a prayer of gratitude that you and your family don't live anywhere near the shunned, malodorous village of Dunwich.

CHAPTER 1

FORMULA FOR DUMMIES

Article from student newspaper *The Miskatonic University Scholar*, September 1, special Welcome Back edition for first semester of the new academic year:

DEALE DEALS OUT ANTIQUITY SECTION

Called 'Roadblock' to Modernization

by Quinn Bisque

If new university president Armand Deale has his way, the Antiquity Section will be a memory. "We already have a rare books department," said Deale. "There's no need to devote precious resources to a special collection of esoteric books that serve no visible purpose."

By amended charter, the Antiquity Section is virtually autonomous. Only a majority of the Board can abolish the section and its Special Collections Library. However, President Deale isn't waiting for Board action. He vowed, "Before week's end, I will request that Professor Morgan voluntarily disband Antiquity for the good of genuine scholarship. His service to this institution though misguided, hapless, and unnecessary has been consistent. He and his staff will be absorbed into other areas of the Miskatonic community."

Antiquity Chairman Professor Conrad Morgan disagreed, "Unlike President Deale, there is nothing faddish, lightweight, or trendy about the Antiquity Section. Our scholarship serves to ensure that a wider world still exists for President Deale to foul up with his feckless educational experiments."

Located on campus above the Henry Armitage Memorial Library, the Antiquity Section was founded in 1934, and has been the center of controversies ever since. Some observers insist the Section is a quasi-religious cult where strange mystical practices called "formulae" are practiced. Others claim the Section provides deniable cover and assistance to assorted law enforcement agencies who, over the decades, have investigated communists, the Mafia, and attacks by misguided individuals such as those behind the Boston Marathon Bombing. Still other observers assert that the Antiquity Section is an elaborate scam in which three families have siphoned off millions of dollars in donations and grants by claiming to safeguard Earth from a deadly cult. For almost a century, the section's Special Collections Library has purchased, or otherwise obtained, very expensive rare, exotic books on such peculiar subjects as sorcery and ritual magic. The books are thought to be worth a fortune to collectors.

Some observers have speculated that these valuable magic books, or grimoires, are a moral hazard that attracts thieves. In 1964, Antiquity Section Curator Lawrence St. John was slain by a knife-wielding assailant. This tragedy led to the section's transfer to its current location on the library's second floor. In addition, a number of alleged burglars have been killed or wounded attempting to break into the library. The most recent violence took place in 1987: a gunshot victim fled across the quad, trailing a foul-smelling yellowish-green substance that some speculated was blood of an unusual nature.

Arkham Police records list most captured burglary suspects as residing in the depressed region around Dunwich. Under questioning, several of these suspects have expressed a fierce desire to obtain one book in particular: the Necronomicon.

Written in 730 C.E. by a mentally distressed man of possible Arab descent, the text contains incantations and magical spells whose purpose is the summoning of titanic, star-born entities—the 'Old Ones' or 'Great Old Ones.' These 'Old Ones' are said to want humanity eradicated from the planet, and Earth dragged into another dimension, for exotic purposes. Long thought to be a diabolical compendium of butchery and chaos, the Necronomicon *is now viewed by contemporary scholars in a more sophisticated light. Miskatonic Professor of Post-Structural Hierarchies Audrey Klumm-Weebner believes the* Necronomicon *is "an intricate cry for help from an oppressed group, marginalized for practicing an unpopular faith by the surrounding dominant society."*

In fact, an accusation that the Necronomicon *and other arcane books were illegally removed from Dunwich has been gaining widespread attention over the past decade.*

Professor Angelo Silent Feather, Associate Vice Chancellor for Contemporary Oppression Modalities, feels that "Poor hungry people had their sacred books wrestled away from them. If my ceremonial raven urine were confiscated from me, I would stop at nothing to retrieve it."

And while the Antiquity Section has operated without incident since 1998, many faculty and administrators tend to agree that the section serves no functional purpose, if it ever did. Professor Carter Fong, Chairman of the Critical Weather Studies Department, feels that "There's no 'there' there. Seriously, dude, where's the beef? I say close it [the Antiquity Section] up and give the space to wicked cool new stuff like critical weather studies."

Chief of Campus Diversity Enforcement Dr. Leo Hameyes believes the Antiquity Section's autonomy may lead it to defy diversity protocols. Said Dr. Hameyes, "For some reason the section won't allow me to take samples of their laughter. How am I to clear them of inappropriateness and exclusion? They could be on university property right now, laughing freely, without social oversight."

President Deale concluded, "Above all, I'd like to see closure with the oppressed people of Dunwich. Let's face it: this university desperately needs more administrators, plus additional parking for administrative staff, not a clique of Dark Age book wardens."

In early September, the campus dozed like a drunk in a hammock. A few students sun-bathed on the quad grass, or tossed around a football, or read on Kindles, almost reluctant to acknowledge the start of the semester. Red brick buildings surrounded the quad in an ivy-covered rectangle, while the town of Arkham, in turn, enveloped the campus in all four directions. Above, a peaceful blue and white sky stretched across eastern Massachusetts as wind-pushed cirrus clouds slid through the heavens. In the midst of this tranquility, Mercy O'Connor walked quickly, a notch below running, checking her text messages.

One from Professor Morgan: 'Tardy.'

Two from Joe Bong: 'You are late.' and 'You are more late.'

Her low heels clacked on the sidewalk as she angled toward the library and fished around in a side pocket of her purse for more breath mints. There'd been a glass of wine before lunch—then a frozen vodka lemon slush, but that was Erin's fault for buying it. A third Chablis with pasta, and a Jell-O shot after leading a toast for Brianne. What was Mercy supposed to do? Abstain at a friend's bridal luncheon?

Actually, that was exactly what she was supposed to do—fast and abstain. Today was Pirandello's Aegis, which probably meant multiple pressures, which meant she'd probably go home tonight with a few bruises. *No, wait.* She was meeting Erin for beers at that new place over in Kingsport with the cute bartender—hopefully minus facial bruises.

Beautiful features had passed by Mercy Bernadette O'Connor in small ways. Her hazel eyes were a bit too wide apart, her legs somewhat short and stumpy, heavily muscled from years of sports. Her weight was not what it should have been. Some of her friends, such as Brianne, were tall graceful women who would glide into a room. Mercy tended to burst in, as if surprising a burglar.

Pulling open the heavy wooden doors, she entered the cool interior of the Henry Armitage Memorial Library, thoughts piling up like storm waves on a reef. Pirandello was Italian, but all his stinking formulae were in Greek. She hated Greek. How were you supposed to remember it, let alone recite it under stress? Why couldn't you say the spell in Latin or English and get the same effect?

Absorbed in self pity, she didn't notice a short, round older woman falling into step next to her, waving a rolled up newspaper.

"Did you read the *Scholar* today?" whispered the woman. "They say terrible things about the Section."

"No. I was at lunch."

"Until now? Must be nice."

"What is it, Lisa?"

"Someone at the administration building says you're about to have company this afternoon."

"Lisa, I haven't got time to tease this out of you. Be direct. Be blunt. Be a guy."

The older woman frowned. "I don't know if I should tell you now."

"Don't."

"Armand Deale is coming over to make Professor Morgan close the Section."

"Now? This afternoon?"

Lisa said, "That's what I heard."

"Wicked. Gets me out of formula."

Leaving a puzzled Lisa behind, Mercy entered the stacks at the back of the building, moved passed rows of books to the back wall, and approached a heavy locked metal door covered by a security camera. A laminated ID hung around her neck from a lanyard. A card swipe later, Mercy entered a dusty hallway with a filthy tile floor, another security camera and a disabled elevator. Stairs led up to a landing, then up another flight to the Antiquity Section. Climbing the stairs, it was all Mercy could do to keep from whistling. Deale's visit would mean no formula, which meant no Greek—at least for today. And if Special Collections stayed quiet, Mercy might even squeeze in an afternoon nap.

Joseph Bongani sat tall and straight behind his metal desk. After checking his two monitors, he scowled at Mercy as she ascended to the second floor. Soft country and western music sounded from a Bose radio, bringing a tale of honky tonks, whiskey, and a woman too drunk to care. Mercy could smell the WD-40. That meant Joe had cleaned his pistols again. He was *Paul Blart: Mall Cop*, if Blart were a tall, skinny, heavily-armed Zulu with a Type A personality. The guard's dark hands turned over homemade flash cards of sinister looking men, some quite deformed, all with very unsettling expressions as if they knew things that would cause your sphincter to void in fright. He was close to Mercy's own age of 25—yet he acted as if he were her guardian and Mercy were a frivolous teenager he'd been stuck with.

"Go at once to Baba Morgan."

Mercy unwrapped a fresh packet of Certs and popped two into her mouth. "If you don't mind, Joe Bong, I thought I'd hit the bathroom, then drop off my purse."

"Don't call me that. Why are you late on a day of formula?"

"What do you care?"

"What if the next horror is to come?'"

"You're worse than Professor Morgan."

"Baba Morgan knows evil. He readies himself."

"He watches his *Patton* DVD, psyching himself up for a desperate fight against long odds. I've heard him say that."

"The stars align for Hallow Mass. The whippoorwills flock in numbers. Obed Whately is said to have returned in July."

"That's before you started here, Joe."

"Yes."

"The old guard used to bring me coffee after his shift. Would you mind doing that?"

"Yes."

Mercy sighed. This stiff absolutely refused to flirt. Gay? An African nerd? Worse. An African redneck with his mandolin and banjo crap.

"I'll bet you've got a flashcard on Obed Whateley."

"Yes."

Mercy found a photo thrust into her hands: a 1973 mug shot from the North Aylesbury PD. Two images: on the left was a small, skinny, hippie man in his early 30s with long dark brown hair and a Col. Saunders moustache. To the right was a computer-simulated mockup that made him appear around 80 years old. But Whateley's green eyes were the thing: mocking, cynical, contemptuous, a combination so prevalent in the Valley of the Miskatonic as to be called the

Dunwich Look, even by people who knew nothing of Dunwich, formula, or random, inexplicable carnage. But Whateley added a subtle infernal accent to his gaze. If eyes were windows to the soul, than Obed Whateley had the soul of a wasp. Disturbed, Mercy flipped the card back on the table.

"I'm an Armitage, and even my bizarre family would not make flash cards for Dunwich warlocks."

"They are not all warlocks."

Joe Bong frowned, his skin so black it almost seemed blue. Lanky, his gray uniform shirt bagged out over a polished Sam Browne belt, heavy with handcuffs, mace, a nightstick ring, and a freshly cleaned .45 caliber semi-automatic. He turned away from Mercy, checked his two monitors, then returned to his flashcards.

Mercy leaned in over his shoulder, giving him a good whiff of shampoo and bath oil.

"Where'd you snag the mug shots? Off the Web?"

"A friend in the police obtains for me the photos. He says there have been offerings on the hills in August. Monstrous things summoned."

"They haven't got the *Necronomicon*." Mercy leafed through the cards, stopping on a thick-faced, dark-skinned man in his late thirties who looked like he masturbated to Islamist execution videos. "Who's this ugly suck head?"

"Chester Sawyer is part human, part Outside."

"What's 'HSF' mean?"

"Hybrid, knows some formula."

"Like what? Blood Fountain? They teach their kids that one."

"Do you know it?"

"I haven't bothered. What else can old Chester throw?"

"The Ring of Haroun. The Indescribable Inversion."

"Shit. That's black stuff. Morgan demonstrated those for me on rats. It's the only time I felt sorry for a rat. But seriously, you think these bad boys are threatening the planet? Whateley and Ahaz Johnson and the rest probably died out in the Dunwich backcountry years ago, cooking crystal meth. Or else they're spending their twilight years on 8Chan downloading bogus copies of the *Necronomicon*."

"They wait and prepare. We must do this also." He held up Whateley's flashcard. "I will know their faces upon sight. But you must not drink so much, and also you must practice more."

Mercy flipped him off. "Practice minding your own business, Joe Bong. I thought your uncle was the priest, not you?"

She spun around, her ash brown hair swirling. She really was attracted to his voice—mellow, melodic, with all manner of neat tongue clicks and kloks. She'd be enjoying it even more if he weren't such a jerk.

Behind her he said, "Do not call me 'Joe Bong.' And there will be a great evil soon."

Crinkling her fingers over her shoulder, Mercy sailed down the hall toward the washroom. She passed the many notices on the Special Collections door: No Photographs, No Scanning, No Loan Outs, Silence Cell Phones. She missed the previous security guard, who knew the basic elements of his job: joke, flirt, and fetch Mercy Frappuccinos. So what if the guy got drunk on the job one day and pulled the fire alarm? It's not like he had interrupted much.

Past the door to the Special Collections Room stood an old-fashioned red-and-white Coke machine that had once dispensed eight-ounce bottles. (Drink Coca-Cola!) Like a maestro bowing to a concert audience, the massive vending machine was bent almost ninety degrees, top half facing the floor. A band of melted metal encircled the machine at the bend. A few yards past the oddly deformed vending machine, Mercy turned left and burst into the Ladies Room.

Brushing her hair in the mirror, Mercy spotted all the defects on her face, and none of the assets. That put her in sour mood. Between Joe Bong's pissy scolding and Morgan's training zealotry, she was reconsidering her plans to learn formula, then sell it. Her cousin Erin, a marketing major, felt they could make a fortune hawking a few basic formula moves, plus upsells, to the Ophra Winfrey-Eckhardt Tolle, spiritual-but-not-religious demographic. Mercy had convinced Erin it would be abnormally easy.

But that was before Mercy had known anything about formula. She thought it would be all Harry Potter point-the-wand and say-some-Latin. But Greek was the easiest language she'd encountered. There was a smattering of Sumerian, Coptic, Arabic, High German, and a mall-load of other tongues, living and dead—plus runes, symbols, charms, and cryptology . . . and then the formulae themselves, plus abstaining from food, drugs, alcohol, and sex for superior execution. It was worse than joining a convent.

A few minutes later, Mercy doubled back down the hall, opened the door with many notices, and dropped off her purse at her desk in the Special Collections Gallery. She checked phone messages and cursed. Professor Arns would be coming in forty-five minutes to check out *De Vermis Mysteriis* as well as *The Discourse of Pedro Zom*. From her semi-circular work station, Mercy glanced back at a locked cage that ran the entire length of the room: inside were the special collections stacks. She'd have to wade in there and pull both books. Mercy couldn't say why, but the grimoires disseminated a creepy vibe. Handling certain tomes left her feeling soiled and indecent, as if she'd lingered on a website watching someone pose children with brain cancer in sexy ways.

Text. Morgan. 'You're very tardy.' She growled in exasperation.

Turning left out of Special Collections, Mercy passed the bowing Coke machine, the Ladies' Room, the Men's Room, and then a bulletin board covered with maps of north-central Massachusetts, astrological charts, a joke in Hebrew, saucy hieroglyphs, strange vowel-less words spelled out phonetically, and a notice for a Red Cross blood drive. Speeding down the hall, shoes clicking on the tile, she walked by an unusual drinking fountain to her right. Mounted on the wall, crafted vintage white enamel with a metal side handle, the drinking fountain's bowl was oddly warped. Enamel rippled in layers as if heated white hot, and then cooled rapidly like candle wax. But it still dispensed water if you didn't mind a little on your clothes.

Mercy passed closed office doors with old-fashioned, pebbled glass panels. Some doors were stenciled with names and titles of long-gone Antiquity Section academics: Armitage, Rice, Morgan, Doucette, St. John. For some reason, she thought of her Great Uncle Louis Armitage, sitting on his porch, chain-smoking with a thousand-yard stare. Then there was the wasting death of Galen Morgan, who'd been acolyte to Uncle Louis at the

'91 Horror. Galen's mind sizzled during the clash, leaving him a docile idiot at 27, buried at 34. Mercy had been a little girl at his funeral.

Flipping back her hair, she thought of Kingsport and a bar stool with a view of the sea, a chilled Lime-a-Rita, and a yummy bartender.

At the hallway's end, Mercy stopped before a closed door. On the pebbled glass, under the title of Antiquity Chairman, was the stenciled Latin phrase: *Ignis Aurum Probat*.

Mercy popped in two more Certs, rapped twice on the "Aurum," and stormed inside.

She almost tripped over a barrel marked "Powder of Ibn Ghazi," atop which lay an industrial paint sprayer. All around were parchments and scrolls in Tibetan, French and Latin. Astrological charts. Translated English pages from *The Emerald Tablet*; books and scrolls by Cornelius Aggrippa, Hermes Trismegistus, Heinrich Kramer's *The Witch Hammer*; the Kabbalah. There were squares and circles and six-pointed Stars of David, and five-pointed pentacles mixed in with a rack of running medals for distances ranging from 3.1 miles to half-marathons.

A raised oak tabletop held a version of John Dee's Sigillum Dei Aerneth or "Seal of the Truth of God," a bewildering decoder of mystic lore consisting of heptagons encasing a pentagram surrounded by the names of planets, and angels, and the seven names of God. On the floor of the huge office, yards of carpet had been ripped up and the wood underneath covered in white and pastel chalk marks outlining Pentagrams new and long-since-smudged.

In one corner stood a dozen metal waste bins, bunched together like penguins. Their openings had been melted shut, making them appear like large, pinched-together Dixie cups. Mercy couldn't help beaming in pride: that had been her finest hour in formula.

Behind a cluttered desk, Mercy could discern the outline of a computer screen and the neatly cropped, greying hair of Professor Morgan. An acerbic voice arose from behind the clutter, "How can you show so much interest in formula, and so little interest in the self-discipline necessary to excel? You are crippling your chances to advance, and jeopardizing us all right before a critical Hallow Mass."

"Sorry, Professor. I got tied up in traffic."

"You fasted, of course, and abstained from alcohol?"

"Absolutely. Though I might have had a small glass of wine."

"Your indiscipline will cost you, and possibly the planet."

Mercy blocked a major eye roll. She really wanted a nap. "Oh, Professor, Armand Deale's on his way over. And Professor Arns will be in Special Collections any minute. I still need to pull his books. Could we pick this up tomorrow morning first thing?"

A piece of blue chalk flew up and over a mound of papers. Mercy snagged it one-handed. With three older brothers, she was good at catching things thrown suddenly in her direction.

"Levi's Tetragrammaton. Quickly, please."

Glaring at the chalk, Mercy scanned the floor, located a relatively clear patch, knelt on an old shop rag and began drawing Eliphas Levi's Tetragrammaton Pentagram.

Conrad Morgan slid back his chair. Runner-thin, in his early fifties, with his sharply pressed dress shirt and slacks, an orange-and-black Princeton tie, polished shoes, and a Marine Corp

Eagle, Globe and Anchor ring, the professor looked less like a mage and more like an insurance company actuary. He watched Mercy chalk in capitols T and E.

"Place a numeral one over the T and a two over the E."

Mercy drew in the numbers, smacking down the chalk extra hard.

Morgan said, "I was in my third year of study before your great uncle let me tackle Pirandello. If Louis ever answered my phone calls, I'd tell him to be proud of you. Does he still watch the Red Sox?"

Mercy chalked in a T R A with 1 2 3 above each letter followed by a cup. "I'm not sure, though he has mentioned the 1990 season."

Morgan's smile was bittersweet. "Roger Clemens, Tony Pena, Wade Boggs. The stinking Oakland A's. My reserve unit deployed that summer."

"Desert Storm."

"Desert Shield, then Desert Storm in January when the shooting started."

Mercy slowed in her drawing of G R A M. She didn't feel well. Mixing drink styles had that effect. Her brother Kevin always said, 'don't mix paint with bleach.' But he worked in a hardware store and his aphorisms tended to reflect that. Mercy always grew experimental when someone else was buying. Could she run out the clock and keep Morgan talking until Deale arrived?

"Aren't you worried about Deale?"

Morgan stood, paced, mind elsewhere. "He's got a reputation for playing nasty, but we're protected by our charter, not to mention great friends like the Isaac Levinson Foundation."

She chalked in eyes representing spirit. "And why do I have to keep drawing the Tetragrammaton?"

"You mean, other than your life depending on it?"

"Well, I was wondering: if the Pentagram were drawn out ahead of time on a large piece of thick paper, would it be effective protection, or would I need to physically draw it out each time?"

Morgan still paced, shifted his jaw, lips together. "Intriguing. Could be effective; might be; should be tested first. Are you thinking of some sort of ready pentagram in case of emergency?"

Mercy thought it best to avoid mentioning that Erin wanted to mass produce pentagrams as an upsell, like yoga mats. She'd also lined up an IT guy, a videographer, and was split-testing catchy marketing phrases such as 'wicca with balls.' Erin had a money guy interested in underwriting their business venture, but wanted to see a little formula sample before committing. But for all her cousin's excitement, Mercy reflected that Erin wasn't the one on her knees drawing boring ancient shit. Mercy answered, "You know, Professor, that sounds like a good idea."

Morgan adjusted his bifocals, sliding them down his nose as he picked a parchment off his desk, "Ready-made pentagrams. I've missed having someone around here who thought ahead. Outstanding idea. You might work out, Mercy, despite your breezy, half-assed approach, and complete disbelief in our mission."

Mercy chalked in A and M and a sword beneath the letters. She decided to fish for formula compliments "Aren't my invocations stellar?"

"You're excellent at sealing. Rotten at Selective Inferno and struggling with Pirandello's

Aegis because of an overall lack of self-discipline and will."

"I'm a 21st century chick. Fasting and abstinence went out with the Middle Ages."

Glancing up, Mercy noticed the wrinkles around Morgan's eyes, spreading out like cracks in lake ice as he said, "Sadly, your attitude is not uncommon, even within our families. It's been a challenge to keep curators and acolytes and a high caliber of guards. And ever since Andy St. John left for Stanford, there's been no one even remotely adept at formula. The flame of vigilance was almost extinguished. I'm so glad I didn't terminate you."

Mercy stopped her chalking. "Are you kidding? For what?"

"For setting a record calling in sick on Fridays and Mondays."

"I had post-masters degree depression. It's real. You can look it up. You'd fire someone for being depressed?"

"And flirting with the guard on company time."

"You took care of that big time."

"I approved his hire. Sloppy of me."

"Great. So now we have a heavily armed Zulu redneck. Oh, uh, what does 'baba' mean?"

"In Zulu culture, it's a title of respect. Nothing you'd be interested in."

"Hey, you know Joe Bong made his own flashcards of Dunwich warlocks? Freaky, huh?"

Morgan stood tall, "Really? I must commend him. His Uncle Father George Manqoba is a dear friend. He used to have a parish in Dean's Corners near Dunwich, converting the heathen."

"In Dunwich?"

"Massachusetts. One thing at a time. Now he works down the block at St. Mary's hospital. Did

Joseph ever tell you what happened to his fiancée in Natal?"

"Seriously? What?"

"Ask him. Pirandello's Aegis."

"Can I finish the pentagram first?" Drawing the interlocking five-pointed star, Mercy kept the lines wide in order to add the necessary Hebrew words. She willed Armand Deale to knock on the door and save her from sloppy preparation. Mercy selected a juicy conversational tidbit, guaranteed to draw Morgan out.

"Why did they keep you in Kuwait after the war ended?"

"Landmines. We were an engineering unit disarming landmines, landmines beyond counting. That's what I was doing on Walpurgis Night when Louis and Galen faced Obed Whately." Morgan's head bowed. He removed his glasses and rubbed the bridge of his nose. "Galen was a curator like you. He was eager, but too green for acolyte. Never fasted; often had wine with his lunch; more than one glass. Obed Whateley crushed his mind like a tuna can in a vise."

Mercy shifted uneasily. "I remember Galen gave everyone potholders for Christmas."

"Simple crafts were a blessing for him."

Mercy paused in her chalking. "They say Uncle Louis conducted a desperate defense."

"The odds were long." Morgan opened and closed his fingers rapidly. "He faced Whateley alone after Galen fell. Checked him. Paid the price." Morgan slapped the side of a tall, thick safe. "I had the will, the imagination. My presence in Dunwich could have been decisive. But, no. Instead I was up to my chest in Soviet PMN mines, 240 grams of TNT. They'd take your leg off. Plus wind and sand shifted entire minefields so they weren't where the map said. You have to spot a dead camel first. Then there's our own Rockeye cluster bomblets—up to 30% never detonate. Pain in the ass."

"That's a lot of ordnance."

"Vital work. Important. But not what I was bred for by blood, location, or desire. Now years have passed and I feel like a Swedish admiral—all the theory in the world, but no combat experience."

"But you were under fire in the Gulf."

"In battle against men, not a contest for the fate of Earth, with life and sanity in the balance; with only a single individual standing between the indescribable terrors of another dimension and a quiet night's sleep for an unsuspecting world. To be an Antiquity Section mage is to embody the flame of vigilance."

Oh, brother.

Mercy chalked in the conjoined symbols of Venus and Mercury. "Joe Bong and his cop buddy think Obed Whateley's back. But I think he probably died ten years ago somewhere in the bush. You know, like Pol Pot."

Morgan said, "That's why we must accelerate your training. Hallow Mass is almost upon us. It may pass by without a whisper. Or it may signal world's end. You must be prepared as acolyte."

"I'm going to a party on Halloween. Drinking. Chasing boys. All that 21st century stuff."

"The stars are right. This Hallow Mass could be decisive.

"They haven't got the book."

"There are no mulligans for fumbling a threat to the world. By the way, if you ever hope to head the Antiquity Section, consider the Ancient Languages Ph.D. Then I can be your faculty mentor. We could start at once on your dissertation."

Mercy encircled the Pentagram with chalk, stood and wiped off her palms, brushed off her slacks. The idea of heading up the Antiquity Section for the next twenty-five or thirty years was about as appealing as moving to Saudi Arabia and opening a Forever 21 Burqa franchise. She felt guilty for playing Professor Morgan. He wasn't a bad guy. But Erin was right: he was waiting for a train that no longer ran. Mercy planned to learn formula, sell formula, and earn enough money to get out of debt and move into her own place again. Never again would Mercy be pressured to follow someone else's dreams like that whole Boston College thing.

"I'm still, uh, deciding on my doctorate."

Morgan's desk phone sounded. Mercy cheered inwardly. But the professor ignored the ring and pointed a finger toward the Pentagram. "Pirandello's Aegis."

"You might have to walk me through the Greek."

Morgan's mouth opened in disbelief. "Learn the words. They subdue the conscious mind, freeing up the imagination and will."

"I know, I know. Things have been hectic."

Standing in the Pentagram, she wished she hadn't had so much to drink at lunch. Mercy's head was fuzzy; her mouth was cottony. Focusing was a problem. She watched Morgan cross to the office window, past a tall, massive standing safe with a combination lock. Outside, to the north, faint traffic noises drifted up from Church Street. A jackhammer sounded as the City of Arkham finally got around to filling in last year's potholes, three months before this year's winter. Between the office buildings across the street, Mercy caught a glimpse of the ancient Miskatonic River, sunlight flashing on the surface as it flowed slowly to the ocean. Morgan pulled the blinds, dimming the room. "Your will is like a credit card. There must be ample funds to cover all eventualities: attack, defense, protection. Otherwise, you'll never survive a clash."

"Professor, I'm a little sick today. I think it's, you know, a chick thing."

"Now is the time to prepare. You said so yourself."

"I think Joe Bong said that."

The desk phone rang.

Pushing aside papers, a framed photo of his wife and teenage sons, then a finish line photo of himself arms raised, setting a new 10K personal record, the professor located the phone, checked the flashing light. To Mercy's intense disappointment, he ignored the call and flicked his wrist. "Now. Go."

"That could be Professor Arns."

"He knows our work and approves."

"What if it's President Deale?"

"He can wait for us 'Dark Age Book Wardens.' Isn't that what he called us in the paper? I like it. I'll have T-shirts made up."

Mercy felt queasy. She flung out her arms, verbally stumbling and stuttering as she mangled the Greek words.

Morgan made a strangled sound, "Terrible. You're thinking and not forming the shield. The pentagram alone will not save you against an arch warlock. You'd be violently murdered by now. Repeat after me: *'Énas toíchos gia empodísei tin tromokratía apó ti nýchta.'"*

Mercy stumbled over the words.

"Discipline is freedom. Again."

Mercy repeated the Greek phrase three more times. Somewhat confident, she flung out her arms.

Morgan drove on. "Say the words while you imagine, focus the will, project, and create."

Mercy remembered an old animated film, *The Incredibles*, in which a teenage girl with special powers protected herself by forming a force-field bubble. Mercy embraced that image, saw it in her mind's eye; projected the bubble image with her will, surrounding the Pentagram with her protective bubble.

More ringing. It sounded like Morgan's cell phone, a tune by Nine Inch Nails.

"Defense and attack will be simultaneous." Morgan rummaged again on his desk, found a tennis ball and lobbed it at Mercy. The ball bounced off her cheek. And while not thrown hard, the impact snapped her concentration. She lost the bubble.

"The aegis only defends against formulae and entities such as Those From the Air. A human being can knock you out with a length of pipe. Master Pirandello and we'll advance to more sophisticated protections. Is your shield still in place?"

"Yeah, yeah, super strong," said Mercy, then mumbled the Greek phrase, trying to reform the shield.

But she was too slow.

Morgan flung out his arms and shouted in Vedic. Mercy felt as if she were in a fast car speeding in reverse. Her feet left the floor and she slammed into the office door so hard the pebbled glass shattered with a deafening crash. Dazed, with a pain in her back, Mercy slid down onto her butt.

A worried Conrad Morgan rushed over. Footsteps sounded outside on the hallway tiles.

"I thought you were protected. Are you hurt?"

Mercy muttered something inane as the professor guided her to his desk chair. He checked her eyes for concussion, then gently probed the back of her head, locating a tender spot via Mercy's 'oww.' She felt light-headed, still shaken by the raw power of Morgan's formula.

Glass crunched in the hallway. Mercy peered up to see the concerned face of Joe Bong peering through the shattered window.

Behind the guard flashed the sardonic grin of Miskatonic University President Armand Deale.

CHAPTER 2

HOME IS THE WARLOCK, HOME FROM THE HILL

"The wind gibbers with Their voices, and the earth mutters with Their consciousness."
— Abdul Alhazard, the Necronomicon

"No single work approaches Paz Encanto's ground-breaking text, Gangsters and Geriatrics. *Recall how Professor Encanto introduced violent street criminals into a retirement home, thus proving that when we expect a particular behavior from a group, we not only find that behavior, but also create situations eliciting that behavior."*
—Lecture by Miskatonic University Associate Vice Chancellor for Contemporary Oppression Modalities, Professor Angelo Silent Feather

Poised outside the Massachusetts College of Art and Design, Jasper Frye let several students walk past, infuriating his companion.

"Since when are ye so choosy about sacrifices?" said Hutchins. In his mid-twenties, he wore a tank top in the late summer heat. Even in the twilight, a casual observer might have noted his chest was reticulated like that of a crocodile. In addition, Hutchins' shoulders were black and yellow, similar to the skin of a coral snake. One might be excused for missing the outline of a 9mm pistol stuck in his waistband under his shirt.

Frye tensed at the approach of a student. This one would do nicely. "Set yourself, Malachi."

A young man rode a skateboard toward the two waiting men, his eyes locked on his smart phone. Wearing a T-shirt with the phrase "A Flash Mob of One," he had his blonde hair pulled up into a man bun.

As Hutchins readied plastic handcuffs and duct tape, Frye reached into his shirt pocket, removed a sugar packet, and emptied it onto his tongue. In his early thirties, he was a powerfully built chinless man with a chinless wife and three chinless children. As Flash Mob drew even, Frye extended a thick forearm, clotheslining the student.

"Gaaaak." Swept off his board, Flash Mob fell backward to the pavement. His skateboard continued on down the sidewalk as if ridden by a specter.

Hutchins and Frye leaped on Flash Mob, binding arms and legs, sealing his mouth with duct tape. Frye glanced around, spotted the student's iPhone.11.4, and wedged the phone into his shirt pocket, mashing down the remaining sugar packets.

Frye and Hutchins lugged Flash Mob across the street and stuffed him into the back of a stolen dark green Toyota Sienna minivan. Frye made sure to remove the student's wallet. Per prior arrangement, he and Hutchins would split the cash, with the credit cards going to Hutchins and all smart phones to Frye. Flash Mob struggled next to the bound, wriggling form of another male undergraduate in a teal polo shirt with a short-brimmed straw fedora. Frye struck Short Brim in the kidney, and the wriggling ceased.

Slamming the back door, Frye climbed behind the wheel. Riding shotgun was Chester Sawyer, a tentacle from inside his shirt reaching out to wrap around a cup holder.

"Ye take yer leisurely time. We must pick up the Little Man."

"Aye. Some help with the sacrifices might hasten matters," said Frye carefully. Mr. Lord High Boss Man with his Outside ways. A healthy fear kept him from beating the wits out of Chester. Though pushy and indolent, Sawyer could throw dark formula, and Frye had no desire to end up like a darned sock, turned inside out.

Sawyer ignored Frye as a second tentacle snaked out between his button holes, a mouth on the tentacle opening and closing like a lake perch. Motoring north through Boston toward Arkham, Frye set the radio dial to the PBS News Hour. A gentle voice filled the minivan, chronicling a woman tuba player's struggle for equality and acceptance in a field dominated by portly men.

"Know ye the Dho formula, Malachi?" asked Chester.

"As well as ye," said Hutchins.

"The Little Man said we'd learn tonight if Dho is sufficient to survive the Great Cleansing."

Frye listened intently. His life might depend on the answer.

Opening another packet of sugar, he poured the crystals on his tongue, maintaining the speed limit through evening traffic, enroute to St. Mary's Hospital.

Through the open room door Deale could hear muted PA calls summoning this doctor or that nurse to the phone. Carts rattled down the corridor. The nearby elevator pinged. A white-haired priest with skin so black his white Roman collar appeared to float like a disembodied square poked his head in the room and asked if the university president needed anything. Deale dismissed the man.

African or something from the sound of his voice. The Catholics probably have to recruit priests in Africa. No one with any intelligence would squander his life on bingo and child molestation.

In his private room, surround by beeping equipment, a rack for IV and blood pressure equipment, oxygen hookup, a hospital tray, bottles and pans for bodily waste, plastic carafe of ice water and clear plastic cups, a big crucifix on the pastel-painted wall, air smelling of three or four disinfectants with a TV mounted high across from his bed, Deale sullenly watched a quirky but brilliant computer technician unearth a vital clue for a crusty young British detective and his affable older colleague as they hunted a serial killer in the Northumbria countryside.

Deale's smart phone sat muted on the hospital tray. He couldn't stand fielding another phone call, explaining what had happened, listening to one more incredulous *'what?'* Most of the campus had witnessed him crossing the quad from the library to the administration building, taking tiny little steps, his legs wrapped together like a barber pole.

In the Emergency Room that afternoon, it had been necessary to cut away his trousers and socks. A burly intern in a blue scrubs had complimented Deale on his legs. 'Good muscle tone. Athlete?'

Deale swelled with pride. In his early forties, at six foot, he kept his trim body in excellent shape.

'Lacrosse in college. Racket ball nowadays.'

'So how did you get your legs wrapped together so tight. I mean, were you trying something new?'

Bristling at the implication that he was somehow responsible, Deale snapped, 'If you ever get your medical license, maybe you can tell me.'

Naturally, the medical staff tried prying his legs apart, lowering him into a whirlpool, and feeding him muscle relaxants. X-rays showed zero wrong with Deale's bones and tendons. Tomorrow he would be given an MRI. And because they could find nothing, the questions kept popping up, 'What exactly were you doing?' 'Were you attempting Pilates?' 'Did you reach for something and whip around to keep from falling?' 'Was drug use involved?'

Legs wrapped together, stretched out on the bed in front of him, Deale ruminated on the one question vexing him: what *had* he been doing? He'd been trying to shake up musty Miskatonic; showing people there was a new breeze blowing from the west. Perception was everything. Marching over to confront Morgan sent the message that the old ways were on the chopping block. But then . . . this?

Crossing arms over his chest, he thought back several hours to Morgan's office. Dropping into a chair facing Morgan's junk-piled desk, Deale had put his feet up, crossing his ankles, establishing himself as the alpha. The O'Connor woman had been across from him in Morgan's chair, still acting dazed from whatever theatrics they'd pre-planned. Morgan paced his office like a caged leopard.

Deale said, 'You're killing my fundraising, Conrad.'

'How so?'

'There are serious people in Boston, New York, and Philadelphia with serious bucks. I want their money for my Miskatonic Master Plan. But I can't mention this university without hearing about 'Dunwich,' 'monsters,' 'burglaries,' 'magic.' People think it's all *Supernatural*, *X-Files, Mysterious Dunwich* over here. You're a joke and you've made this institution the punch line; and that's ending today.'

Morgan raised a forefinger, "You forgot *Dunwich, Devils and Death* by Aquarius Fomble. For a book dismissed as popular tripe, he got a surprising number of things right."

"Who cares? Once you and your legacy section are gone, I'll be able to sell Miskatonic as a respectable academic destination."

"Numberless math? Critical Weather Studies? Really, Armand, this isn't California."

Deale chuckled, "Young children, academics and the media are easily bored. They love the illusion of progress. No one wants to appear backwards. Present company excluded."

"Time moves more slowly at Miskatonic," said Morgan. "Tradition still has a place. Honor is not a dead word—"

"—Yes, it is," said Deale. "Your honor and my fundraising do not mix. You are a millstone upon my Miskatonic Master Plan. Seriously, I didn't come east to preside over one of the most backward institutions in the country. You're like Texas A&M without a football team. Think a moment: we're inside the Henry Armitage Memorial Library. What does it memorialize?"

Morgan's voice was calm, as if telling a teenage boy why driving a Camaro with a bucket over his head was a bad idea, "That knowledge is power and not always benign. That not everything new is good, and not everything old is worth discarding."

Morgan recrossed his ankles, "Professor Fong was right. We memorialize three families who have carved out a niche claiming to protect the world from evil magicians, and monsters, and predatory towing companies, etc., etc. I admire you. You made a career for yourselves and wrapped it up as saving the world. Nothing wrong with that. I'll take care of you. But the generational gravy train ends now."

Deale expected Morgan to erupt, maybe even order him from the office. Either would play well on Gabby Face. But instead, the professor crossed to the windows, opened the blinds and let in the afternoon light, then leaned against the massive safe. "What do you offer?"

Deale's smile was sweetened by the look of disbelief on O'Connor's hapless face.

"Conrad, I can insure you the softest of landings: a corner office in the new administration building, a graduate assistant or two, no teaching, no publications. In fact, you don't even have to show up on campus anymore. We'll mail you the checks and keep the bonuses flowing."

"And Mercy O'Connor?"

"We'll find her a spot."

"Joseph Bongani and the other guards?"

"I'll tell campus security to keep them on."

"And the Special Collection?"

"We can dump a few books on Harvard or Brown, sell the rest at private auction. And you'll get 20% of that. But first, cull out the Dunwich books. They have to go back."

"Would you please remove your feet from my desk?"

"No. Professor Silent Feather recommended some form of symbolic gesture from you. Do you know Angelo?"

"Yes. He implied my predecessors were thieves."

"That's just for the media. He really respects you. Anyway, because of all the blood spilled historically, yada yada, there should be a remedial act. He thought you could meet with a representative from Dunwich. We'll dig one up— just kidding. Give peace a chance sort of stuff."

Morgan toyed with his Marine Corps ring. "Wouldn't such a meeting signify that the threat was no more? And that both sides were equally at fault?"

"Not really. It's just saying both sides want to move forward. And it would be great optics if you could personally return one of their books, especially that one called the *Necroharmonica*."

Deale watched Morgan walk casually toward him, "I know you think it's fiction, Armand, but the dangers posed by the *Necronomicon* are real. There are certain parties in Dunwich, and around the world, who would use that book's unholy knowledge to open dimensional portals. Through those portals would ooze hideous beings that aren't interested in sampling the wonders of numberless math. Humanity would be massacred. Dunwich must never get that book."

"Conrad, it's only a book."

"Call a scorpion a kitten and you'll die trying to cuddle it."

"Call a kitten a scorpion and you'll look stupid and cruel keeping it in a glass cage. I'm offering you an easy way out. Don't play hardball with me. I'll slime you on social media so bad you won't be able to find work shoveling horse shit after a parade."

Moran nodded, as if considering the consequences, then said, "Last chance: would you kindly remove your feet from my desk?"

Deale shook his head more in sadness than anger. "Or what? Violence, Conrad? Seriously? It would be one of the biggest mistakes you ever made."

Morgan raised his hands above his shoulders, muttered something low in a foreign tongue. Deale recalled feeling unsettled, the hair rising on his arms. And he didn't like the sudden look of glee on O'Connor's face. Clearly, they'd worked out this little skit in advance.

Deale said, "Is that your answer? Rattling chicken bones? So sad to witness a grown man capering around like a goof."

Deale anticipated lifting his feet off the desk and strolling out, leaving behind a final snarky, cutting remark. Morgan disappointed him; such a passive-aggressive weakling. Deale had faced tougher opposition from the Mathematics Chair at Mountain View State. A little more pressure and Morgan and his department would crumble like stale bread, signaling to the rest of the faculty and administration that President Armand Deale was for real. That was catchy. He should have Carter Fong launch the hash tag #dealeforreal.

For some reason, Deale's ankles refused to uncouple. Like a boa constrictor sliding around a tree trunk, his right leg wrapped itself tighter around his left leg, stopping right on the line between discomfort and pain.

Deale mentally commanded both legs: unlock. Nothing.

Morgan and O'Connor watched, faces neutral, as Deale nonchalantly leaned forward and grabbed his shins. Every tendon stood out on well-defined arms and shoulders as he struggled to wrench his legs apart.

Deale stopped, face red, His legs were cemented in a spiral, spot-welded together, a single unit.

"Is anything wrong, Armand?" asked Morgan.

O'Connor looked to the floor as if reading something on her shoes, but Deale spotted the gleeful lift at the corner of her mouth. It infuriated him. Before he could stop himself, he'd hissed, "What did you do?"

Morgan's face showed concern. "Very little, some capering. Shall we call for medical assistance? A wheelchair?"

Using his hips, Deale swung both legs like a massive club, knocking over a stack of papers before setting his right heel on the floor. Using the arms of the chair, he stood, discovering forward motion possible only in little penguin steps.

"What fascinating eccentric people you are," said Deale, face twisted and scarlet. "This has been like a visit to a carnival. I'll be in touch."

Penguin-walking, Deale left the office, crunching across broken glass with tiny steps.

Halfway down the corridor, he heard Morgan, O'Connor, and their stupid guard erupt in laughter.

That's the way they want to play? Fine. It's freaking on.

"Swaddled your legs, did he?"

Deale's consciousness returned to the present. A little old man in pressed suit pants and a collarless shirt from the 1990s stood beside his bed. The man's green eyes were intense, mocking, disturbing in ways Deale could not articulate, so he watched the British detectives instead. "You have the wrong room. Please leave before I call the nurse."

"Call ahead and ye will never rid yourself of the Antiquity Section."

"What is this? International Talk Like a Pirate Day?"

"That is September 19. Look ye here, Deale, Morgan twisted your legs. They will be untwisted tomorrow I wager, but ye still crave revenge, yes?"

Deale risked a look at the old man. "I'll be normal tomorrow? Says who?"

"Morgan used half formula to make a point. I would've used all and no more talk."

"I have zero idea what you just said. What do you know about Morgan and my legs and the Antiquity Section?"

"The *Necronomicon* is mine."

Of course. The old clothes, the disturbing look, the funny talk like that of a Quaker who'd been to junior college. Audrey Klumm-Weebner had described it all in her masterful work, *Old Ones, New Values: Fresh Insights on the Population of North-Central Massachusetts.* He could use her wisdom. Talk to the experts, then make the best decision.

"We share a common opponent," said Deale. "Professor Conrad Morgan."

"'Enemy' suits me better. Look ye here, Deale: fetch me the *Necronomicon.* Ye shall be rewarded."

"I tried. It's tougher than it looks."

"Who is Morgan's acolyte?"

"I have no idea. Some woman named Mercy O'Connor takes care of his special collection."

"Say what ye know of her."

"Not much to tell. Joe Six Pack family; electricians and firemen, not very bright. Good soccer player; a scholarship to BC that she promptly blew by getting kicked off the team; barely graduated with a degree in English— there's a moneymaker for you. Buried in student loan debt, somehow managed to grab a Masters in Anthropology at Miskatonic, probably because she's related to the Armitage family; started working at the Antiquity Section almost a year ago. Basically, a party-girl, a lightweight, a crêpe."

Deale shifted in discomfort, not liking the man's eyes. They put him in mind of a preying mantis about to pounce on a grub.

"Splendid. Can ye move at speed and return my book before Hallow Mass?"

Deale hesitated, "That's your fall religious ceremony, is it not?"

"Aye. With book in hand, this year Earth will finally be cleansed of all polluting life."

"Then we have much in common. I, too, favor an unspoiled environment."

"Scoured of pests."

"Filthy corporations."

"Scrubbed of humanity."

"Population control. I agree."

"Though some may go to the city at the poles."

"Of course. A reasonable destination for any thinking man."

The old man swung the hospital tray around until it touched Deale's chest. Reaching into his trouser pocket, he emerged with something closed in his fist.

"Then we have a pact. Ye return me the *Necronomicon* by October 31st."

"I don't know your name."

"Leland Janus." Janus opened his fist over the hospital tray. A round object clacked onto the plastic surface next to the smart phone. Deale picked up a coin, examining it carefully. "Twenty dollar gold piece?"

"Aye. Liberty Double Eagle. Worth $6,500 given today's gold price."

"For my agreement?"

Deale ventured another glance at Janus' eyes. They seemed especially contemptuous, bordering on the pity you'd give a child delighted at seeing a blender work for the first time.

"Say a marker for yer agreement. Fetch me the book in time for Hallow Mass and ye may have a sack of the same coins."

Janus held out both hands as if indicating the size of a medium pumpkin.

Deale's mind raced. He needed to consult his experts, formulate a plan. Placing a hand over the coin, he said, "Done. You'll have your book."

Janus extended a hand. With the slightest reluctance, Deale shook the cool dry skin.

Deale said, "Oh, wait. I mean, how will my legs be fixed?"

Janus said, "Know ye not? Morgan will undo his work."

He walked from the room, leaving Deale to mull over his last sentence. It made him uncomfortable. More seemed at play in the world then he cared to admit. But then, with the book returned to Dunwich, and the world undestroyed, there'd be no need for an Antiquity Section other than nostalgia. Closing it out would be a matter of diplomacy with the Board and a few of the foundations.

Then let the cash dam break.

Armand Deale pictured himself fundraising at the Ritz-Carlton in Boston, the Four Seasons in New York City, the Hay-Adams in Washington D.C. Anywhere but the Arkham Best Western. With his annual bonus structure tied to donations,

Deale could be pulling in seven figures by this time next year. Having turned an academic black hole like Miskatonic into a white-hot sun, he could write his own ticket. He should think of a book title now.

Humming along with the closing credits of the TV show, Deale opened a pocket on the back of his smart phone case and hid the gold piece.

Frye drove the van north, crossing the Miskatonic on the West Street bridge, then angling northwest back to Dunwich. On the radio, WGBH Greater Boston featured Jim Braude moderating a roundtable discussion on a state ballot initiative to improve educational opportunities for farm animals. Frye hid his smile at the memory of the Little Man standing outside the van staring at Chester Sawyer. Tucking tentacles back inside his shirt, Sawyer had climbed out of the shotgun seat and into the back with Hutchins and the sacrifices. But that bit of humbling didn't stop Chester from playing warlock's pet.

Sawyer asked, "Is Deale in accord?"

Leland Janus, also known as the Little Man, also known as Obed Whateley, grinned a sinister smile, "Morgan swaddled Deale's legs with the Translucent Python."

Frye laughed with the other three men.

"Old Deale must have been a picture," said Hutchins.

"Aye, he was that," said the Little Man, turning around to face Chester, his green eyes blazing with malicious eagerness. "Look ye here, Chester, I'll cook up something pleasant. Ye must administer it to Morgan. Frye and Hutchins will help."

"Draw upon my strength and cunning, Obed," said Chester.

"My strength and cunning," thought Frye.

"A most painful poison?" asked Hutchins.

Whateley shook his head. "A solution to keep him alive but helpless until a day beyond Hallow Mass. He will recover in time to die screaming in the mouth of Hastur."

Whateley's face grimaced in hatred. Frye felt fear scamper down his chest with freezing feet. Whateley's knowledge of diabolical formula made Chester seem impotent by comparison.

Fury pulsed from the Little Man like hot air from an exhaust fan. "All my life have I worked for the Great Cleansing—hunted by cops, checked by the vile nose water calling itself the Antiquity Section. I was a youth in the Devil's Hop Yard when that living glob of vomit, Julian Rice, forced Sirac Bishop to annihilate them both. Thirty-five years later, a walking slab of excrement named Louis Armitage killed my shoggoth and forced me to flee. Now the stars align once more and Conrad Morgan, that pool of bile, will not stop me from opening the gate once and for final."

"Well said, Obed," whispered Frye.

"Aye, 'tis time," said Hutchins.

"Would that your skills wrenched open the door this very night," said Sawyer.

Whateley collapsed in his seat as if he'd given a long, passionate speech at a political convention. Frye relaxed, always a relative term around a warlock. Drawing a sugar pack from his shirt pocket, Frye poured it on his tongue, dropping the paper to the floor mat. His mind turned to practical matters. And as sure as there were sixteen more sugar packets in his shirt pocket, Frye knew he'd be stuck handling the details of poisoning Conrad Morgan. Tricky. He needed intelligence on the man, and thought he might know where to turn, as Whateley said, "Frye, stop ye at that Burger King up ahead. I crave a tender crisp salad for after."

Frye nodded his chinless head. "Think it wise with sacrifices in back?"

Hutchins said, "They won't eat much."

To chortling and chuckling, Frey turned into the drive-through window of a Burger King. He ordered Whateley's post-ceremony salad, his own chocolate fudge and caramel sundaes with extra sugar, a double Cheese Whopper for Sawyer, and a Tendergrill Chicken Salad Sandwich for Hutchins.

Frye paid for the food. Once again, no one offered to reimburse him. Not. One. Penny. Driving away, Frye marinated in resentment as Sawyer cooed, feeding his tentacles bits of Cheese Whopper.

Whippoorwills cried and the bullfrogs along the Miskatonic rasped out their grinding calls. Distant dogs howled and fireflies winked as Obed Whateley summoned Those From the Air. From the safety of a pentagram, with Sawyer beside him as acolyte, Whateley concluded the opening portion of the ceremony, "Something for something. Take for thee one youth and allow forth the Darkness From Without."

Twenty yards away, safeguarded by Whateley's power, Frye and Hutchins watched the transaction. If the top of Sentinel Hill were a clock with 12 to the north, Frye stood at 9 with Whateley's pentagram at 11. Facing northeast toward the stone alter at 2, in the hill's innermost circle, Frye watched Straw Hat struggle. Arms and legs bound, Straw Hat lay at the base of the alter in flickering torch light, among an untidy pile of human bones. The young man twisted around as best he could, then peered up as if someone on a ladder were baiting him. Frye felt the hair on his arms and neck rise up.

"Chow time," whispered Hutchins.

A moment later, something unseen snipped off the back of Straw Hat's thigh. Screaming, the student twisted and bucked in pain, blood thick as paint spouting onto the dirt. Moments later, the student was chopped up by invisible entities in a series of huge sharp diagonal bites. Frye thought it like watching a fat mouse dropped into a piranha tank. In moments, only a straw hat and a bloody espadrille remained.

In the light of a nearby bonfire, lashed to the stone altar, Flash Mob hollered madly.

"I was taken from a certified safe zone. You did not have my consent."

The frightened student said more about microwaved aggressions and triggering. Frye wasn't sure what the kid meant.

An outer ring of stone pillars surrounded the hill, massive obelisks eleven to twenty-five feet in height. Next came a narrow ring of rocky soil enclosing an inner ring of smooth dirt, marred by deep, long jagged fissures. In the center of the third ring stood the stone altar, chest high, slightly concave. Four iron loops held the ropes that bound the wildly jerking Flash Mob. If Frye knew anything, it was how to tie a knot. This kid wasn't going anywhere except into the tummy of whatever shambling obscenity Obed Whateley was summoning.

A soft voice, sexless, ageless, whispered from the air outside Whateley's pentagram. "So sweet the squeals. Allow us the one upon the table."

In a commanding voice, Whateley said, "Extend not your reach, least ye anger a greater. Make way by power and will and ancient bonds. Make way for the Darkness From Without."

A mighty hiss from the hillside was followed by a rumble. Sentinel Hill jolted, causing a tall obelisk to wobble like a bowling pin.

The stench of Outside rose and Frye's eyes watered. Something new, ominous, frightfully dangerous had seeped into being near the stone altar. Frye and Hutchins exchanged fearful glances.

Even Chester Sawyer appeared nervous as he handed Whateley a silver sword. Whateley pointed the blade toward a space above the stone altar, using the blade to focus his will.

"Receive a bounty for my traffic," he called in dominant compelling tone, "Grant me that knowledge known to thee on thy travels, cloaked by time and distance."

From above the stone table answered a voice that sounded as if a colossal centipede were experimenting with English through vocal chords designed only for chittering.

"Chance and fortune color all deeds. "

Flash Mob screamed, his voice climbing several octaves into a thin piping wail as something large and invisible peeled open the student's stomach and sucked out his intestines.

Whateley said, "May I affect the Great Cleansing without the book?"

"No. Even with stars aligned, The Lurker at the Threshold cannot pry open the gate. Certain offerings must be consummated with the right words at the right time for the Old Ones to emerge."

Flash Mob's lungs were ripped upward, flapping like a bloody crow.

"Might the Great Cleansing occur this Hallow Mass?"

Bonfire crackled, whippoorwills piped, and a wet popping sound of bones crunching sounded from above the table. Finally, speaking with mouth full, the Darkness From Without said, "Yes. Your enemies are divided. Your path to the book is clear. But success is clouded by ambiguity."

"How so?"

A foot with a running shoe vanished into the air. With each bite, the Darkness From Without grew more distinct. Frye thought he glimpsed a great pointed mouth filled with needle-like teeth.

"Forces align to oppose the Return."

"Name them."

Bones crunched, followed by a slurping sound like a youngster eating an ice cream cone.

"Vagueness; chance and fortune."

"Conrad   Morgan?"

"His formula is deft and powerful."

"Louis Armitage?"

"Once great, he now sits in lassitude since your clash."

Frye noted a hulking, bat-winged form gradually looming into view above the stone altar. He looked away after it tried making eye contact with him.

Whateley stood silent, sword pointed, then said, "After the Great Cleansing, will the inner city at the two magnetic poles accommodate those with knowledge of Dho?"

Frye thought briefly of his wife and kids. He loved them well enough, but in Dunwich it never paid to grow too attached to anyone. They would understand.

A leering Moray Eel-like face snapped up a head with a blonde man bun. "All who know the angle of the planes and all the formulas between Yr and the Nhhngr will break through, but must be transfigured. Those with much of Outside and knowledge of the Dho formula may break through. Those with excessive humanness will die in peals of fright, serving the Old Ones with their final shrieks."

Next to Frye, Hutchins smugly slapped his crocodile chest.

Whateley quizzed the Darkness From Without on formula and the stars and the book, and Miskatonic University, but Frye paid no attention. He'd heard what he needed to know. Without Outside traits, he lacked all capacity for mastering the angle of planes. Even with knowledge of the Dho formula, Frye would die a keening wretched death along with most of humanity.

In less than sixty days.

If Whateley recovered the *Necronomicon*.

Jasper Frye began mulling over various actions that would ensure the survival and betterment of Jasper Frye.

CHAPTER 3

EVERYBODY'S WORKING FOR THE WEEKEND

"To better foster diversity, I stop students and deconstruct their humor through a ruthless critical lens. The process takes forty-five minutes. Any failure to cooperate means Diversity Tribunal, then expulsion. As a result, undergraduates stop laughing when I approach. I accept the compliment."
—*Miskatonic University Chief of Campus Diversity Enforcement, Doctor Leo Hameyes, from his acceptance speech at the Oberlin College Iron Boot of Tolerance Award*

"Be wary of anyone who says weather may not be studied outside the realms of 'meteorology' or 'science.' You are hearing the wounding snarl of exclusion."
—*Professor Carter Fong, from his book,* Weather Thou Goest: Critical Weather Studies and the New Atmospheric Paradigm

In the gloom, Mercy saw an endless row of old wooden desks, rusted sewing machines, tipped-over wooden chairs, and wads of paper on a faded maroon carpet, spread atop the concrete floor, extending past brick walls and huge windows each with sixteen, mostly shattered, glass panes. Once the factory had made dresses for short wide woman, as well as ladies with prosthetic limbs. Patterns lay on the floor for one-legged pantsuits and dresses that would fit any woman the height and width of a child's pool. Tall wooden shelves still held colored bobbins of string in orange, scarlet, and lemon. Dress dummies stood facing each other like armless women chatting at a lawn party. Overhead, rusted fluorescent light fixtures in rows of five hovered above the smell of mildew and decay. Mercy hadn't seen rats, but they were certainly around, skittering in the shadows.

Bongani had really got on her nerves with his hurry-up-and-practice more BS. He'd been especially hemorrhoidal today, sniping at Mercy as she left early for the shoot. That had stirred up unpleasant family memories that, along with today's fast and alcohol abstinence, plunged Mercy into a sour temper.

Her stomach rumbled and she felt angry, frustrated, sore. Focus was the problem once again today with Pirandello's Aegis. Morgan had shoved her off the pentagram twice, knocking her once to the ground. Mercy took the day's negative emotions and kept them on a low boil like a turkey broth, intending to fling them into formula. Tonight was for the money. The ruined factory around her was located in a triangular no-man's land between Dorchester, Roxbury (often called 'Glocksbury,') and South Boston. Despite the nearby expressway traffic, they were alone here in a huge space with no one around for blocks around them. Except rats and possibly drug addicts.

Twelve feet away, Erin supervised the IT and Videographer in setting up and clearing a filming space on the carpet. A box of gluten-free pizza rested on a battered wooden sewing table next to several bottles of chocolate ale. Erin looked very stylish in her flannel shirt, teal colored beanie, extremely short denim cut offs and Doc Martens.

Next to her, thin, androgynous men in little hats, younger than Mercy, connected portable lights to battery packs, then hooked up cables to a 17-inch Mac PowerBook and a Sony HDV pro camcorder perched on a tripod.

The Videographer was a sophomore from Tufts. He wore a Supreme varsity jacket and had bangs falling across his eyes. He sounded languid and ironic, "Are we really going to use just the camera mike?"

Erin pushed aside a wooden swivel chair, making more room on the maroon carpet. "Forget sound tonight. We'll sweeten the whole thing in Final Draft. I know exactly what I want."

Video shook his bangs, "We should mic her. I mean, aren't there words to her spells or something, you know: 'Expecto Baronum'?"

The Internet Technician was a freshman at Boston University. He wore skinny jeans and Chukkas with statement socks that tied his look together. "It's 'Expecto Patronum,' fool."

"Oh, pardon me, your fandom rocks. Still dreaming of a date with Hermione?"

"Still dreaming of being Hermione?"

Erin adjusted her oversized glasses, "Be bitchy on your own time. Use the camera mic for ambient sound and room tone. And make sure you shoot that pentagram solo."

IT glared at Erin, but said nothing. Video responded with a sassy lilt, "Can we use a Dutch angle?"

Erin tugged on a curl hanging out of her beanie. "Shoot the footage and don't aggravate me."

At another dusty sewing table, Mercy unrolled a round, plastic pentagram. It was about the size of a large bath mat that two people might uncomfortably stand on. She spread it out, comparing the mat markings to a diagram of Levi's Tetragrammaton Pentagram. Mercy carefully ensured all symbols were present and in the right positions. She fretted about her dark plum PT Cruiser, parked outside in the paper-strewn parking lot, as a female hand rubbed between her shoulders.

"So, Cuz, how's the mat shape up?"

"So far, everything's looking correct and in the right spot. Could we not have found a place without working indoor plumbing?"

"I wanted urban and edgy. With music, sound effects, and voice over, it'll look super hot; like it's an ancient secret that must be carefully unveiled in secret to a select elite."

"These actually *are* ancient secrets."

"Make sure you use the mat."

"Pirandello's Aegis only protects against other formula."

"Yeah, but it looks hot. Oh, listen, I know you probably don't, but the money guy wanted me to ask if you have spells for falling in love, weight loss, or golf swings? He said any one of those are golden."

"Here's the menu: Pirandello, the Selective Inferno—

"—that's the fiery one, good—

"—and the Forge of Nin-Agal."

"Love the name."

"He was the Assyrian god of smiths."

"Of 'Smith?'"

"Like blacksmiths? That's the sealing one. By the way, I'm starving. Can we start now?"

Erin ignored the question and clapped her hands together. "Okay. Remember: you can't go too big. This is gonna be wicca without embarrassing nudity or poison ivy; perfect for the indoor enchantress. The journey is the destination.

If our buyers never seal a wastebasket, or light a scented candle, we say it's because they haven't fasted enough, or focused enough, or whatever. Then we upsell them. This could be a post-modernist cash machine."

"I'm already onboard, Erin. But listen: even though I fasted and all, this formula stuff is more of an art than a scientific law."

One of Erin's perfectly plucked eyebrows raised. "Performance anxiety?"

"Not exactly." Mercy struggled for the words. "You're using will and imagination and focus. Sometimes you get a little, sometimes a lot. I'm not experienced enough to tease out exactly the right amount. And when you're setting something on fire, that's a good thing to know."

"Merse, chill out. I've got wine coolers in the car."

"Not now. Later, hell yeah."

"You're going to be great." Erin inclined her beanie toward the squabbling Video and IT. "Afterwards, we'll ditch them and go to Cambridge. I know this excellent little place. We'll positively gorge on finger food and drink way too much. I'm buying."

"It's just that I don't know what I don't know."

"That sounds like a sports saying. Don't ever use it again. We're doing this. How about starting with the shield thing standing on the mat?"

"Pirandello's Aegis, on the pentagram, in Greek."

"Beautiful. Then we'll ease into the fiery one, then you can seal a 50-gallon steel drum."

"Wait a second, that's too much—"

But Erin was back among the techs, chiding them, overcoming objections, pushing the pale thin men to begin.

Mercy craved a cocktail.

A quarter hour later, Pirandello's Aegis wrapped and Mercy felt like an idiot. She performed the spell several times as the camera recorded her from different angles. Erin stood out of frame yelling, "bigger." Then Mercy moved aside while everyone reset for Selective Inferno. Finally, with the camera rolling, Mercy called out the Hebrew formula and ignited a cinderblock. A greenish flame scorched it black, but failed to reduce the block to embers—her intention. But no one else knew that, and they were impressed as hell.

"Wicked awesome," said Video.

Said IT, "She just torched the sucker."

Erin called, "You guys give me hand staging this drum."

Confident now, Mercy mentally rehearsed the Chaldean phrases for the Forge as Erin arranged a green 55-gallon drum with peeling paint. Mercy estimated she'd have to seal about two feet of metal. How long would it take? How long could she hold formula?

Video crouched behind his camera. "Cue the sorceress."

Erin led Mercy by the arm to her mark. "You're up again, Merse. You've been amazing. You're gonna nail this shot."

"I think the Forge was designed for sealing up dimensional openings and doors and gates. Maybe it's not a good one to teach indoor enchantresses."

"You're so sweet to say that. But I'll worry about marketing. And don't move a single inch from this spot."

Stomach growling, Mercy stood seven feet from the barrel. Throwing out her arms, she repeated the Chaldean words, focusing on one edge of the barrel, recalling how her brother Kevin once set a Tupperware dish on fire. In her imagination, she saw the plastic melting and curling. She grabbed for the day's negative emotions and fed them into her will, reaching out with her mind, sensing cold metal, willing it hotter, malleable.

An orange-reddish flash.

A strong odor of burning metal.

A plume of gray-black smoke, growing thicker.

"Holy shit, the hair on my arms stood up."

"Same here. Suh-weet."

Mercy released the spell.

Video held a tight shot on the smoldering lip of the barrel as IT played back downloaded footage for Erin.

Said Erin, "Again in slow motion."

Mercy joined her cousin, standing behind the IT as he reran the digital frames. Mercy observed the metal rim growing more flaccid, curling inward, fiery drops of molten orange dropped off into the barrel, igniting the trash below.

IT shook his head, "I just saw it and I don't believe it."

"Wicked awesome," said the Video. Brushing aside his bangs, he looked at Mercy. She saw surprise and, for an instant, fear. It delighted her no end.

"We are golden," said Erin, hugging Mercy.

Minutes later, wine cooler in hand, Mercy drank deep. She relaxed for the first time that day. IT and Video both found reasons to touch her arm and shoulder as they broke down equipment and loaded it into a RAV4. As the wine soaked her neurons, Mercy basked in the good feelings. If rats showed up, she'd set their filthy little rodent asses on fire.

In no time, Mercy's Cruiser hugged the back license plate of Erin's Volvo S40 as the two vehicles wheeled from the factory parking lot. Mercy turned on WFNX and sang along with Corn Whole's latest hit, "Abuse Me for Love." A wine cooler was parked on stand-by in her cup holder and the rolled-up, plastic Pentagram mat occupied the back seat. Mercy felt like hot shit.

Before long, the cousins were perched on stools in a Cambridge bar. Mercy chowed down on fried zucchini and bacon-wrapped hot dog bits, while drinking Champagne Sangrias, then Raspberry Martinis, then Pink Starburst Cocktails, courtesy of Erin, then some Brandeis associate professor of something. Erin's excitement was incandescent as she repeated how freaking impressed the IT and Video had been. "Knocked the 'jaded' right off 'em."

Mercy said, "You can tell me more things like that if you want."

Mercy's PT Cruiser didn't arrive home until early Saturday morning around 1:30 a.m. Leaving one tire up on the curb, she wobbled to the front door, fumbled with her keys, then stepped into the living room. A lamp still burned. In his leather chair, her father sat reading a Kindle. Stocky and balding with a fringe of grayish hair atop rough, weathered skin, Tim O'Connor wore a Boston Bruins jersey and sweat pants. As Mercy staggered past him toward the stairs, he put down his Kindle.

"S'up, Dad?"

"You drink too much."

He probably stayed up just to tell me that. Mercy clutched the banister tightly on her way up to her room. She really needed to get out of the house . . . again.

Armand Deale timed a putt beautifully.

He sent his ball through the windmill, past the spinning arms and onto the green where it gently bumped a concrete curb, rolling to a stop three inches from the cup. As his four companions watched, Deale raised the putter in triumph as if on the cusp of winning the Masters. Running a hand through longish wheat-colored hair, Deale turned to his four peers. "So how do we get the book and move Morgan out in less than two months?"

"Pull a fire alarm and when they evacuate, drop the book out a window," said the only woman in the group. Her tone was silky, aggressive. Ten years younger than Deale, the woman's coppery brown hair was pinned back from her face and neck, exposing smooth fleshy skin. Despite a Rubenesqe figure, she carried herself like a model, exuding femininity in yoga pants and a short-sleeved peach silk top that clung tightly to all the right curves. Whenever male eyes lingered upon her, the corners of Professor Audrey Klumm-Weebner's mouth rose in a little smile, similar to the one on a leaping dolphin tattooed on her right bicep. She gestured around the Arkham Fun Putt. "By the way, excellent spot for a strategy meeting. This place is so delightfully obtuse."

Audrey was almost divorced; he was separated. Deale wondered if he were reading too much into her little comments. Still, Audrey, or KW as she liked being called, had knowledge of Dunwich, and a scent that left Deale as flushed and confused as a teenage boy.

On the green, Deale tapped his yellow ball into the cup, then held up the golf ball as if acknowledging applause at Augusta. Putting from the tee, Audrey's lavender ball rolled slowly past the spinning arms, through the windmill, and onto the green where it barely missed the cup. All around the Arkham Fun Putt, families and couples enjoyed the warm Saturday afternoon as antique pop serenaded the golfers: Dave Clark Five, the Monkees, ELO with their signature string section playing "Strange Magic."

"Hey, I'm sinking a hole in one," said a young muscular man. He wore a funny Jon Stewart shirt, knee length shorts, and Saucony Triumph running shoes. On his right calf was a tattoo of a storm cloud and lightning. The young man pointed skyward with the handle of his putter. "Check out those big puffy clouds. Amazing."

"'Cumulus,'" said Audrey.

"'Cumulus,' yeah. Gotta download that," said Carter Fong, rocketing his ball toward the windmill. But with a sharp click, the blue ball struck one of the slowly spinning arms and rolled back.

Cursing, Fong stepped aside to allow a thin, intense man in his mid-fifties to occupy the tee. In a pink Lacoste shirt, gray suit slacks and thick-soled black shoes, the man sported stubbly red hair along thin, delicate arms, ending in fingers that seemed rodent-like in their furry dexterity. Leo Hameyes carried no putter. He crept forward from the tee as if sneaking back home late at night, bending low to roll his orange ball through the windmill opening. He gestured around at the crowd. "So much inappropriate laughter. I want to rush around and question them all."

"Chill out, Leo. Enjoy the weekend." A pudgy middle-aged man with gray-black hair in long braids adjusted a synthetic eagle feather in his hair. Dressed in a blue work shirt and relaxed-fit jeans, he sat cross-legged behind the tee. Reaching into a deerskin bag, the man pulled out a seven-inch buck knife and sliced himself a sliver of pemmican. Born Angelo Luigi Brancato to wealthy Italian-American parents in Philadelphia, he'd changed his name in 2000 to Angelo Silent Feather. From that point, his academic career took off. Chewing pemmican, Silent Feather gestured to Armand Deale with his knife. "Not to be a noodge, Armand, but how do we know this Leland Janus is really the book's owner? He might be trying to con a copy, to sell it. "

"He seemed genuine," said the university president. "Besides, it's insensitive and exclusionary to question the sincerity of an oppressed religious minority."

His colleagues nodded solemnly. Deale choose not to mention the gold coin, as it might cloud matters. Still, he had to admit, Janus had been right: Conrad Morgan had visited around lunchtime on Thursday, wishing a sullen Deale well. At the door of the room, the Antiquity Section chairman said some strange words in an indecipherable language. The next thing Deale knew, his legs unwrapped. Back to normal. Good as new. The medical staff was dumbfounded. They wanted to run more tests, but Deale checked himself out. And though troubled by the implications of wrapping/unwrapping, one needed to embrace life's many political and social contradictions. Once the book was returned, and the Antiquity Section dissolved, Deale need never trouble himself with anomalies like formula.

"Once the Antiquity Section bounces, who gets their space on the second floor?" asked Fong. "I nominate Critical Weather Studies."

Audrey said, "I claim the second floor for the Post-Structural Hierarchies Department."

Deale drew a deep breath. The way she'd said 'Post-Structural Hierarchies' had left him with a severe trouser disturbance.

"I think a contemporary modalities of oppression museum would fit in well," said Angelo.

"We need a large anti-inclusion pit," whispered Leo Hameyes. "And soundproofing."

Deale threw out his arms, "Does anyone NOT want the space?"

They all guffawed except for Leo Hameyes, who never laughed. Instead, he pressed his lips together, emitting an amused *mmmmmmmmmmm*.

Two more hard-hitting swats saw Carter Fong finally knock his ball past the windmill arms. Strolling along the little path to the green, he asked, "Hey, Armand, seriously, what happened to your legs? Did Morgan taze you or something?"

Deale smiled like a good sport taken in by a practical joke. "As I said, theatrics. They staged the whole thing: the breaking door glass, that O'Connor woman's injuries, the dark room, all the clunky magic props. They really got into my head, psyched me out."

"Enough to braid your legs," said Audrey. Was she being droll? Challenging him? He couldn't get a read, but Deale had been the subject of Audrey's attention all afternoon . . . and basked in it.

"Plus they had an African-American guard listening to country and western music. I mean, what's up with that?"

"Sounds like the guy is burning up in a weirdo fire," said Fong.

Armand watched Audrey, Carter and Leo putt out. Angelo rose, adjusting his deerskin bag. Still cutting pemmican slices, but not offering any, he joined the others as they trooped over to the

11th tee. There, Deale tapped his ball—but it struck a metal pole obstacle and bounced back. "By the way, have any of you ever been up to the Antiquity Section? In the hallway, they had an old-fashioned Coke machine that must weigh a ton. But it was bent in half, doubled over as if punched. Then further along, you saw this incredibly bold, retro drinking fountain made to appear melted. Very hip."

"Very Dali," said Audrey.

Leo tiptoed past the tee almost to the aluminum bend before releasing his ball. The orange golf ball clipped one of the pipes but angled into the green a yard from the cup. He was delighted and erupted in a robust *mmmmmmmmmmmm.*

"What's Dali?" asked Fong.

On the 16th hole, Deale was distracted by Audrey's cleavage and unable to knock his ball through the hippo's mouth. He took a six as Fong birdied. Audrey birdied. Leo eagled. Angelo reached into his deerskin bag, removed some provolone, and sliced off a chunk with his knife, remarking, "I'm going to suggest we remove Morgan using Mountain View State rules."

"We had five months to crack that old math department goon," said Fong.

"We've got a hard deadline. We need to up our ante," replied Deale.

Audrey said, "Sounds deliciously naughty. Tell me about Mountain View State rules."

Said Leo, "Pressure above from faculty, administrators and regents."

"Pressure from below from student demonstrators. My specialty," said Angelo.

"And a continuous attack on social media," said Carter. "My specialty. In fact, let me create a hashtag."

Leo crept around quietly, "Afterwards, Morgan will face diversity tribunal. In a soundproofed location."

At the 17th hole, Deale tapped his yellow ball, watching it hit an obstacle just hard enough to carom right, coming to a stop four inches from the cup.

Audrey hit next, her lavender ball coasting to a stop very close to Armand.

"Our balls are near," said Deale, then felt stupid and fifteen years old.

Audrey's mouth rose in her dolphin smile.

As the others putted or rolled, Audrey said, "Did Leland Janus specify the Dee *Necronomicon*?"

Deale blinked. "We have more than one?"

"There's the 17th century Latin translation, by Olaus Wormius. Then there's an incomplete English translation by John Dee. That's the one the authorities handed to old Armitage back in 1928."

"Morally disgusting," said Angelo. "It would be like someone giving away my ceremonial bat breasts."

Fong said, "Why would cops hand a Dunwich book to the university?"

Audrey continued, "A Dunwich religious figure, Wilbur Whateley, owned the Dee version. But he wanted to copy a passage from our Latin edition for sacred reasons. Henry Armitage denied his simple request out of spite. Somehow, Wilbur later became confused and wandered into the library at night. There, a guard dog attacked and killed him for no reason. Cops searched his Dunwich farm, found the books, and handed them over to Armitage."

"Which probably means this Janus is a Whateley relation," said Angelo.

Carter Fong and Leo Hameyes finished putting and rolling as Audrey continued, "Of course, Mr. Privileged Class Armitage set out to smear Wilbur Whateley."

Leo nodded, "Once again, confirming the scholarship of Paz Encanto."

Audrey continued, "Precisely. Armitage claimed Whateley's body was a freakish patchwork quilt of different species. Then, conveniently, this mutated body was said to have dissolved in front of Armitage and two of his crony academics."

"Rice and Morgan," said Angelo.

"Fortunate, wasn't it?" responded Deale. "A claim, but no proof."

In a knot, they walked slowly to the 18th tee as Audrey continued, "So our three reactionary professors then drove out to Dunwich and later said they fought off some ghost monster connected to Wilbur Whateley's faith."

"Dominant culture bastards," said Angelo. "Make up a story built around a nontraditional faith practiced by a shunned, voiceless people, then spend the next hundred years milking it for all it's worth."

"That's pretty much what I told Morgan," said Deale.

"Go ahead and finish, Audrey," said Fong.

"Take your time, Audrey," said Deale.

"Well, that's about it," she replied. "When we return a *Necronomicon*, it should be the John Dee version."

Angelo sipped from his creek water flask, "Audrey, in your Dunwich scholarship, have you ever learned why the Whateley family never filed suit for return of their property?"

"Been there, lost that," she responded. "Over the decades, Whateleys have sued in state and federal courts under the Religious Artifacts Act and the Non-Traditional Religious Freedoms Act and many other laws and statues. While it isn't their fault in the least, Whateley plaintiffs often appear misshapen, stink, and possess robust criminal records. Miskatonic University ends up looking like the only grown up in the room."

"I've got a sweet hashtag," said Fong, looking up in triumph from his smart phone. "#givebackthebook."

"Good," said Deale. "We'll start the campaign next week. I'll talk to Autumn Cryer. I think we need an article in the *Scholar* to kick things off. "

They paused outside the restrooms as Fong dashed inside.

"I understand that the eschatology of Dunwich is a response to oppression," said Leo. "But how did a non-traditional creed written by an Arab take root in North America centuries before diversity?"

Audrey gestured with her putter to Angelo. "When in doubt, ask a Native American."

As attention shifted to him, Angelo rushed to finish chewing his provolone. Mouth partially full, he said, "The *Necronomicon* and the Old One creed were established around Dunwich long before the caustic arrival of Europeans. However, instead of converting the Dunwich Pocumtuck Native Peoples to Christianity, certain English found themselves converting to the ancient faith of the Old Ones. Is it any wonder the other English suppressed them? For three hundred years, Dunwich has paid the price for being better salesmen."

On the 18th tee, Deale hit his ball underneath a menacing Tiki figure. The yellow ball bounced off the back wall of the green and rolled into the cup. Armand roared with laughter and accepted the congratulations of his peers, especially Audrey—whose touch lingered on his forearm.

"Wicked, Armand," said Fong, wiping his hands on his shorts. At the tee, he smacked his ball so hard it struck the Tiki and ricocheted back, almost hitting Angelo.

"Beautiful," snapped Silent Feather, "whack an Indian. He won't mind."

"Sorry," said a chastened Fong. "This putter is broken."

"Why don't you give me a blanket infected with small pox?"

"I said I was sorry."

"Make me walk to Oklahoma."

"Hey, I'm oppressed myself, so back off."

Positioning her lavender ball, Audrey raised her voice, overriding Angelo and Carter, "I'd love to have my graduate assistants interview some Dunwich women for a new paper I'm writing."

"What's the topic?" asked Leo.

"Gender stratification in underserved communities; specifically the only way a Dunwich woman can advance socially is by interbreeding with an Old One and producing a hybrid child like Wilbur Whateley."

Angelo asked, "Isn't Obed Whateley also a hybrid?"

"Just a warlock."

"Like Mr. Wizard?" said Deale.

"A religious title," said Audrey, "like 'rabbi' or 'minister.'"

Leo crept up to the Tiki and rolled his ball through. "The religious beliefs of Dunwich will fade once they have access to a living wage, light rail, and common sense anti-smoking programs."

"We should be the ones returning the *Necronomicon*," said Fong. "I mean, it's their book but we're gonna make them drive to Miskatonic to pick it up?"

"Janus seemed pretty eager," replied Deale. "He won't mind."

Audrey tapped in her ball and moved close to Deale as Carter Fong and Leo Hameyes struggled to find the cup. She brushed her hip against the president. "Carter's right. University representatives should restore the religious text. Morgan gives the book to us. We give the book to Dunwich. Better politics, don't you think?"

Deale almost blurted out a series of unique carnal requests, but instead said, "You're the hot new Dunwich scholar. You think that's the right play?"

Audrey lowered her voice. "I think you should give me the second floor of the undergraduate library."

As Fong and Leo finished putting, Deale's fingers pressed against Audrey's bra strap through the thin silk of her top. "You guys have convinced me. A socially vetted contingent from the university should return the book to Dunwich."

"Hey, score for my plan," said Fong, pumping his fist.

"I'm in," said Angelo Silent Feather. "As an oppressed person, I'll relate very well to the locals."

"They've got some crazy weather there," said Fong. "I'd love to see fat lightning from one of their thunder clouds."

"Thunderheads," said Angelo.

Leo added, "I must study their laughter which, no doubt, contains equal parts bitterness, frustration, and rage."

Deale said, "Excellent. Let's meet in in my office next week and coordinate our plans."

After several 'good-byes,' 'see-you-laters,' and a 'have a nice weekend,' Deale and Audrey found themselves alone in the parking lot, standing within each other's personal space.

Audrey smiled, "Perhaps if the second floor were assigned to someone, they could check out their new space, and scout out the security arrangements."

Deale felt lightheaded. "Future ownership has yet to be determined."

"Morgan won't let Leo into his section. Can you imagine Angelo or Carter being subtle? You should put your trust in Post-Structural Hierarchies."

Deale couldn't help himself and gasped at Audrey's pronunciation of impenetrable academic jargon.

"I'd better get home and change," whispered Audrey. "I have to be somewhere tonight."

Walking toward her electric blue Dodge Neon, Deale thrilled as their fingers intertwined.

The university president felt all control slipping away, "Audrey, I have a very unusual request: please say the name of your department."

In a husky voice, she breathed, "Post-Structural Hierarchies Department."

Deale blurted, "That was lovely."

Audrey knew what to do next. "Discursive construct is a form of mute facticity."

"My god."

"Reinscription accentuates anthropological cultural subversion."

"I've been thinking," said Deale, voice thick with need, "that the Post-Structural Hierarchies Department might nicely fill the second floor of the undergraduate library."

Her finger nails lightly scratched his palm, "How tragic that I have to be somewhere this evening. I can think of something else that needs filling."

Audrey slid behind the wheel and started her car. Pulling out, she rolled down the window and said, "Remember that attempting to disambiguate notions of identify is a matter of social subjectivity."

Deale watched the Dodge drive away, blood howling through his veins.

CHAPTER 4

STRATAGEM

"Not in the spaces we know, but between them, they walk serene and primal, undimensioned and to us unseen."
—*Abdul Alhazard*, the Necronomicon

In a good mood, pockets full of cash, Frye stopped at Golden Day Donuts in Lowell. From a middle-aged Cambodian cashier he bought a large coffee and four frosted cake doughnuts. As he saturated the coffee in sugar, he glanced above the counter and noticed a little structure high up near the ceiling. At first, he thought it was a birdhouse. But then he realized it looked like a little Buddhist temple, with lotus flower pillars in colors of light yellow and green.

Noting Frye's gaze, the cashier said, "That spirit house. Keep spirit happy."

Frye capped his coffee, grabbed the white bag of pastries, and headed for the door. "Ye know nothing of spirits."

On a dark side street, he ate his snack in his car, dirty fingers sticky with frosting and crumbs. Big screen TVs glowed within the houses, a Fed-Ex van drove slowly down the street, hunting an address. Frye left the radio on, enjoying WBUR and *All Things Considered*, relaxing to composer and trombonist Wycliffe Gordon's theme. Host Penn Feye introduced a humorous segment on Japanese humanoid robots, employed for the first time at a Los Angeles Social Security Office.

Sipping his coffee, Frye chuckled knowingly as correspondent Logan Gom said, "in addition to being lifelike and ethnically diverse, these humanoids are capable of standing behind a counter for minutes without acknowledging the next person in line. In addition, several models have been engineered to rest a hand on one hip, or appear to be viewing smart phones."

The smart phones he'd sold tonight had earned Frye almost a thousand dollars, but spying on Morgan was a money suck. Using his own car to avoid complications, Frye reflected that no one—not the Little Man, Chester, or Malachi—had offered to pay him for gas as he drove between Dunwich and Arkham and around the Boston area, following Morgan to his sons' sporting events, as well as 5K and 10K races. Still, shadowing Morgan had proved easier than Frye imagined: whatever the man possessed in formula, he forfeited in street smarts. Frye nonetheless exercised caution; he had no desire to alarm an Antiquity Section mage. He recoiled at the thought of the full Translucent Python, his entire body twisted tightly like a damp rag.

What happened to Morgan must seem an accident.

Today was Wednesday, and Frye hadn't heard back from his nephew. At fifteen, the boy had three arrests for burglary, possession of stolen property, and identify theft—a good lad, cagey with the Web. Sipping his coffee, Frye started up the rust-streaked Toyota and drove a short distance to Chelmsford.

At a Walmart, Frye bought a candy bar—and a disposable phone. He got back into his car and drove to the rear of the huge parking lot, passing a silent Winnebago. There he cut his lights and coasted into an unlit patch of asphalt. Turning off the engine, Frye drank the rest of his coffee. As he scraped up the extra sugar from the Styrofoam cup bottom, he listened to Nina Totenberg's opinion on an upcoming Supreme Court case that addressed the civil rights of four chimpanzees and a plastic blow-up sex doll.

A moment later, he called a number in Athol that was answered by a teenage boy.

"Score, Uncle Jasper. I went back like forty something years. If you total 'em all up, it's $268,000."

"Generous enough. Tell me, has Morgan any races next weekend?"

"Hang on." Keystrokes. "Yeah. A 10K up in Newburyport."

"Remember, our business is between you and I alone. And look for an envelope in your mail drop tomorrow."

"Thanks, Uncle Jasper. Any time."

Yawning, Frye left the parking lot, heading west. Over the decades, Whateley had amassed over a quarter million dollars in private rewards for his arrest and conviction. But that ruled out notifying the cops. With his criminal record, Frye could easily be pressured into renouncing all claims on the reward money. And trust the cops to botch the whole matter, letting Whateley escape, knowing who had ratted him out. Frye shuddered.

Which left the Antiquity Section.

Morgan seemed savvy and might drive a hard bargain. But this girl, O'Connor . . . according to the Little Man she was simple, a sot. Manipulating her, Frye might claim over half the rewards. Maybe all. Morgan would be poisoned by next week. After that, Frey could devote time to O'Connor, guiding her to direct the police to the right spot at the right time.

Deep in thought, he passed through Dean's Corners, on his way into a lonely, despised country.

The following morning, in the Miskatonic University Administration Building, second floor, Office of the President, coffee cups and spoons clinked as the meeting got underway. Seated in an ergonomically fitted, executive work chair with deep eggplant cushions, Armand Deale slapped the padded arms. "Where is Leo?"

"Enlightening a student," said Carter Fong, gesturing out the window.

Deale rolled his chair over. Down below in the quad, Leo Hameyes confronted a freshman. From this distance, he appeared to be making the young woman laugh multiple times, long and short, loud and soft. At last, the woman burst into tears and covered her face.

"What about KW?" said Fong.

"Undercover," said Deale. He gestured across the quad to the second story of the library. "She'll be scouting out the Antiquity Section this morning. In the meantime, I want to hear your progress. Also, Leland Janus will be calling today. I want to introduce you as the group that will be returning his book. Angelo, start us off."

"Our activists have registered with Student Life," said Angelo Silent Feather. Seated cross-legged on the mulberry cut pile carpet, he reached into his deerskin bag and pulled out a flask of creek water. "They're called Students for the Liberation of Underserved Groups, or SLUG. Juniors Honna Pegler and Barry Gristleman will be the public face of the group. I'll be faculty advisor."

"Good. Get with Autumn Cryer and work out a press release. We'll run it as a story in the

Scholar. And coordinate with Carter so the social media kicks off at the same time."

"Not to be a noodge, but shouldn't our students be the ones returning the book?"

"Excellent point, as always, Angelo. Let's say Honna and Barry will officially return the book. The rest of you will accompany them to Dunwich as advisors. Professor Fong, you have the floor."

Fong reclined on an ivory Aristocrat classic sofa with ruffling, buttons and tufting. "Now that Angelo's group has a name, we'll set up a web page, and launch accounts on Facebook, Twitter, Snapchat, Glee Puss, Gabby Face, Have You Seen My Lunch Pictures?, all the top sites. Do we have a start date?"

"Let's say the Tuesday after next, the third week of September. That gives us all next week, plus the following Monday to synch up. I've already talked to several sympathetic board members. I'd say we're on track."

Leo hurried in, crossing to the coffee.

"Very chilly today."

"That's because some other clouds and wind showed up," said Fong.

"Low pressure front," said Silent Feather.

Fong added, "Then the cold air rises."

"Sinks," said Deale. "Cold air is heavier. So, Leo, keeping the campus safe from inappropriate laughter?"

"All laughter really," said Leo. "And isn't that the safest way to prevent wounding? *Mmmmmmmmm*."

As Angelo and Carter brought Leo up to speed, Deale let his eyes drift across framed photos and awards covering one wall and half of another. They were testimonials to the drive of Armand Deale. *This is what a visionary's office looks like.* Corporate PR photos captured Deale shaking hands with Larry Ellison, CEO of Oracle, and Google Co-Founder Sergey Brin. There were honorary academic awards from San Francisco State and Stanford, along with staged political grip-and-grins with former Governor Jerry Brown and former Senator Barbara Boxer. Ranks of charitable awards, academic awards, citizenship awards, environmental awards were arranged around a photo of Armand Deale in hiking shorts and boots, planting a tree in the Santa Cruz Mountains, face solemn with awe and reverence. The newest wall photo featured Armand Deale at a fundraiser, shaking hands with Brie Spine, Mayor of Arkham.

And plenty of wall space remained.

Leo Hameyes joined Carter Fong on the couch. "I've already begun the paperwork for diversity tribunal proceedings against Morgan. Once his section closes, he'll be like a lobster without a shell."

Near the wet bar, not far from the entrance to Deale's private bathroom, stood the future of Miskatonic. A 3D plastic model of the Master Plan spread out across four feet of table. Deale's farsightedness addressed the most important aspects of modern education: students would enjoy three rock climbing walls and an STD clinic. A growing body of part-time faculty could relax in their own lounge: a pre-fab aluminum shed with a lunch cart outside. Towering over all would be the new administration building. Every lush office would house bold, far-seeing administrators with long, sexy titles, big staffs, six-figure salaries, reserved parking, gym membership, bonuses, and access to the administrator wine bar. Their rulings and policy would shape the world in which students lived, the way an aquarium defines the limits of Angelfish, preparing them for post-college life in America.

And the basement would belong to Dr. Leo Hameyes and his soundproofed anti-inclusion pit.

Phone for Deale. Gleason Fundament.

"In a meeting now, Gleas."

The high-pitched voice of the university legal counsel went up a notch. "Just wanted to check on something. This Dunwich person you've been talking to is definitely not Obed Whateley, correct?"

"He said he was Leland Janus."

"Good. Obed Whateley has an extensive state and Federal rap sheet. You don't want anything to do with him."

"He's an activist, Gleas. Disorderly conduct? Failure to obey a police order? We've all got those."

"Let me finish. Obed Whateley's record goes back decades, and includes murder, attempted murder, suspicion of mass murder, multiple charges of kidnapping, mutilation, aggravated torture, and eating a police dog."

"He ate a police dog more than once? Must be an acquired taste. Listen, this can't be Janus. My guy is some little old duffer, probably close to 80."

"Same age as Whateley."

"Seriously, Gleas, how do we square reconciling with the Dunwich community, then calling their representative a murderer? I'll handle this."

Back at his champagne colored executive desk with its glass top, Deale hung up his desk phone.

"Anything?" asked Fong.

"Legal with legal worries. We're fine."

Intercom. A young female voice: "President Deale, Mr. Janus is on line two."

Deale put the call on speakerphone. "Mr. Janus, great to hear from you. You'll be delighted to know we're all pistons firing when it comes to returning your book."

"Look ye here, Deale, there's more."

Deale said, "We understand you want back the Dee version of the *Necroctagon*."

"*Necronomicon*, ye steam wit. But more is needed. Ye must include a copy of page —"

Deale heard nothing beyond 'steam wit' and fought to keep from snapping. Angelo noticed the university president grinding his teeth and jumped in. "Mr. Janus, I am Professor Angelo Silent Feather. As a Native American and victim of oppression, I know the urgency you feel for justice. We're all working to the same end."

"Ye are Mohawk?"

"Nipmuc. Hundreds of years ago, my people lived alongside the Native Americans who worshipped your creed."

"Our Pocumtucks would have drug ye blubbering for mercy to the nearest stone circle. Ye would have perished emptying your lungs in terror to the sky."

A long strained silence followed.

Carter Fong said, "What a colorful, metaphorical way of speaking."

Tension broke, and everyone but Deale smiled and nodded.

Janus said, "Who are ye?"

"Professor Carter Fong. I head Critical Weather Studies."

"Fong? Mind your own affairs, Chinaman. I need no shirts pressed."

A much longer, strained silence followed.

Deale carefully said, "Mr. Janus, please, we understand the strain you've been under from an uncaring society, but as a point of etiquette . . . . "

"Ye do nothing, Deale, and ye do it well. More is required to summon The Opener of the Way. All must be in readiness by Hallow Mass eve."

"That's October 30. You're changing the terms of our agreement."

"Ye gab like a woman. Fetch me the Dee version and the page from Wormius that I requested. And ye shall have what was agreed upon."

Janus hung up.

Silence. Outside Deale's office, a woman laughed, a keyboard clacked under rapid typing, a copy machine beeped for more paper. Inside, three pairs of eyes settled upon Armand Deale.

"I think a lot of that was oppression talking," said Fong.

"His religious beliefs, the core of his life, have been spat upon by the dominant culture," said Angelo Silent Feather.

Added Leo, "His voice contained a large measure of contempt, leavened with, what I can only call, genuine menace."

"Certainly colorful," said Deale, instead of his first word choice: '*pissy little asshole.*'

"Not to be a noodge, but what agreement was he mentioning?"

Deale thought rapidly. "He would receive back his book, then allow us to photograph his ceremony."

Deale put on a good face as the meeting broke up. Hameyes, Fong, and Silent Feather congratulated him for his sensitivity in asking permission to film the religious ceremony. Deale reminded the three men to RSVP for the party at his house the following weekend. Alone, he stood at the window, staring across the way at the Antiquity Center. O'Connor appeared to be moving around, talking to someone. Audrey? He needed to speak with Audrey about Janus, as well as communicate a number of robust carnal needs.

What was the stupid page number again?

Across the quad in the Antiquity Section Mercy crossed to her desk, set aside a Dunkin Donuts cup and rechecked the day's printout. Doctor Chatterjee was driving up from New Haven to study fragments of *The Book of Eibon*. Professor Klumm-Weebner would be here shortly to examine the Dee *Necronomicon*. Quite the stranger to Special Collections, yet she'd written a big deal book on Dunwich and loved to snark the section. This would be interesting.

Mercy buzzed Morgan. "Did you know Klumm-Weebner has reserved Dee for this morning?"

"No, fascinating. Her grad assistants did all the heavy lifting for her last book. Stay alert. Something may be up. Oh, and today we begin your mastery of Selective Inferno, so sharpen up your Hebrew."

"No lunch again?"

"A late lunch. Did you call Environmental Services about my office window?"

"Yeah. That jerk, Barney Reznicek, said they had to order pebbled glass. How come you don't have interns to make calls and coffee and otherwise be helpful?"

"Would you intern here?"

"Good point."

Hanging up, Mercy listened to the rattle of pages as a balding, jowly professor studied *Unausprechlichen Kulten* by Friedrich von Junzt. She fought back a temptation to call Erin and wheedle more compliments about her formula, or ask whether the Money Guy absolutely loved the digital video. Almost a week and no word. Mercy couldn't stand much more of Morgan's training, fasting, living at home, and owing $40k for an English degree. She was amped up for major life changes.

Twisting her hair with one hand, Mercy wrapped it with a scrunchi. Opening a far right hand desk drawer, she removed a key ring with a large and small key. The ring was attached to an old braided leather key fob. Mercy felt slightly unsettled: hadn't Galen Rice also crafted key fobs?

Turning, Mercy stood at the special collection cage. Using the large key, she opened a two-sided Schlage lock on the wire door. Once inside the cage, Mercy followed procedure and relocked the door behind her. Pushing a miniature shopping cart, she scanned the shelves, locating the *Book of Eibon* near the *Eltdown Shards* and the *Pnakotic Manuscripts*. Setting *Eibon* down inside the cart, Mercy choose the small key on the braided leather fob. Key in hand, she pushed the cart along to a locked glass case containing two books. Lying side-by-side were the crown jewels of the Special Collection. Mercy knew their lineage well, rehearsing it in case Klumm-Weebner had questions.

Written by a mad Arab poet, Abdul Alhazred, the book(s) were his legacy. He had lived for a decade in the vast deserts of Arabia—*the Roba El Khaliyeh*, a mysterious realm where few ventured. The "empty space" was a legendary home to protective evil spirits and monsters. Alhazred claimed to have seen the fantastic City of Pillars, and to have explored the ruins of a nameless town. Within the antediluvian rubble, Alhazred unearthed evidence of a terrible race, malignant, hostile, older than mankind. In 730 C.E., the poet moved to Damascus, writing of what he found in the sand, and calling his manuscript *Al-Azif.* A jack Muslim at best, Alhazred's insanity was confirmed after he admitted worshipping heterodox entities called Cthulhu and Yog-Sothoth. In 738 C.E., Alhazred died or disappeared—accounts vary—with one version describing him being devoured by an invisible monster in a Damascus street before panic-stricken onlookers.

Mercy selected one of the books, placing it in the cart. She relocked the glass case and rolled the cart toward the door.

A few hundred years later, Theodorus Philetas of Constantinople acquired a copy of *Al Azif,* translating it from Arab into Greek. He renamed the book the *Necronomicon*. In 1228, Olaus Wormius transcribed Philetas' Greek into Latin. Shortly after, Pope Gregory IX banned both Greek and Latin *Necronomicons*. For possessing one, you and your copy would be burned alive. In the 16th century, English court astrologer and mathematician John Dee translated a Latin version into English. But it was fragmentary and incomplete. One such Dee document was found in the effects of Dunwich warlock Wilbur Whateley. Puzzled authorities presented it to Henry Armitage in 1928. The Dee version joined Miskatonic University's own, more complete *Necronomicon*, a Wormius edition from 16th century Spain.

Mercy pushed the Dee version in her cart. Not many scholars asked for a *Necronomicon*. And no one from Dunwich had tried stealing the books since she was in second or third grade. Maybe it was just a book. That was the rational view, and Mercy considered herself a rational woman with a great deal of expensive rational education.

And yet she disliked touching it.

Bound with a thick buckle, the *Necronomicon* <u>felt</u> disturbing, as if a befouling corruption dripped from the pages, burrowing into her pores. To clutch the *Necronomicon* was like gripping a plump five-pound sewer rat with fleas hopping from its dank fur onto your arm. That wasn't rational. But it was accurate.

Lifting the books from the cart, Mercy held them against her chest, unlocking, then locking the special collections door case. Mercy's desk phone rang. Rushing over, she set down the books and picked up.

Joe Bong said, "Klumm-Weebner is here. She is not to be trusted."

Mercy sighed. "Is she standing right in front of you?"

"Yes."

"Stop being subtle."

A moment later, Audrey Klumm-Weebner sailed into special collections, looking fresh and well-coordinated. Mercy envied her bright autumn scarf. On KW's right arm, extending out from her shell, Mercy spotted a leaping dolphin tattoo. Approaching the desk, Audrey signed in on the clipboard, saying, "Well, you're certainly security conscious around here. Are you one who buzzed me in?"

"No. The guard does that from his desk."

"Then he checks my I.D., says I'm untrustworthy, and directs me here where I sign in again?"

"We do love our protocol. And please excuse Joe. When he arrived from Africa, the airlines misplaced his manners."

Audrey smiled, "And he listens to country music? Fascinating."

"Garth Brooks is very big in Natal."

Eying the wire door, Audrey asked, "And is that the Special Collections area?"

"Yes. Always locked." Mercy tinkled the keys, then placed them back in the far right hand drawer.

Audrey glanced over at the balding, jowly professor, then lowered her voice, "Don't you ever have to pee? If I were shut in this room, I'd have to go all the time."

Mercy rolled her eyes in mock dismay. "I've been thinking of keeping a coffee can back here."

To Mercy's surprise, they laughed quietly together. She'd been prepared to dislike Klumm-Weebner. The woman's friendly, confident manner threw Mercy off-guard. Nevertheless, Klumm-Weebner did have an annoying habit of peering around the room like an owner appraising a newly purchased property.

Mercy gestured to the thick, buckled book on the desk. "On our website, you reserved the *Necronomicon*." Mercy decided to see probe Audrey's openness. "I guess you've handled it before, given your book on North-Central Massachusetts."

Audrey placed both hands in front of her mouth. "Busted. I had a part-time assistant professor and two grad students do all my research. But I'm starting a new paper about the women of Dunwich and, this time, I'm determined to do my own research—or, at least, make a good attempt."

That was a pretty disarming. Mercy rattled off her standard newbie speech. "As you may have gathered, there are a few rules. If you like, you can leave your bag in the coatroom back near the door. And please silence your cell phone. No photos or selfies with the edition. I'll give you a sheet of rice paper in case you want to follow along with the text. So pop into a seat, and I'll bring you the book."

Leaving her purse in the coat room, Audrey sat in a dark, padded oak chair behind a walnut desk with a green glass banker's lamp. On the desk, Mercy placed a wooden reading cradle. Then she set the *Necronomicon* in the cradle, undid the buckle and laid out a sheet of rice paper. "So, in case you haven't heard enough rules: no microfilms, scans, copies, photos. When you turn pages, use your thumb and forefinger. Also, no food or drink."

"Oh, darn," said Audrey. "I have a pot roast in my purse."

Mercy laughed. "Great. I'm starving. Oh, and please don't touch any illustrations. I'll give you scratch paper for notes, but only write in pencil. No ink."

"So this is it," said Audrey. She gently touched a page. "So much terrible tragedy, so little understanding. Have you ever been to Dunwich?"

Mercy recalled a wild drive in a car full of laughing teenagers and a staggering amount of pot smoke. "Once, long ago." Mercy decided to probe again. "You must have spent time there when you researched your paper."

"Embarrassed again. I never set foot in the place. But, full disclosure: I did watch every episode of *Mysterious Dunwich*."

Double disarm. Mercy decided to like Audrey. "I loved *Mysterious Dunwich*. Christopher Walken was so adorable."

"He was the shit."

For a few minutes they chatted quietly about the show. Premièring on cable in 1999, *Mysterious Dunwich* had purported to explore the horrors, disappearances, legends, murders, and creepy lore surrounding the olfactory-challenged village in the Upper Miskatonic Valley. Actor Christopher Walken worked hard to make it all scary, but he was hampered by a lack of visual material. A handful of media were used over and over, including newspaper articles about the 1928 Horror, black and white TV footage from the Elaine Milano kidnapping that triggered the 1956 Horror, a tape recording of police interviewing the only survivor of the 1973 Funwich Commune, 1980 video footage of a trailer court where 22 people vanished, Beta Cam aerial shots of Sentinel Hill where the TV crew was vaporized in 1986, and amateur 16mm film footage of the Massachusetts State Police blocking the road to the Big Luck Casino as the 1991 Horror unfolded.

Mostly the low-budget production leaned heavily on old letters, artist renditions and popular true crime books such as *Dunwich Devils and Death*. But for most viewers, the show's main attraction was Walken's charming attempts to sell even the trite and banal as ominous and spooky. Despite production values so bad they were good, the show lasted two seasons.

Audrey said, "Wasn't Professor Morgan the chairman back then? He's not even mentioned."

"He said that the producers were pissed because he and Uncle Louis and the other families wouldn't cooperate. So they downplayed the Antiquity Section. Still, it was pretty funny."

"Oh, my God, yes."

Mercy gestured toward the *Necronomicon*, "Whenever you're finished, leave the book on the table. I'll put it back. And, if you would, please, sign out on the clipboard. The washroom is down the hall to your left. There's a drinking fountain near by, but it's a little twitchy. Any questions, I'll be right up at my desk."

Audrey beamed, "This has been wonderful, talking to you."

"By the way, love your ink."

"That's so sweet."

After the balding jowly professor signed out, Mercy returned his book to the cage. She failed to note Audrey watching as Mercy removed the key from the far right-hand desk drawer, opened Special Collections, locked the door behind her, returned Von Junzt to his proper place, unlocked and locked the cage door, and dropped the braided fob back in her desk.

At one point, Audrey strolled over to the windows.

"These are old school."

"Pretty old. Originals, I think."

"No screen or anything. Do they open?"

"Yeah, just push on the bottom. But why open windows when you've got climate control?"

Audrey shrugged, "A breeze might be pleasant."

Returning to the text, Audrey took some notes as Mercy emailed a request to the Harvard Library to borrow a book for Professor Morgan. Back in the day, her parents absolutely forbid her ever going to Dunwich. That guaranteed a visit. With her brother Kevin driving, she had set out with him, Erin, and a guy Erin lusted after. When they'd passed the turnoff where Uncle Louis and Galen Rice traveled to their fate in 1991, Mercy remembered laughing loudly, drawing deeply on the bong. It distracted her from the disturbing round hills that grinned down at them like lunatic faces in an attic window. At one point, Kevin wheeled down a side road, parking near a barren, rocky patch of dirt called the Devil's Hop Yard. Mercy recalled that her maternal grandfather had died there as acolyte to Julian Rice. During a wild magic brawl, several participants, Thomas Armitage among them, vanished at the height of a violent storm that produced massive hailstones.

In the pot-fogged car, on a pleasant spring day, Mercy couldn't help feeling uneasy. As Kevin finally drove off toward the rank village of Dunwich, she wondered what had bothered her. Ghosts? A premonition? Maybe the Devil's Hop Yard was what her grandfather had instead of a cemetery. Finally departing Dunwich that long ago day, Mercy remembered feeling giddy, delighted to escape the sensation that someone— something—malefic watched you always: scheming, calculating, poised to spring on your back like a starving panther. Kevin drove the long way home to Arkham, and no one complained.

Mercy shuffled some papers so it wouldn't be too obvious she was mentally drifting. Of course, the Devil's Hop Yard reminded her of Fomble's book. A few years before her Dunwich trip, Mercy had read *Dunwich, Devils and Death*. She and Erin had phoned each other, reading aloud passages that mentioned Thomas Armitage. But in Fomble's narrative, Mercy's grandfather didn't exactly over perform. In fact, the author indicated that Armitage was a playboy who talked a good game, but cracked in the face of danger during the 1956 clash.

Of the Rice, Morgan and Armitage families, a quarter of the members disliked the Antiquity Section, half could have cared less, and another quarter kept the Antiquity Section afloat, especially the Rices, who'd paid heavily in blood. Mercy's mother was a committed disliker. Asking her to clarify Fomble had been a huge mistake.

'Don't read that muck. It's like eating something you find on the ground in a zoo. Old Francis Morgan

wouldn't even speak with Fomble, that muck peddler. Your grandfather died gallantly, fighting gangsters.'

'Did Francis Morgan say that?'

'How would he know? He managed to get conveniently shot and miss the showdown.'

'How do you get shot conveniently?'

'Ask Francis Morgan.'

'He's dead now.'

'Convenient, isn't it?'

'But why would Aquarius Fomble write something that wasn't true?'

'Money. Don't you know anything yet?'

'But they weren't fighting gangsters. They were chasing warlock Sirac Bishop and Obed Whateley —'

'—who were kidnappers, which means they were gangsters. Go to your room.'

'But I didn't do anything.'

'Go to your room at once.'

'But I have soccer practice.'

'When you come home, go to your room.'

Audrey Klumm-Weebner smiled down at Mercy as she signed out. "All finished."

"Oh, uh, great talking to you. Come back again."

"I will. And thanks, Mercy, for making me feel at home."

CHAPTER 5

FACES OF FRUSTRATION

Mid-September blog post from Birds of the Northeast, *by Emily Stoatman:*

"More notes on the Eastern Whippoorwill or Caprimulgus vociferous. *From the family of Nightjars, these robin-sized friends are a leaf-brown with a black throat. Nocturnal, they generate a noisy, rhythmic whip-poor-will that is repeated over and over. Found in dry, open woodlands and canyons, the Eastern Whippoorwill — much like my husband — sleeps by day, nesting among dead leaves. (We've touched on Mr. Stoatman's alcoholism in other posts.) See a whippoorwill in your car headlight, and its eyes will reflect red. Perhaps that is why these lovely night birds were once associated with witchcraft. Whippoorwills feed on insects and will swarm around livestock, leading to the belief that they sucked dry the udders of goats. (Hence their name from the Latin* capri and mulgus, *or "goat-milker." Ugh. I hope not. :D)*

"In legend, the Eastern Whippoorwill has been labeled a psychopomp. Traditionally, psychopomps (from the Greek psyche and pompos, *breath or soul and guide), were thought to be non-judgemental, compassionate entities who ushered the dying into the afterlife. However in North-Central Massachusetts, psychopomps — our whippoorwills — have a scary reputation. They synch up their cries to one's dying breath, waiting patiently to grab one's soul upon expiration. If successful, the whippoorwills erupt in a diabolical cackling that lasts until dawn. Should they*

miss a quarry their normal night cries sadly trail off, much like my children's attention when chores are announced.

"Not surprisingly, these fables are most common around Dunwich, where whippoorwills have been reported this year in record numbers. Whatever else may be said of Dunwich, whippoorwills embrace its rounded hills and deep ravines, forest, fields and copses, often lingering there long after migration has emptied the rest of the region."

As the Little Man lavished praise on Chester Sawyer, Frye and Hutchins exchanged dour glances. Around them in the woods, the whippoorwills shrieked and the bullfrogs belched out their Monday night chorus from the nearby river. As the stars rose above, a young prisoner kneeling between Frye and Hutchins commenced to shake like a dog passing a coconut.

Said Whateley, "Aye, Chester, ye used his love of running against him. Now Morgan is infected. Within the week, he will be shackled within his own body, a slug waiting for the boot that will crush it flat."

"I tried to think as ye might think," said Sawyer.

Hutchins whispered to Frye, "Your plan and our risk. But ye wouldn't know it from this jabbering woodchuck."

Emptying another sugar packet, Frye said, "He should have multiple lips instead of tentacles. Then he could suck rump without rest until the Great Return."

Busy snarking on Sawyer, their attention strayed. Before they could react, up jumped the kneeling man. He bolted for the river.

Hutchins produced a semi-automatic pistol and fired three times. *Bap-babbap!* One round punctured the running man's greasy coveralls, striking him in the right calf. Grabbing at the wound, he toppled into the grass and tried crawling off.

Chester turned to Frye and Hutchins, "Ye addled geese. Be more watchful."

Biting back a sharp remark, Frye, with help from Hutchins, stood up the wounded prisoner. The gunshot man tottered on his one good leg. Whateley approached. Chester scooted up behind the Little Man, a tentacle poking from his shirt as if anxious to observe events.

The wounded prisoner said, "Obed, by the roiling face of Cthulhu, I told them nothing."

Sawyer did the talking, "Ye had the Sienna to dismantle, but drove it to Boston, bought crystal meth, and were apprehended."

"I said not a word."

Sawyer continued, "How is it that, with your past deeds, ye were released anon?"

"I was in jail all night."

"Others say ye swapped knowledge of our sacrifices for a quick discharge."

"I said not—who told you such a thing? My sister-in-law? She is a liar and a turnip-eating whore who would dally Those From the Air, if possible."

In his reedy voice, Whateley said, "What think ye, Chester?"

"The Indescribable Inversion."

"Too quick for a chatterbox. The Skull of Atlas."

The prisoner cried out, "Obed, please, no, by the Thousand Young of Shub-Niggurath."

"Foul snitch," snarled Frye, and kicked at the man.

As Whateley threw up both arms, crying out in Medieval Latin, Frye felt the hair on his neck rise. In the light of a waxing crescent moon, the wounded man shrieked in terror as his head began to grow. First it swelled to the size of an exercise ball, then ballooned to the circumference of a college football mascot head. Palms under his chin, straining to keep the weight of a massive cranium from snapping his neck, the prisoner hopped to a tree and thrust his chin atop a branch the thickness of a man's leg. There his head expanded yet more, snapping branches above, finally stabilizing at the height and width of a Smart Car.

Chester Sawyer giggled. Frye blocked a snort. Hutchins covered his mouth and looked away. Whateley laughed and the others followed in his wake. Frye had to admit: A human Bobble Head was indeed a risible sight. With the branch under his chin crackling, the wounded man blinked big eyes in desperate fright as Frye and company walked from the stand of trees into a field of waist high grass. Around them the piping of the whippoorwills changed, slowed, seemed to find a new erratic rhythm. Less than a minute later, a thick branch broke behind them with a loud *Kraaaack!* followed by a softer dry pop.

The whippoorwills erupted in a cacophonous gale so loud all conversation ceased. The four men exited the grass onto an unpaved dirt road, lit by starlight. In the distance, across the Miskatonic to the northwest, lights still burned at Osborn's store and Ye Great Olde Inn. Walking with Hutchins, Frye considered his own recent intrigues. Discretion was vital.

Ahead of him, Whateley murmured something to Chester Sawyer, who turned to Frye and Hutchins, "As the Great Return nears, Obed and I have need of younger, more innocent sacrifices. Their unsullied life force is most vital for our formulae. Botch it not. And Frye, henceforth ye dispose of all vehicles."

Frye nodded. In the poor light, Sawyer could not see his jaw muscles tighten. *More risk, no compensation.* Jasper Frye again thought of the O'Connor girl at the Antiquity Section. Whatever arrangements they might make must now include the removal of Chester Sawyer.

Two days later on a Wednesday morning, Mercy blocked a yawn at her Special Collections desk. Her eyes felt scratchy. She'd rub them but didn't want to smear her mascara. Last night had turned excessively festive. While out clubbing with Erin Doucette, she'd heard that Money Guy was ecstatic over the video they'd shot in the old factory. He wanted Mercy, Erin, IT, and Video to sign non-disclosure agreements. But Erin refused, insisting the agreement be sweetened with an advance. Money Guy had the next move. *Gutsy call.* Mercy would've just signed.

At Chez Bazaar in Kingsport, Mercy swigged Poinsettias—like a mimosa but with cranberry juice—served by the yummy bartender. On his break, they'd made out in the back room. With curly hair and fascinating lips, the bartender told Mercy he desperately wanted sex with her tonight after his shift. But then he added that they shouldn't ever date, since dating was hypocritical and sexist.

(*"So we can have sex, but you can't take me out?"*

"I respect you too much.")

Defenses down, her libido inching into the red, Mercy had almost agreed. But when the bartender returned to work, she made Erin drive them to another bar. Erin was blasé about the bartender's stance.

("I'd do him. When did you turn so picky?"

"I liked it better when guys spent money on you, then lied.")

At Klunkheimers, Mercy got hammered, yelling over the band that everyone should fly to Crete and party.

She'd come home late to her father once again waiting in his chair.

("Is this what you want to do with your life?"

"Actually, I wanted to go to Italy. Remember?")

Last night's brief exchange with her dad kicked Mercy down the slide into a murky pool of tainted memories. Sitting at her Special Collections desk, she exhumed her resentment-rich past, recalling high school soccer days. Back then, Mercy had been a terror, wracking up trophies and awards. While she had talent, her parents were relentless in pushing her to achieve more. Nothing was ever good enough. And so, over time, her athletic interest waned. Mercy made plans with a girlfriend to spend a summer in Italy. At lunch, they'd chat about hostels and other inexpensive places to stay, shopping in Rome on the Via Condotti, meeting guys on the Spanish Steps. It would be fantastic. Mercy recalled Thanksgiving dinner of her junior year. With high school playoffs over, she'd announced: *"I'm not playing club soccer this year. I'm absolutely soccered out. I want a job after school."*

Dad: *"Are you crazy? You've got talent. Don't piss it away."*

Mom: *"Language, Tim."*

Dad: *"We're not the Doucettes. We don't have a money tree growing around this place."*

Mercy: *"But I want to save money. Courtney and I are going to Italy after graduation. Remember? We talked about it."*

Mom: "But, Sweetheart, when you first mentioned that we thought you had a fever. Europe's not going anywhere. Think how much happier you'll be with a scholarship. You just need to try harder."

Mercy: "I can go to college later. What's wrong with Miskatonic? You told me I'd hardly pay a thing because Grandpa Thomas and all our relatives were big shots."

Mom: "He died gallantly fighting gangsters. I don't care what kind of muck you read."

Dad: "You want to see Italians? I'll take you to work with me. You can see some Italians. You'll be grateful for college."

Mercy: "All I've done for the last eight years is play soccer—club soccer, soccer camp, cross training for soccer season, league games, league championship, Northeast tournament games. I feel like an unpaid center midfielder. I want to do something else."

Dad: "We haven't got a cash tree around here."

Older Brother James: "Believe me, Merse, I felt the same way about hockey. I still think about tearing a shoulder my senior year and losing a ride to Michigan. Now I'm digging ditches and learning wiring codes. Not that there's anything wrong with that."

Dad: "I was hoping you'd say that."

James: "At least I have a job. If I were you, I'd grab the full ride."

Middle Brother Clancy: "Seriously, Merse, if you don't go to college, what else you gonna do?"

Mercy: "Go to Italy."

Clancy: "For life? That's a job? 'My job is going to Italy.'"

Mercy: "Can anyone hear me? Soccer stopped being fun."

Clancy: "Try the army for a few years. You'll be amazed at how many things you do that aren't fun. Make that life-threatening and not fun."

Dad: "Who told you life is fun?"

James: *"Mine's no St. Paddy's Day."*

Mercy: *"Why isn't anyone listening to me?"*

Youngest Brother Kevin: *"We listen, but you don't. I told you not to date a spud like Kevin Mulcahy. He dumped you flat."*

Mercy: *"He did not, and at least I date human beings. How much time do you spend online checking out Russian babes?"*

Mom: *"Kevin, is that true? We didn't buy you a laptop for muck."*

Kevin: *"Shut up, Merse."*

Mercy: *"No."*

Clancy: *"Play soccer. Earn a scholarship, Merse."*

Kevin: *"Look, if I were as good at X-Box as you are at soccer, I'd take the free ride."*

Dad: *"You'd better get your grades up, Kevin, or you'll get a free ride over to Boylston Street. You can play X-Box with the rest of the bums."*

Clancy: *"That's funny. Bum X-Box."*

Kevin: *"Why don't you back off?"*

Clancy: *"Why don't you back me off?"*

Dad: *"Finish your dinner or go outside, but you're not fighting at this table."*

Mercy: *"Will everyone stop talking to me like a child? I'm not playing soccer."*

James: *"You're the baby of the family."*

Mercy: *"I'm old enough to make my own decisions."*

Dad: *"Eat your turkey."*

Mom: *"We respect you for the young lady you've grown into. Now eat your turkey."*

And in the end, she'd eaten her turkey and bent to the pressures of guilt and shame and manipulation and praise from family, teammates, and coaches. The summer after high school graduation, she had watched Courtney fly off to Italy with another friend while she played club soccer. That fall, during freshman year at BC, as

Mercy's commitments increased, so did her presence at many a jovial kegger.

After an hour of unpleasant family memories, Mercy walked down to Morgan's office and failed at the Selective Inferno. In the bottom of a pail of water, Morgan had placed a chunk of river rock. Mercy was charged with incinerating only the rock. Instead, she evaporated all the water, leaving the rock cool and untouched. Clouds of steam drifted out into the hallway through the empty space once filled by pebbled glass.

"That sucked. Professor, I think I'm still drunk from last night."

Morgan nodded, rubbing his left bicep. "I did sort of spring this on you. Your Great Uncle Louis used to take me to the seashore near Gloucester and have me torch boulders sticking out of the waves. Great for your concentration."

"Professor, why do you keep rubbing your arm? Weights?"

"No. It was that crazy pile up I told you about last Sunday. The gun goes off, the race starts, then someone trips and there's bodies falling all over the start line. Including me. Someone in the crowd must've been wearing jewelry, because I got this sharp little cut on my bicep. Ah, it'll pass in a few days."

"I can't hack all this training. I mean, you keep upping the ante."

Morgan rolled his left shoulder as if working out a kink. "Come over here, please."

Morgan opened the tall safe. Mercy had never seen inside before: shelves with ledgers and journals, envelopes and check boxes full of pens and paperclips, and a strange greenish piece of melted glass. Morgan handed her the glass, then rummaged around more. He held up what appeared to be a thin navy blue yearbook.

"This is a special commemorative volume on the Miskatonic 1985-86 basketball team."

Mercy detected a pair of spectacles melded into the greenish glass. Very eerie. "The team that knocked off UMass in the NIT?"

"My senior year. Our guys advanced to the quarterfinals. An astounding feat for the War Scholar net men."

"Then they lost to Fordham in double overtime."

"My heart was punched out. We came so far, never to taste that heady air again."

Morgan was silent for several moments. Mercy said, "Professor? Was there something I should notice about this glass?"

"Trinitrite. I've been pushing you hard, Mercy. Please take the next two days off."

"You're shitting?"

"I'll handle Special Collections. In fact, you can leave immediately. Relax, have a few stimulating drinks, and read a bit of this if you get the chance."

Returning the glass chunk to the safe, Morgan handed Mercy a very old tan ledger. News clippings, printouts, and papers white or yellowed with age stuck out of the pages like a bad haircut.

"It's not very well organized. What is it?"

"You'll see. It'll make sense in its own untidy, mostly chronological, way. You'll even learn about trinitrite."

"Well, thanks for the time off."

"See you Monday. We'll tackle the Inferno again. You'll be excellent in no time."

Puzzled and delighted at four days off, Mercy departed with the ledger, leaving Morgan to pace, rubbing away at his left bicep.

On Friday evening, several miles northeast of campus, in the French Hill section of Arkham, laughter permeated an upscale living room. Through large picture windows, one could see a well-manicured lawn. Beyond grass and flower beds to the southwest, above rooftops shone the university clock tower. To the northeast, away from the weekend glow of Church Street, moonlight radiated off the Miskatonic River.

A sculptural metal frieze dominated one wall of the jubilant living room. On the frieze, a hand-hammered intricate metal wing tip extended up from verdigris bronze waves. The work was titled, "A Long Day for Icarus." Beneath the frieze, the polished hardwood floor was topped with a cream and beige area shag. An oversized chaise longue faced a thick, glass-topped coffee table. On the floor past the coffee table were velvet throw pillows covered in Aegean, poppy red, and peacock blue. Dominating the space beyond the pillows was a mocha Italian leather sectional couch.

Armand Deale sat on the chaise longue next to Audrey. Their legs touched as they used Deale's smart phone to play the online version of Answers Against Decency, eleventh expansion. For each round, a different player would be Overlord. The Overlord would then read a series of fill-in-the-blank questions. There were four possible answers. Players could win points for choosing an answer that the Overlord ruled either funniest, most indecent, or both.

On the Italian leather couch, Carter Fong smiled vacantly, eyes two red slashes as the hash deepened its smoky embrace. He and his date examined their possible responses on a tablet. Fong's trouser leg had risen, exposing the cloud and lightning tattoo on his calf. But Fong's ink was nothing compared to that on his companion, a freshman from the Berklee College of Music, dressed all in black except for the white lining of her Converse sneakers.

Berklee College had a unicorn tattoo on the inside of her right forearm. On her left forearm was inked the image of singer Miley Cyrus dry humping a parking meter. On her skinny neck in drop caps were the words "Corn Whole." Earlier that evening, over pasta and Chablis, Berklee College had informed Deale and his guests that her body would be completely inked over by year's end. Then she lifted her tee-shirt to model a detailed tattoo of the sinking of the *U.S.S. Houston*, engulfed by Japanese shellfire, sinking by the bow, guns blazing, in the Sunda Straight of her breasts. This drew a polite round of applause.

A cushion away reclined Leo Hameyes and his wife. Using a laptop, the couple scrolled down to the next game question. Ms Hameyes seemed uncomfortable, brown eyes darting around if seeking an exit from a room fast filling with water. Deale suspected she had once known beauty, but now she took refuge in cotton and flannel and heavy socks with Birkenstocks. At one point, Mrs. Hameyes had laughed out loud. But one glance from Leo restored her to *mmmmmmmmmmming*.

Angelo Silent Feather sat cross-legged on the floor, deerskin bag slung across his dress shirt. He used his smart phone to select responses. Deale couldn't remember the name of his date, a clingy Harvard grad student from the Kennedy School of Central Planning.

Fulfilling his role as Overlord, Deale read out loud the next fill-in-the-blanks statement: "I quit taking Viagra after . . . " With Audrey breathing against his cheek, Deale checked the screen as the other players selected their answers:

Fong and Berklee: ". . . screwing a woman with diarrhea."

The Hameyes: ". . . realizing my mother was ugly."

Angelo and Kennedy School: ". . . making a hobo blow me for snack food."

Deale reread statement and answers, to much laughter and *mmmmming*. Pausing for effect, Deale announced, "I'm awarding both the humor point and the indecent point to the hobo answer. That puts Team Silent Feather in second, passing Team Fong but still behind Team Hameyes."

"*Mmmmmmmmmm.*"

Fong giggled again. But he'd been doing that for two hours and no one noticed.

"All the teams are named after men," whispered Audrey in his ear.

"That's because I can't remember anyone else."

"Because they're women."

"I remember your name."

"That's because I support post-modern intercostal reductionism."

"Sultry bitch."

After a few more rounds, the Hameyes were declared winners and the party finally broke up. Acting as hostess, Audrey remembered everyone's name, thanking them for coming as well as ensuring that Berklee College drove Carter Fong home. Deale sank deeper into the chaise longue, glancing at the blonde walnut media center with its plasma screen mounted above, Apple TV box, and framed photos. One photograph featured a young Deale in his lacrosse uniform, while another picture showed a mature Deale on a beach, lying on a blanket next to a thin, intense woman with a challenging stare.

With the 'drive safes' and 'see you Mondays' completed, Audrey closed the front door, plopping onto the Italian leather couch across from Deale. He shook his head in astonishment. "Can you believe Fong? Were does he get these chicks?"

Audrey laughed, "Was she even eighteen?"

"Barely. He was a terror at Mountain View State. At least this one's out of high school."

Audrey said softly, "Any word from your wife?"

Deale sighed. "Laurel was livid when I told her about the Miskatonic offer. She felt the Boston area was saturated with colleges the way cable TV is saturated with shows about hillbillies. What possible success would I have in fundraising against Harvard, MIT, Brandeis, Tufts? But I said that if I could sell Miskatonic in this market, the sky was the limit."

"Didn't share the dream?"

"No. Plus she was having an affair with our State Senator. Anyway, we're still cooling off. I figured a vast boring nation between us is plenty cool."

"Think you'll reconcile?"

"Don't know that I want to now."

"Good answer, Deale."

"Any word on your divorce?"

Audrey's shoulders sagged, "Other than 'inevitable?' Zachary used to be so much fun. But when he latched onto an issue, he was passionate to the point of obsession. Two years ago he was out in Wyoming working on light pollution. In solidarity with the light-saturated, he refused to use headlights when driving. That night, I don't think he ever saw the buffalo. Since the crash, he's never been the same."

"For selfish reasons, I can't say I regret your loss."

"I'm getting over it. You giving me the second floor of the library was delightfully exciting."

"When Fong heard, he threw a fit, but then forgot about the whole thing. With Angelo, I had to convince him the choice had nothing to do with his being a Native American. Leo can be tricky. You never know which way he'll hop. I'll make it up to him once the Master Plan is approved. By the way, splendid scouting report on the Antiquity Section. Did you pass it on to Angelo?"

"Yes. And I worked up a rather daring scheme to secure the book. Angelo loves my plan, provided I call it 'our' plan. But with Morgan now gone, it's only a matter of time before we have the book."

Deale scratched at his chin, "Hard to say. Just because Morgan checked himself into the hospital today doesn't mean he's dying. Some kind of numbness in his arm and leg, from what I heard. It could clear up in a day or two. We must assume he'll fight like hell to protect his livelihood."

"The Antiquity Section has indeed been a money maker."

Flexing his fingers, Deale closed them in a fist, "Last time, I underestimated Morgan and ended up waddling across the quad like I had a rake up my ass. Starting next Tuesday, the Antiquity Section gets the full-court press."

"It would be funny if Morgan hurt himself with his own formula."

"I was thinking about that."

Audrey's hands went around the back of her neck. "You think formula is more than hypnosis, don't you?"

"Let's suppose it's something like Indian swamis sitting on a bed of nails or levitating. Call it channeling the body's electro-chemical energy; mental manipulation of electro-magnetic fields; chi, ki, prana, whatever. I admit I felt something just before my legs locked. But it doesn't matter. We're closing 'em down. Morgan can find carnival work."

Audrey crossed her legs. "And we're giving the book to Mr. Bluntness?"

"Social justice aside, if Janus weren't so old I'd seriously consider kicking his wrinkled ass into another time zone. We're restoring his sacred text and he insults everyone in the room. Oh, I forgot to mention: Janus wanted a page copied from another of the *Necrooreos*. Does that make sense?"

"Yeah. The Dee version is pretty chewed up. If he calls back, let me know. I can always ask my new BFF, Mercy O'Connor."

"What do you make of her?"

"I don't think O'Connor even wants to be there. I mean, she spent most of her time daydreaming. She's nothing. The security guard was on to me from the jump. He might be trouble."

"Angelo's kids will wear him down." Deale's voice grew hoarse. "I haven't shown you the rest of the house."

Audrey smiled sadly, "Please, Armand. I don't want anything complicating the divorce."

"Who's going to tell your ex?"

"Please."

Purse in hand, she crossed to the front door. Deale hugged her good-bye as Audrey whispered, "Cartesian dualism is corporeal stylization."

Deale felt carnal merriment. "You can't leave."

She breathed, "My pre-linguistic inner essence is a contingency duality."

"You hot little whore cat."

"Call me tomorrow," she said. After a nimble head turn that left Deale kissing her cheek, Audrey wriggled free. Deale watched her Neon move down the driveway, his groin district awash in a dam burst of hormones. Retreating to an exercise bike and a furious workout, a sweat-drenched Deale began to wonder if Audrey Klumm-Weebner weren't playing him, big time.

CHAPTER 6

PAST PERFORMANCE GUARANTEES FUTURE RESULTS

Third week of September, article from the *Miskatonic Scholar:*

STUDENTS SOUR ON ANTIQUITY ARROGANCE
By Quinn Bisque

Honna Pegler has strong opinions, and she's not afraid to state them. On the subject of the Antiquity Section holding sacred Dunwich texts, the junior stated, "You know, it's wrong for them [Antiquity Section] to loot religious books and not return them. Suppose someone took a bible from a church? There'd be shooting and killing."

One of many on campus who want to see the Necronomicon *returned to its rightful owners, Honna co-founded Students for the Liberation of Underserved Groups. Working closely with Resentment Studies Major Barry Gristleman, Honna and SLUG hope to raise awareness on campus and social media about what they call "the Antiquity Section's criminal possession of non-traditional religious text."*

"Suppose someone grabbed a Buddha statue from a temple?" said Gristleman, a junior who tweets out the hash tags #istandwithdunwich and #givebackthebook. "There'd be knifings and a fire." Gristleman, Pegler and SLUG want pressure brought on Antiquity Section

Chairman Professor Conrad Morgan to return the Necronomicon *to a Dunwich representative. In addition, they insist Morgan attend several months of weekend inclusion workshops, as well as a mandatory diversity tribunal. Said Pegler, "You know, if he's done nothing wrong, he's got nothing to fear."*

Another staunch critic of the Antiquity Section, Professor Angelo Silent Feather, Associate Vice-Chancellor for Contemporary Oppression Modalities, called for calm. "I empathize with the justified rage of the Dunwich people. Suppose someone swiped a Koran from a Mosque? Well, that's a bad example. Nothing would happen because of Islam's historical tranquility. Perhaps he [Morgan] could surrender one book, the Necronomicon, *from those seized a century ago. Such an action would demonstrate that the Antiquity Center has joined the 21st century and is sensitive to minority cultural modes of faith."*

Autumn Cryer, Vice President for Public Affairs and University Relations, was quick to add, "Let no one confuse legitimate concerns with shaming or bullying. Yielding the Necronomicon *won't destroy Earth, but it will make our planet a better, friendlier place. Hopefully, Professor Morgan will choose to unite with the majority of students and faculty in saying 'oh, hell, yes' to healing and reconciliation."*

Professor Conrad Morgan was unavailable for comment as he is hospitalized at St. Mary's for testing. Medical insiders have linked his treatment to possible prescription drug abuse or an STD.

Coffee in hand, Pentagram mat under her arm, purse on her shoulder, eyes on her phone, Mercy couldn't believe she was being trolled on Twitter.

Honna. @Pegler_H
@MerseBabe7 You stink and so does your evil breath! #bringbackthebook #istandwithdunwich

Rhoddie Lamquay @RLcares2

@Mersebabe7 Check your privilege, elitist b**ch! #givebackthebook

The Gristleman @activFist

@Mersebabe7 Hey, stupid! Ever think to #givebackthebook? But then who would you oppress next? #istandwithdunwich

On the library's first floor, Lisa arose from her desk and waved a copy of Tuesday's *Scholar* like a construction warning flag. "Be careful. Two undergrad guys just asked where to find the door to Special Collections."

"Odd. We usually don't get men under sixty."

"Did you read this? I'll bet they're protesters." Lisa helpfully inserted the school paper under Mercy's arm, above the mat. "How's Professor Morgan?"

"Not too good. I saw him last night. They're moving him to Mass General for more testing. His body is locking up in weird ways. Is Joe Bong on duty?"

"Yes and my friend at administration says you're getting picketed this afternoon."

Mercy rolled her eyes and thanked Lisa. Heading into the stacks, she thought of formula and the chances of the world ending on Hallow Mass: the odds were in her favor as long as they held the *Necronomicon*. Swiping her card, Mercy unlocked the door leading to the Antiquity Section, pushed it open and paused to notice black spray paint over the security camera lens.

Out of the stacks charged two undergrads.

The Tall Guy wore a tee-shirt reading, "This is What Dunwich Looks Like." The Bearded Guy held up his smart phone. Arms full, Mercy jammed a heel into Tall Guy's knee. Toppling back into the stacks, he flailed and fell on his back, clutching his kicked right knee. Bearded Guy shoved ahead, knocking Mercy into the Antiquity Section and emptying her arms of Pentagram mat, school paper, smart phone, purse and java. Dunkin' Donuts coffee splashed her possessions, including the hem of her dry-clean-only pants.

"Asshole," she yelled as Bearded Guy bolted up the stairs toward the Antiquity Section, whooping, "Give back the book."

Mercy hollered, "Joe, coming your way."

Bongani flew down the steps, but then dropped his nightstick, fumbling to pick it up. Bearded Guy stopped on the first landing, filming the whole thing. Mercy raced up the steps, grabbed the protestor by his belt and pulled him back down.

The student yelped, "Oww. I want everyone to know I'm under attack by the Antiquity Section for no reason."

Mercy slammed Bearded Guy into the metal door. Before shoving him outside, she said, "You spilled my coffee, jerk. That's the reason."

Bongani glanced at Mercy, then over to her soaked things. He sprinted upstairs, taking them two at a time. Mercy shook her head in exasperation. *All this hard guy, Mr. Preparation 'tude, and he drops his stinking nightstick. Now he's probably worried he'll miss another song about drunken engineers and ghost trains.* But the guard returned with a roll of paper towels. Kneeling, he helped Mercy dry off her possessions. In his brown eyes, she spotted the tiniest bit of respect, the way her brothers looked at her after she'd fought back against their bullying. Mercy beamed: finally something other than nagging.

Twenty minutes later, cleaned up and back in Special Collections, Mercy read the coffee soaked article in the *Scholar*, scrolled through more Twitter trolling from SLUG, then checked her phone messages on the section line. Some guy wanted to talk about Obed Whateley. 'Ye' this and that. Dunwich. And he'd asked for her by name. Someone from Dunwich knew there was a Mercy O'Connor. Not cool. When she updated Morgan today, Mercy would seek his advice.

In the meantime, she called Environmental Services about the painted-over security camera.

"Yeah, well, we'll get to it."

"Like you're getting to the pebbled glass window? Mr. Resnicek, we're supposed to be picketed later today."

"Then they'll paint it over again, so what's the point?"

Mercy finally extracted a promise to have the camera cleaned, then rang up campus security.

"Hi, Chief Underkrammal? This is Mercy O'Connor over at the Antiquity Section? Back in the spring, we met at the mandatory celebration for the Yes Means Expulsion campaign."

"I remember. You had twice as much wine as anybody else."

"It was a long event. Just so you know, two students tried forcing their way into the Antiquity Section this morning. One was ejected from the premises."

"They were just here. Traumatized. I have their report plus smart phone footage."

"Did you want to interview the guard and myself?"

"Why?"

"Context? See, sometimes there are two competing sides to a story. So you check out stuff like evidence and past behavior to help reach a determination. We have a camera inside the door to our section. I believe it filmed the entire incident."

"The report is already finished."

"You'll be getting a little addition."

Mercy dashed off a statement on the incident, signed it, and then passed it on to Bongani for his signature. She caught him examining some kind of pretty homemade bracelet, which he quickly stuffed in his pocket. Interesting. Turning down the volume on a song about soft summer days, a first love and big city coldness, Joe Bong agreed to send the statement and the security cam footage over to Campus Security.

Back at her desk, Mercy updated Morgan via his cell phone. "I think the SLUGs were testing us. Speaking of which, how'd your tests go, Professor? Are you at Mass General?"

Morgan sounded worried, distracted, "Yes, but now they want to send me to Beth Israel Deaconess. I prefer St. Mary's so my family doesn't have to drive all over hell and Boston. And, thank you, my tests have been extensive and fruitless. I don't have cancer or Tay-Sachs, or Lyme disease, or rickets, or Dengue Fever. Did you know my hair is falling out?"

"You told me yesterday."

"Ah, yes. Thanks again for visiting. Of course, hair loss means samples are available for the next step: an ongoing barrage of toxicology tests. They scan my DNA using gas chromatography-mass spectrometry. Do you know what that is?"

"Not really."

"Neither do I. But so far, I've tested negative for Arsenic, Cyanide, Strychnine, Lead, Mercury poisoning, as well as antifreeze. I was positive it was antifreeze."

Mercy laughed. That was more like the old Professor Morgan.

Morgan continued, "There was a giant snake movie my sons loved. In it, this spider venom paralyzed you. You couldn't run, then giant snakes would slither up and eat you alive."

"*Anaconda Three: Blood Orchid*. My brothers memorized it."

"Whatever the case, I am definitely turning into a sentient manikin. I'm holding the phone right now in my one useable hand."

"Jesus, Professor."

"Please say a prayer in case there really are giant snakes."

Discussing the morning's raid, Morgan thought Deale was probably pressuring the other campus departments. Mercy shouldn't expect much cooperation. But he would talk with key board members and see what could be done to chill Deale.

"Then Joe Bong charges down the stairs and drops his nightstick. All the grief about how I should practice formula and he can't even hold a club."

"Did you tell him that?"

"Not yet."

"Think about what will make you a better team. Will that be it? Because he could be all you have to count on for the next few days."

"I'll think about it."

Morgan seemed more concerned about the Dunwich caller.

"Call back, but don't meet him. It's too dangerous. Hear him out on Whateley. You might try and find out what they poisoned me with."

"You sure it's Dunwich?"

"Sitting here staring at my IV, I recall a similar incident with Warren Rice. Did you read any of the journal I gave you?"

"Uh, I was busy this weekend."

"Throw any formula?"

"No."

"Mercy? If they know your name, they might decide to probe you on formula."

Her stomach felt airy, packed with agitated moths as she recalled rats twisted like taffy, or furry bodies inverted, or with football-sized heads, pink little legs vainly scrabbling.

Morgan continued, "But you're running things in my absence. So only practice if you want."

"Maybe I'll get up to speed on the Inferno."

"If you like."

They agreed to speak Wednesday, sooner if something came up. By now it was late morning. Mercy called Bongani and updated him on her morning's chats, alerting him to the Dunwich call. In the background, Mercy heard a ballad about revenge upon an unfaithful lover that involved You Tube and water-based paint.

A half hour later, Erin called.

"Merse, lunch. My treat. Pick you up on Church Street."

Mercy automatically grabbed her purse, but then sat back down. "I can't, pretty girl, Morgan's still in the hospital and we're about to be picketed."

After a short version of the morning's events, Erin said, "Sounds like Mr. Crabby Pants really is Paul Blart."

"I thought I'd be able to count on him. I guess I'll be doing this solo."

"Okay, you do your work stuff. All I can say is that things look sweet with the Money Guy."

"Fun cash for us?"

"Maybe, baby.

Mercy felt a twinge of guilt, "I'm a little worried about formula for the masses. Like I said, there's more to this stuff than I knew."

"Don't overthink things. Indoor Wicca could be bigger than The Secret. I won't say 'bye,' 'cause I'm already gone."

Connection broken. Mercy couldn't shake a growing discomfort over the idea of selling formula. Of course, every woman had her price.

A soft splat.

Mercy glanced around, puzzled.

Splat-splat.

On the windows, yellow egg yolk rolled down the outside glass.

The protesters were early.

Mercy skipped lunch and practiced formula in Morgan's office. Using her Pentagram mat, she set up the Aegis, then practiced the Selective Inferno on a bucket of water containing a chunk of granite. This time she completely incinerated the bucket. The water washed across the floor, erasing chalked-in pentagrams and leaving a burnt plastic smell. Mercy cleaned up the mess, sprayed the air liberally with air freshener, then checked in with Bongani. He'd eaten his tuna sandwiches listening to protesters banging on the downstairs door, yelling obscenities at the blacked-out camera, and then chanting out in the quad for an hour or so.

"They want back the book," he told her.

"They're not getting it."

With the protesters gone by mid-afternoon, Mercy convinced Lisa downstairs to smuggle her up a salad and yogurt. Eating quickly, she thought of things to ask the Dunwich caller. Why talk to her? That was a good question. What about Whateley? Who poisoned Morgan and with what? Was anyone in the Miskatonic administration in touch with Dunwich?

Mercy dialed the Dunwich number. No answer. She left a message.

With the camera lens still blacked out, Bongani ran down the stairs and opened the door for that afternoon's scholar. Mercy pulled *The Alchemy of Saturn*, set up a reading desk, and handed the scholar his rice paper. Soon it was 4:30 PM. The swing shift guard arrived, reporting no protesters visible. Then, for the first time ever, Bongani stopped by to say 'good night.' Mercy met him at the Special Collections door as the elderly professor inside continued reading Marco Chakraborty's cabalistic tome. Mercy said, "Time flew past like a great bird today."

"Yes. And you practiced formula today."

"Tell you, Joe Bong, you might consider practicing a bit with that nightstick."

He winced. Direct hit. Mercy thought he might be blushing. She felt bad and said, "Hey, sorry. But reap what you sow is my family motto. What if you call me 'Mercy' or 'Merse.' What do you think?"

"What if you don't call me 'Joe Bong.'"

"How about 'Joe B?'"

"Okay . . . Mercy."

Mercy smiled. "Whew. Breakthrough. Next stop is sex on top of Morgan's safe."

Bongani stared for a moment, then grinned.

Twenty minutes later, with the old professor signed out and "Alchemy" secured in the Special Collections cage, Mercy searched the Web. She found a number of videos and stills from Sunday's Newburyport 10K. On one smart phone video, she saw the start line: an arch of balloons above and a rubber timing mat on the ground. From her own handful of races, Mercy knew all runners wore a chip. Once they passed over the mat, the chip was activated and their time digitally recorded. Mercy replayed all forty-three seconds of the footage. Four yards behind the start line, a few people lay flat on the ground while other runners dodged, hopped, side-stepped as they hurried to reach the mat.

Something seemed odd.

Mercy ran it again.

She selected another video.

This new one showed the pile up and a man with his back to camera. The man wore a matching tracksuit of royal blue, probably polyester, with white stripes. No one wore track suits like that anymore except the New York Mafia, who never seemed to read their fashion memos. Mercy re-ran the footage, focusing on the guy. Almost out of frame as he reached the starting mat, Track Suit darted into the crowd instead of onto the race course. Mercy played the footage again. She couldn't see a complete face. But ducking out of the race wasn't why you paid an entry fee. Mercy shut down her desktop computer.

After saying 'bye' to the swing shift guard, Mercy made her way out of the undergraduate library. She felt good about Tuesday. She'd roughed up a SLUG, thrown some formula, melted the ice with Joe B., followed up on things, took responsibility. A lot of loose ends, but it'd been some time since Mercy had accomplished this much at work, other than sealing waste bins shut.

At home, her mother was cooking stroganoff, her father reading a mystery on his Kindle. Tim O'Connor glanced at his daughter and said, "What time are you going out tonight?"

"I might stay in."

"Broke again? Sick?"

"Maybe I want to bask in the love of my family."

"You're pregnant?"

"Yes, Daddy. The father is a bisexual socialist who believes professional football should be banned and the money used to build a monument to world harmony."

Her father grunted and returned to his Kindle. Mercy ran upstairs to her room as he muttered, "He's not Italian, is he?"

Later that night, Mercy lay on her bed, examining possibilities. Someone from Dunwich might test her. Wow, what would that be like? No theory. No tennis balls on the cheek, or shoves across the room. She could die in unusual, disturbing, and graphic ways. And even if you win, you lose—like Great Uncle Louis or Galen Rice.

Mercy opened the old journal from Morgan's safe. Different styles, seemingly all male penmanship. Clippings and papers and book reviews mashed together, some articles in Ziploc plastic bags, others bundled in Saran Wrap, others brittle and yellow with age, extending back almost a century. On the first page, in faded ink, she read:

"We must counter-meddle."

Afterwards, there was a series of statements related to formula:

"Precision is vital."

"The greater the formula, the more unbending the concentration."

"A small distraction can unravel all."

Then a series of questions:

"How wide a dimensional door will spell doom for Earth?"

"Other than Yog-Sothoth, what other great diabolical entities may be summoned without the Necronomicon?*"*

"Might formula be used for practical commercial tasks such as welding?"

A few more passages revealed these were observations and queries from Mercy's distant relative, Henry Armitage, whose name graced the library. Very cool. Reading more fragments, pithy asides, notes, and conclusions, it became clear that her relative had "counter meddled," along with Warren Rice and Francis Morgan. Together, the three Miskatonic academics had studied formula as if it were an unknown pictograph without keys, aiming to fight fire with fire. Atop Sentinel Hill, they'd checked the 1928 horror. Now their goal was to stifle the growth of all that was baleful and apocalyptic, slinking out of Dunwich.

Flipping ahead to 1935, Mercy spotted new handwriting—bold, powerful. With Henry Armitage dead of natural causes, there was a new Antiquity Section Chairman, Warren Rice. His views on Dunwich were forthright:

"Tear down pillars and altars, burn the squalid village. Shoot the warlocks, then plow the ground, sow salt and let no man walk those hills for a generation. Otherwise, this devilish carbuncle of a cult will fester and grow in perpetuity."

Warren Rice noted events by month and year. His passion involved stockpiling grimoires and magic texts. Mercy skimmed the entries.

"April, 1937: Off by train to Philadelphia tomorrow to secure a Greek copy of Abominations of the Moon.

November, 1937: Why did I ever have children?

January, 1938: Another foiled burglary attempt. Ha! Those Dunwichers hate the dogs, and vice versa.

May, 1939: A WPA squad of seven men marched into Dunwich to hack hiking trails in the back of Sentinel Hill. They've all disappeared. What a surprise.

March, 1942: Discreetly, the government has asked the Antiquity Section if we might teach formula to the Army. I explained to a committee that a 'magik corps' would require fasting and other checks on the carnal appetites in order to maximize efficiency. They decided to pursue something called atomic energy."

Trinitrite. That word popped in her mind again. Wasn't it something to do with sand? She read on:

"February, 1943: My son now serves overseas in army counter-intelligence. He has uncovered modern traces of the Dunwich cult in Lisbon, deeply entrenched, malignant as ever."

Mercy noted three Rice entries for July, 1944:

"By train tomorrow to Red Hook in Brooklyn. There I will purchase a French translation of Choon Seng's Seeds of the Dragon.*"*

"Ha! Two dirty birds thought to pluck my book. Well, they got more than they bargained for, though one managed to slash me in the calf. So much for New York City's low wartime crime rate."

"My health is terrible. This makes no sense."

That was the last entry by Warren Rice. An obituary recorded his death as 'wartime stress' and listed his burial in Christ Church Cemetery in south Arkham. Only Francis Morgan remained to continue the Antiquity Section.

"Slashed on the calf." "Cut on the bicep." Professor Morgan knew what he was talking about. She wished her Dunwich caller would phone. Mercy flipped ahead, stopping in the 1960s. Inside a Ziploc bag was a *Boston Globe* review of a familiar book.

'Dunwich, Devils and Death' by Aquarius Fomble
by Neil CB Doberman | Globe Correspondent | May 24, 1968

If you're looking for a poor man's In Cold Blood, *please seek elsewhere. This confused pop crime tale attempts to unravel the Elaine Milano kidnapping, tossing in a gunfight, a freak Halloween storm, and the death and/or disappearance of several men, including two faculty members from Miskatonic University. Written in mish mash style that combines potboiler prose with the psychological insights of Laing and Szasz, the tragic story of a never-found 10-year-old girl is not improved by garnishing the tale with Satanism, magic duels, suicide, and an allusion to escaped Nazis. Observe the following passage about a suspected child kidnapper and alleged Dunwich warlock:*

A giant goatish man, abandoned by his father, Sirac Bishop had no choice but to act out his childhood traumas. He found psychological release in magic, comfort in ceremony and routine. Behind that hairy demonic face, he could easily have seen himself as a rebel, rejecting the plastic society that had rejected him. Let us seek compassion before judgment.

Should you be rushing to the bathroom to upchuck your lunch, know that there are many such paragraphs. I never thought I'd write this about a book, but you're better off watching television.

Dunwich, Devils and Death
By Aquarius Fomble
Landcake Press, 280 pp., illustrated, $4.79

Neil CB Doberman is a contributing editor at the **Ponderous Scholar Gazette,** *a recipient of the Wingate Peaslee Fellowship for Excellence in Political Economy, and reviews books for the* **Arkham Advertiser** *and the* **Athol Literary Review.**

Mercy smiled. No one could accuse DD&D of understatement. Paperclipped to the back of the review were several old purple-inked mimeograph pages from Chapter Eleven of Fomble's book. Mercy carefully removed the clips and read:

Irony soaked their every action like a lonely rain. They had come to hunt the outcast Sirac Bishop, little realizing that in Dunwich they themselves were the despised outcasts. Packed into a Massachusetts State Patrol Car, three Miskatonic professors and two state policemen crossed the ancient covered bridge, entering devil-encrusted Dunwich village. It was 2:37 in the afternoon of October 31, 1956. Perdition pressed upon them from all sides, and one is left to wonder if beads of infernal sweat dotted their brows. Bishop's magic might well wrench open a dimensional fissure the way a powerful man with a crowbar might tear open a plywood door. What then shambled into our world could wreak havoc on the scale of a hydrogen bomb. There was no margin to be wrong. No window for failure. Yes, cloying fear indeed.

At 2:42, the patrol car met with three shotgun-clutching locals outside Osborn's Store. Patrol car leading a pickup truck, the eight-man search party drove toward Sentinel Hill, the putrid heart of Hell-saturated Dunwich.

At 2:54, the search party detoured down a side road to check the ruins of the haunted Wilbur Whateley farm, ground zero for the 1928 horror. There the locals, professors and cops encountered young Obed Whateley, armed with an M1 carbine. Shots were exchanged. Sirac Bishop appeared. A preliminary clash of caustic, twisting magic flared between warlock Bishop and Miskatonic professors Francis Morgan and Julian Rice. Bishop broke off the clash and escaped. The police discovered their patrol car radio inoperative. Assistant Professor Thomas Armitage grew highly agitated and waved about a .38 caliber revolver, claiming Dunwich was 'nowheresville.' He attempted to return to

Osborn's, claiming the search party needed more canned goods, but was stopped.

At 3:11, the search party pursued on foot across rough terrain. After fording the Miskatonic River, the pursuers split up. The three shotgun-clutching locals took a short cut to intercept Bishop and Whateley near the accursed Devil's Hop Yard. Rice, Morgan and the jittery Armitage, along with one patrolman, stayed on the trail. The second patrolman drove the patrol car back to Osborn's Store to phone for more assistance. As he departed the Whateley property, the second officer reported hearing approximately eight or nine shots fired from the direction taken by his partner and the Miskatonic professors.

From here on, the next twenty-two minutes remain stubbornly shrouded in a sphinx-like mystery, deeper than an ebony enigma at night. At approximately 3:30 PM, the daylight over demon-drenched Dunwich seeped away, replaced by a foreboding purplish darkness.

Three minutes later, a cataclysmic storm split the heavens.

Fourteen terrifying minutes passed before the furious tempest dissipated. Halloween evening crept in like a black cat in rubber dancing shoes. With sirens moaning, police and ambulance units arrived at Osborn's. A search of the area eventually led authorities to the unholy Devil's Hop Yard and surrounding vicinity. There they discovered Francis Morgan, severely injured, shot as well as battered by freakish hail. The state patrolman who had accompanied the Miskatonic professors was pummeled by hail and in deep shock, his brown hair prematurely turned white. Of the shotgun-wielding locals, two had their skulls crushed by hail, while a third survived but was severely burned on the face and hands as if by some great heat.

There are reports of a single gunshot right before the monster storm. The pistol of Thomas Armitage was

*discovered wedged between rocks, one round expended.
Fired in a desperate bid to escape something foul beyond
our imaginings? Who can tell? His body was never
found. Nor was the body of Julian Rice. Nor was the
body of warlock and suspected kidnapper Sirac Bishop.*

*Obed Whateley was observed very much alive,
fleeing deeper into the Dunwich hills. Perhaps this is
not the place, but rumors persist that teenage Whateley
was, in fact, the illegitimate son of Martin Bormann,
private secretary to Adolph Hitler. Whateley's interest
in the dark arts served only to mask his greater goal of
creating the Fourth Reich in rural Massachusetts. But
more on that at another time.*

Mercy paused. Rereading that passage, she
wished her maternal grandfather hadn't been such
a foul-up. That aside, psychobabble and hillbilly
Nazis couldn't mask the fact that only Francis
Morgan survived the incident with mind and
body mostly intact. Two other men were critically
injured. Four men died taking warlock Sirac
Bishop off the board. And Obed Whateley escaped
to throw formula for around sixty more years.
Super.

On the last page, in crabbed penmanship,
Mercy read:

*Much of this is utter slop and maudlin conjecture,
but Fomble's chronology leading up to the storm is
basically accurate, as is his speculation on the suicide of
Armitage. I heard Tom's frightened shrieks as Julian
clashed with Sirac Bishop. I heard the single gunshot. I
can only hope he shot himself in his big mouth. With
Tom, everything was always 'cool,' and 'under control'
and 'no sweat.' If he'd spent more time on formula and
less time banging cocktail waitresses in Quincy, then I
wouldn't have had to comfort his young wife and
daughter with mendacious lies. We should be more*

discriminating in whom we instruct, for even now, we know not the limits of formula. I sense if we did, we might find ourselves frozen in shock at the dreadful power within our grasp.

It was signed 'FM.' Mercy guessed Francis Morgan, great-grandfather to Conrad Morgan.

'Young wife and daughter' were her maternal grandmother and mom. Now Conrad Morgan was sidelined, leaving Mercy alone. No backup from the Miskatonic Administration, no backup from the Antiquity Section, no cops, no friendly locals. Even Joe B. was doubtful, maybe too uptight to function in a crisis. To face the abominations of Dunwich there was Mercy O'Connor and her three pathetic spells. She realized with fatalistic certainty that Obed Whateley could annihilate her. Far from any sense of continuity or family pride, the journal left her feeling she was welded to a past that demanded complete sacrifice in exchange for, at best, unpleasant victory.

Mercy spent the rest of the evening in brooding depression.

CHAPTER 7

FALL CONVERSATIONS

"Iä! Shub-Niggurath! . . . Their hand is at your throats, yet ye see Them not; and Their habitation is even one with your guarded threshold."
— *Abdul Alhazard*, The Necronomicon
(Latin Version)

Oct. 1

As the PA system called doctors to phones and nurses to rooms, Mercy paced the nearby corridor. For a moment, she thought herself back on the pitch, maneuvering through a defensive backfield as she dodged carts and shuffling patients with IV poles. *I've got a walk-in closet full of questions and now he can't even talk.* A stocky black priest with glasses and a fringe of white hair approached Mercy.

Pointing toward Professor Morgan's room, Mercy said, "Hi, Father George. He lies there and blinks at the ceiling. For the last few days he could at least whisper stuff like, 'I have no idea.' 'Not sure.' 'Could happen.' 'Practice if you want to.' Can't they do anything for him?"

"I suspect the poison is most ancient and subtle. Do you have a moment of time?"

"You mean before I rejoin your nephew back in lockup?"

"He has told me of the protests, and that your scholars no longer wish to be hounded and mocked, and how the protesters follow you about the campus filming everything except their own provocations."

"That's a lot of talking for Joe B."

"But he says you are strong."

"He said that? I don't feel it. I feel like I'm being punished for things I'm not responsible for."

Father George placed a hand on Mercy's shoulder, "Before speech was completely lost, Conrad said to tell you he appointed you the new head of the Antiquity Section. He believes in you. He also said to keep receipts for all expenditures."

Mercy's mouth opened and closed like a bass.

Oct. 3

A house mix heavy on techno music with a baseline as rapid as the beating heart of a frightened bird blasted over the speakers. Mercy munched cheese snacks with caramelized onions from a tray on the bar. Club Swill featured a small dance floor, a deafening sound system and a huge plasma TV dominating the space above the bar. Right now, it was tuned to ESPN for the BC-Syracuse game. On the road, down 14 – 3 in the second quarter, a massive roar from a phalanx of pitcher-drinking fans informed anyone in Suffolk County that Boston College had just scored. Mercy cheered along with the crowd and, for a moment, forgot her troubles.

"Yeah, Eagles. Kick their ass!"

Perfume teased her nostrils an instant before Erin returned from the restroom, wriggled onto the next bar stool, and said, "Continue, continue."

"There's not much else. If I make it to work at 7:30 in the morning there aren't any protesters. But I have to bring my lunch or they'll follow me to the cafeteria with their little cameras. And since they started stalking me, I can't park in the campus lot or I'll get keyed again. Parking around

Church Street is a bitch. I was almost tempted to unleash my brothers."

Erin covered her mouth. "Oh, my God. You can't do that."

"I know. It would totally be velociraptors versus metrosexuals."

Erin laughed. "Good one, Cuz. You need an adventurous new life. What're you drinking?"

"Tonic and lime."

"Are you serious? You mean this whole time you haven't had one decent drink? Do you want an M-Cat?"

"No drugs or alcohol. I've been really nervous lately about losing control."

Erin put an arm around Mercy's shoulders, "Merse, you need to lose control, get wild, jump a guy, sign that release. Did you sign it? Please say you did."

BC fumbled on the Syracuse eight-yard line. An Orangeman linebacker recovered.

Mercy said, "You know that pentagram mat you designed is simply awesome. I've been using it a lot."

Erin raised an eyebrow, "Money Guy wants to pay you five grand. He wants to pay the techs and he wants to pay me. But he won't pay anyone unless the little sorceress is on board. Now's the time to ditch Antiquity, earn some decent money, get out of debt, start living, girl."

Mercy squirmed. "I know things suck at my job, but formula is pretty tricky. I tried telling you before. I mean, most of the day that's all I do is practice formula. With the protestors, it's like being trapped in study hall."

"If anything, all that fasting has made you thinner by at least a dress size. Maybe I should practice formula."

Mercy blurted over the techno music, "Do you know about Trinitrite?"

"It's like ecstasy, but cut with horse endorphins."

"No. It's from the first atomic bomb test in New Mexico."

"What are the effects? Euphoric? Erotic? You know me: I'll try anything."

Mercy upped her game. "It's not a drug. But when they detonated the first nuke, sand got caught up in the fireball, rained back down in liquid form, and then hardened into glass chunks."

"So you suck on the glass? Put it in Jack Daniels?"

"Morgan showed me this Trinitrite in his office. You could see eyeglasses inside, like something embedded in Lucite. I think they're all that's left of Julian Rice. Remember the Devil's Hopyard when we were kids?"

"We were so stoned we'd have laughed at burning old people."

"Right. But I've been reading this Antiquity Section journal. Something terrible and amazing—formula but like a nuke explosion—happened there. Grandpa Tom and others disappeared. But the damage was confined to a small area, less than two acres. How do you even do that? But that's formula: it's very mysterious with a high ceiling on destroying stuff. We can't sell something that dangerous."

"You're babbling. How awful can formula be? Nothing personal, but you learned it. You know, Merse, I set everything up because you said this would be an awesome idea. I used favors, begged, wheedled, bullied, cranked up the charm, and now I'm hearing you're quitting because you took an overdose of Trinitrite and freaked out."

"You don't know what we're messing with. Neither do I."

Erin grabbed up her purse. "Thanks for costing me money and making me look bad. Oh, and don't ever tickle me again on Gabby Face."

Erin wriggled off. Mercy felt miserable, staring at her tonic-soaked lime while some basic guy with a ginger beard and an expensive sports coat hopped into Erin's old seat.

He said, "Didn't you go to Emerson?"

"No."

"I went there. Now I work in Hollywood for Pirate Cyclops Studios." He handed Mercy a business card featuring a cyclops with a pirate patch over its eye. "We're a hot brand, tearing it up in TV animation. Maybe you've caught one of our shows on the networks or cable: *Sea Dentist*, *Awesome Teenage Super Teens*, and *Gert the Toaster*. 'Gert' is pretty cutting edge stuff. It's the first children's cartoon about a transsexual appliance."

"Excuse me." Mercy rose and headed for the exit.

On TV, Syracuse scored a touchdown.

Oct. 7

In the living room, Mercy's parents watched an episode of *Armenian Mechanic*, where each week guests earned money by guessing how much the mechanic would overcharge for basic repairs. In her peach-colored robe, hair drying in a fluffy bath towel, Mercy read the Antiquity Section journal.

"Watch this," said her father, "fifty bucks minimum to change a fan belt." He turned to Mercy, "Why aren't you out somewhere?"

Barbara O'Connor spoke up from behind the colorful glossy pages of *Dumps of New England*. "Kay Doucette said she's spatting with Erin."

Mercy glared at her mother. "Is that public information?"

"We're all family here," said her father. "See? I told you: fifty-nine bucks. Guy's a complete asshole."

"Language, Tim. Mercy, dear, aren't you fighting over the funny little gestures Conrad Morgan was teaching you?"

"No, Mother, you're wrong and I'd rather not discuss it."

Tim O'Connor said, "How come you got all these protesters on yer back? Don't they want some book? You're the boss, now. Have that Italian guy give 'em the book and shut 'em up."

"Bongani is a black African."

"Yeah, yeah.

"He's not Italian."

"I work with 'em all the time. They're not so bad."

Oct. 9

Mercy jumped at a thud from the window, as some large moist object slid down the outside glass, leaving a filmy trail next to last week's rotten tomato stains, next to egg stains from the week before that. Mercy grabbed her smart phone and coffee, walking down to the guard station. Bongani muted his radio in the middle of a song about heartbreak and an old hound dog. Together they watched the monitor as young SLUG faces leered into the poorly-cleaned lens outside the downstairs door.

"Audrey Klumm-Weebner will be here this afternoon for another peek at the Dee *Necronomicon*. She'll text from downstairs and you can let her in. Thank you last time for not calling her a liar and a thief."

Bongani held up his Dunwich flash cards. "She should be in here. She is Deale's great good friend."

"Right now, she's about the last scholar visiting Special Collections."

Four extended middle fingers filled the monitor between black paint streaks.

Mercy said, "Didn't you say you used to play soccer?"

"Yes. As a boy, I would kick the ball against my family's hut. My mother would run outside and try and hit me, but I would escape. But when I came home to eat, my father would punish me."

"You were taking your wild pills back then." Mercy sipped her coffee. "Do you want some? It's a Dunkin' Donuts regular. I think Morgan has hot water cups in his office under a pile of Assyrian toilet paper or something."

Reaching into his backpack, Bongani unscrewed the top of a thermos and held out the plastic cap. Mercy added coffee, saying, "Don't tell me, I remember: defensive midfield?"

"Wing. And you were the midfielder. Run all the time."

"I made the center of the field my bitch. I mean, our strategy was to keep possession of the ball. Pass off, run to the empty space, never stand still."

"So the other could not score."

A loud banging echoed from the downstairs door. Mercy wondered if the protestors would force their way inside. She almost hoped they would. "SLUG has had possession of the ball for two and half weeks. Just saying."

"But we must guard the books."

"If it's so important, how come we're alone? The world hangs in the balance and only five security guards and me show up for the game."

"Baba Morgan and my uncle."

"Eight but Morgan's a scratch; make that seven."

"My police friend, Michael Vitale. He has many guns."

"But only two arms. Eight again."

"Your Uncle Louis?"

"Oh, right, the drunken hermit mage. Still eight. I'm in a sour mood, Joe B. I get cranky from fasting and too many soccer analogies."

Oct. 13

Four days later as Mercy and Bongani ate lunches of yogurt and tuna sandwiches respectively, Armand Deale ordered for two: braised shiitake mushrooms, the sea scallop with white soy sauce, and the salmon tataki with smoked salt. Across a small table near the L-shaped sushi counter, he and his date exchanged intimate glances.

"Such a delightful atmosphere," said Audrey. "How did you hear about this place?"

"I'm from California," said Deale through a mouthful of mushrooms, "I can smell great Japanese cuisine over vast distances." He lifted his Ashai Super Dry in a little toast. "To a Janus-free future."

Audrey twinkled a little dolphin smile, clinking his beer glass with her goblet of Cabernet Sauvignon. "Again?"

"This morning. Did we have his book yet. Then, in between insults, he asked if I'd remembered to copy page so-and-so from the other *Necroheman*."

"What page?"

"I've been deliberately tuning him out. I'll get it next time." Deale remembered the little old man's disturbing eyes from the hospital, glittering with derision and menace. "You were over at

Antiquity last week. How close are they to quitting?"

Audrey absently stroked the stem of her wine glass. Empty gesture? Future promise? Deale wasn't sure, but he had a preference. Audrey said, "After three weeks, the pressure is clearly having an effect. You can see the tension in their faces, especially O'Connor. Oh, and please ask Angelo to make his kids stop slop bombing the windows. They look terrible and SLUG comes across as destructive dweebs."

Deale shrugged, gestured with an open hand. "You know Angelo. Anything remotely like criticism is an assault on all Native Americans everywhere throughout history. I've tried approaching him through Fong, but no luck."

Audrey dabbed scallops off her lips with a coral linen napkin. "I heard Leo was quite the award hog last night."

"Amherst presented him with its Golden Mace of Diversity Award. He's staying over today to teach a workshop on eliminating excluding laugher." Deale sliced into his mushrooms, "Hameye's really turned that excluding laughter business into a niche."

Dolphin smiling, Audrey said, "making Miskatonic cutting edge."

Deale thoughtfully chewed his mushrooms. "Pushback is rolling in from board members, one of the foundations, the alumni association, even some of the media. People say the university comes across as bullying the Antiquity Section. It's not good optics, especially with Morgan sick. And I'm tired of being asked to comment on the same You Tube video of Mercy O'Connor roughing up a protester."

Audrey tilted her wine glass in appreciation. "Was that the one with the delightful shot of the security guard dropping his nightstick? I'm afraid I badly overestimated him."

From a small teapot, Deale poured hot sake into a sakazuki, a flat saucer-shaped cup. He sipped, then said, "I have an idea that might play out."

Audrey finished her scallops and sampled the sake, nodding in appreciation as Deale finished explaining his scheme. She reached across the table and stroked his hand. "I love your marvelous brain."

As the subject changed, they discussed politics and art and popular culture with liveliness and wit. And while Audrey remained flirty, Deale noticed she hadn't once teased him with dense academic jargon. Maybe Audrey no longer felt it necessary.

Mixed signals. But one could be too certain of victory. Deale sensed blood scurrying to a pleasing anatomical area. There were all sorts of ways to play games. Audrey would learn that Armand Deale had not yet begun to maneuver.

Oct. 16

Rain cleaned some of the Special Collection windows, driving protesters inside and stopping the bullhorn baiting and chants. Using tape and wadded up pages of Campus Safe Zone compliance guidelines, Mercy had fashioned a soccer ball. In the hallway, she and Bongani passed and dribbled as best they could with paper on tile.

Mercy said, "So what about the ancestor spirits?"

"Ancestor spirits are everywhere, even dreams. They will bring you much good, but must also be respected. Everywhere you see piles of isivivane stones to honor local ancestor spirits so the people may travel safely."

Bongani bounced the ball from one thigh to the other, then over to Mercy as she said, "And what were those zombies?"

"Tokoloshe, made by the wizards. The people set bricks underneath the bed legs so the tokoloshe pass beneath."

"Dwarf zombies, wicked." Mercy stopped a ball with the inside of her right foot, then kicked it back with her left.

Bongani continued, "And you must not answer a door knock at night. Tokoloshe."

"What about the Old Ones?"

"They have been in Natal longest. It is very poor in the country so many men must go far away to Durban and work. That is when the cult raids and takes sacrifices."

"Is that what happened to your fiancée?"

He kicked the ball hard past Mercy into the bent over Coke machine. *Okay. We're not going there.* Retrieving the ball, she booted it back to Bongani. "You know a lot about the cult?"

Bongani said, "Some. To belong is to give up all. For the cult, you must surrender family, Ubunta—our humanness and ties to others—your ancestors. As Christian, I would have to give up the Lord God Jesus."

"You can do that at Catholic college. They'll teach you Jesus was the first social worker."

Bongani's cell phone rang. He picked up, listened, then turned to Mercy. "My friend, Michael."

"The cop?"

Bongani handed her the phone.

"Sorry to bother you," said a young voice. "But Joseph said someone from Dunwich tried contacting you about Obed Whateley. I was wondering if that person ever called back? Left a name?"

"No, nothing. I even called him back, but never heard a word. Joe says you stay on top of Dunwich doings."

Bongani dribbled down the corridor past the melted drinking fountain toward Morgan's office.

"Yeah. Not many of us. The reason I asked was this buddy of mine is a Boston cop. He said they arrested a Dunwich man on charges of drug possession and operating a stolen vehicle. Suspect claimed this hot Toyota Sienna was used in kidnapping two students back in August. Turns out he was right. Victim DNA was found on the floorboard. Boston PD likes a Malachi Hutchins and a Jasper Frye as the kidnapper suspects. They used to be a team, robbing packies. But then Frye went into Apple picking."

"What's that?"

"Jacking smartphones. Good cash value; unwary victims. My informants say Frye and his pal are associates of Chester Sawyer."

Mercy glanced at Bongani, saw him dribbling back along the corridor toward her. Rapidly, she flipped through his flash cards to Chester Sawyer. "Hybrid, knows some lethal formula?"

"Exactly. I see you stay on top of Dunwich yourself."

"Well, that's our nine-to-five. Is the suspect still in jail?"

"The detectives cut him loose to set up Sawyer, but never heard back."

Mercy said, "He probably skipped to Florida."

"Or got squeezed by the Translucent Python."

Mercy grimaced as Joe kicked the ball up onto the table. "Even death is odd in Dunwich."

"Very true. I'm sure you know that whatever goes down on Sentinel Hill this Hallow Mass is going to be massive."

Mercy rolled the ball around the table with her palm. "How can you be sure?"

"They didn't kill Professor Morgan when they had the chance. I think they left him alive so he'd know."

"Oh. Yeah."

"Plus children have been kidnapped. In the last three weeks, two girls and a boy, all between nine and twelve, in and around Boston."

1956 Horror; Elaine Milano.

Michael Vitale continued, "all those innocent sacrifices mean major formula, Yog- Sothoth at the least."

Mercy fumed, "If the kids are in Dunwich, why aren't the cops tearing the place apart finding them? Don't they even try?"

Vitale's laugh was arid. "Last time the FBI rolled into Dunwich looking for kidnap victims they came out empty-handed. The Bureau hates looking dumb and ineffective. They won't move on rumors and there's no evidence. My guess is the kids are already dead."

Mercy said, "That's horrid."

"That's Dunwich. So keep on keeping the *Necronomicon* safe. If they get that, we're in for the long-expected Old One reunion tour."

They talked a bit, flirted a little, then Mercy handed the phone to Joe. He and Michael discussed a new shooting range in Braintree. Mercy kicked the ball back toward Special Collection, bouncing it off the wall, practicing traps. How weird to hear someone outside the Antiquity Section weigh in on Dunwich and formula as if it were a Red Sox pennant run. And a cop at that. Still, he sounded nice. She should get his number.

Bongani caught up with her and they recapped the call.

"It drives me crazy, Joe B. Eight people, that's all who care about saving the stinking world."

"Our ancestors."

"Super. What are they going to do?"

Bongani thought a moment, then said, "Their lives have built the road we walk upon. Their spirits always remain to help, like the saints. Unless you ignore them. Then they cause trouble."

Mercy kicked the ball into Special Collections and struck the cage. "That's exactly what we need: trouble from dead people."

Oct. 20

Across the quad, Armand could see the stained windows of the Antiquity Section. Audrey had been right. They were messy. Disgusting. The quad beneath the second floor Antiquity Section stood empty that morning of bullhorns and obscenity filled-signs and chants. Leo Hameyes lurked near the bookstore in a warm coat, training a graduate student in identifying excluding laughter. Like a mother eagle instructing an eaglet on spotting torpid salmon, Hameyes indicated a pair of chuckling sophomores. Darting out, the grad student stopped the pair, compelling them to submit to laughter vetting. Deale's chest swelled. Audrey had been right about that too. Soon every campus would be practicing the 'Miskatonic Method.'

With his back to the window, he turned to face Mercy O'Connor, "You're sure you wouldn't like coffee?"

Seated on the ivory sofa, admiring the mulberry cut pile carpet, Mercy declined. Deale noticed she'd dressed up for today: enough makeup to be attractive, but still professional, a mustard yellow suit, taupe hose and low heels, almost as if dressed for a job interview. Excellent.

"How is Conrad?"

"I saw him last night. His limbs remain paralyzed, and he can't speak. The doctors have no idea what to do next."

"Terrible." He pressed the intercom and instructed his assistant to send Conrad Morgan another fruit basket.

"So, Mercy, I know you're thinking 'what does he want?'"

"The book?"

Deale smiled, "Pardon a pun, but we seem to be on the same page. I personally feel this is not your fight."

A body shift, a slight facial rearrangement; could this be a kernel of agreement? Deale pressed ahead, "I admire loyalty, but you shouldn't be obligated by another's decisions."

O'Connor folded both hands in her lap, "You may not have heard, but Professor Morgan placed me in charge of the Antiquity Section. So it would be my decision to retain the *Necronomicon*."

"Correct me please, but isn't the chairmanship limited to those with a Ph.D., or in the process of obtaining one?"

"I'd have to, uh, double check the charter."

"Please do. In the meantime, let's act as if you have authority to dispose of Special Collections property. Suppose there were no pressure on you to return the book?"

"From you or SLUG?"

"This office, of course. And, while wholeheartedly supporting our students' right to free expression, I might be able to convince the protesters to ease off a little."

"And Dunwich?"

"I can understand their frustrations at being throttled by the dominant culture, but that's beyond my brief. Come over here, please."

Escorting O'Connor to the master plan tabletop model, Deale was delighted to see her scoping out his wall of celebrity photos. He said, "You heard me tell Conrad what I want: money. Here's my dream in 3D, the future I'm eager to create. What's your dream? Do you want to remain head of the Antiquity Section, study formula until well into your fifties and sixties?"

O'Connor hesitated, "No, I suppose not."

"I'm guessing your dream is time. Time to figure out what you want in life. Time to earn money and pay off student loans. Time to experiment, try jobs and career paths."

Deale felt like he was hitting home. She stood very still, eyes on the tabletop as he continued, "There might be a place for you in that model. Maybe near the basement to start, but with the potential to advance, gain experience, test your skills, acquire new ones. And it might come with a high five-figure starting salary, benefits, and a bonus structure. You'd be part of a team, with plenty of support and guidance. Then, if you decide building the new Miskatonic isn't for you, you'd depart with a solid salary history, and the most glowing of recommendations."

"You want the book."

"Not at all. Your section keeps the book. All I ask is a loan. Hand me the *Necroomnibus* next week. Two or three days later, I give it back. I vouch for its condition and safe return. Then we'll start to work creating the time you need to dream."

"But you'll hand it over in time for Hallow Mass."

"Yes. A loan. No more."

"It's a very dangerous book."

"Mercy, you're too smart to believe that."

"But if the Dunwichers believe it, and act upon the information in the book, then people die whether it's true or not."

"A literal interpretation of their faith smacks of discredited fundamentalism."

"Human sacrifice smacks of human sacrifice."

"Dominant culture propaganda designed to suppress a competing faith. Read your Paz Encanto."

"I have. And I've read accounts of what happens if you're hauled into those stone circles."

"Folklore, not facts. Our very own Professor Klumm-Weebner sees the whole Dunwich eschatology as psychological; a metaphorical belief system related to self-cleansing and the dragging away of the old person to be replaced by the new. She's given me a number of sources to study. I would be delighted to share them with you."

"Opening dimensional doors and freeing monstrosities can't be fixed with a footnote."

"It's so painful to hear an intelligent young woman say things like that. Opening dimensional doors to emancipate monstrosities is, by all scholarly accounts, a healthy, if primitive, form of group therapy."

"Police reports tell a different story."

"They're attack dogs of the dominant culture. Please reference Dr. Guana Waters-Niquist of Evergreen State College. Watch her TED talk on the Dunwich cult. Waters-Niquist points out that fire, chanting, strange words, and sacrifice might describe any church service. She received thunderous applause."

"President Deale, we're talking past each other. Thank you for helping me clarify my thoughts. And thank you for the job offer. But the *Necronomicon* cannot go to Dunwich under any circumstances. It must remain safely here at Miskatonic."

"I can't believe you believe what you believe," said Deale.

Without a word, O'Connor gathered up her coat and purse and left the office. Deale simmered. *Superstitious bitch. Notify Audrey, Angelo, and the others. Next week, Mercy O'Connor gets her dumb blue-collar ass kicked. And tell Angelo to call Barney Resnicek. For Audrey's plan, we'll need a painter's ladder.*

CHAPTER 8

BATTLE OF THE ANTIQUITY SECTION

"Is Dunwich a suburb of Hell? Oh, please, not that. Show me your data. Show me your studies. And don't say you're relying on oral history or discredited common sense. That diva won't shop."
— *Swarthmore sociologist Dr. Ruth Kornblight, from an article in* The American Journal of Scornful Rebuttals

During an afternoon of opioid painkillers and vodka, a fifteen-year-old boy from Athol blurted out a secret to his peers. Slurring his words, he recounted how he'd been paid by his very cool Uncle Jasper to compile a list of Obed Whateley rewards from the Massachusetts Crime Stoppers Web Site. But he wasn't supposed to talk about it, and no one else should either. Later, one of the boy's peers told an older brother who mentioned it to a friend who declared it to a second cousin who lived in Dunwich. She whispered the news to an acquaintance in Osborn's Store who was overhead by an in-law of Chester Sawyer. Chester's sister-in-law explained to Chester that Jasper Frye was an FBI informant employed by the Bureau to capture Obed Whateley, and that for his assistance Frye would receive four million dollars and a spot in the Witness Protection Program.

This gossip led to Jasper Frye's excruciating agony on the night of October 25. As Sawyer employed the Translucent Python, Frye's body slowly twisted tighter and tighter, rotating on a colorful bed of elm, ash, and maple leaves. Frye's lungs compressed; his shrieks lacked the robust volume of several minutes earlier. Listening to Frye's harsh whispered confession were Obed Whateley, Malachi Hutchins, and a hulking, chinless Dunwicher in a grass-stained windbreaker who seemed to be sexually aroused by Frye's plight.

Said Chester, "Once? Ye called the noxious Antiquity Section and said nothing?"

Over the whippoorwills and bullfrogs, Frye gasped, "Are not my actions of greater weight than one ill-thought moment? Did I not carry out yer plans and obtain the child sacrifices?"

Sawyer glanced at Obed, "He executed my schemes with precision. But I was there to oversee."

Hutchins coughed loudly.

Whateley said, "For faithful service, Frye should not perish slowly by the Python."

Sawyer thrust out his arms, but a tentacle snaked out from within his coat and bit a sleeve, hanging on like a dog playing with a rag. Grunting, Sawyer removed the tentacle, uttered the formula and Jasper Frye unwrapped like the release of tightly wound rubber band, his spinning body making shhhhhing noises in the leaves. Stunned and in pain, Frye sat up gulping air, his shirt covered in white sprinkles from burst sugar packs. "Obed, my loyalty and devotion are yours. Ye know me: never have I even asked for payment, despite long driving miles and meal stops."

"True, but ye have considered betrayal once, and thought is herald to the deed. Chester possesses all the cunning necessary to obtain the book by Hallow Mass Eve."

Frantic, Frye blurted out, "Chester could not find his rump with a flashlight and a dozen more tentacles. Ye have need of me still, Obed."

Chester glared in fury, Hutchins winced sadly, and the hulking Dunwicher giggled and groped himself in inappropriate places.

"Skull of Atlas," said Chester.

Whateley mulled it over, then decided, "Half Flight."

Frye closed his eyes as Whateley cried out the ancient Tamil formula. An instant later, Frye shot into the starry night sky over Dunwich, ascending straight up over a thousand feet as if bound to a missile. At that point, the formula expired and Frye was left to find his own way back to Earth.

"Look ye here, Chester, craft another of your excellent plans and seize this besotted O'Connor girl at the Antiquity Section."

A faint cry of forlorn despair reached their ears, gradually growing louder. Around them, the whippoorwills changed their pitch to a frenetic rhythm. Chester had to raise his voice, "But is not the university fetching the book?"

Walking from the grove across leaves, between Chester and Malachi, Whateley snapped, "All is 'yes' from Deale, but no book. I trust him not to succeed. So much is afoot, fast and preparation, child offerings, mighty formula to throw. Had I time, I would slay Deale over a month and record his screams to play alongside my supper."

Back in the grove, the solitary Dunwicher stared upward, giggling in excitement.

"I will ease yer burden as always," said Chester as a pin wheeling figure plunged into the grove behind them, smashing into the Dunwicher. Bursting like a blood balloon, the remains of Jasper Frye commingled with the devastated corpse of the hulking Dunwicher.

Whateley glanced back, puzzled, "Knew he not to exit the grove?"

Hutchins said, "He was never one to embrace the obvious."

Whateley said, "Were my children out of prison, we would have competent help."

Ceasing their rhythmic chanting, the whippoorwills trailed off into a disappointed, lackluster piping. Whateley clasped Chester's shoulder, "Capture this O'Connor girl. Compel her by any method to deliver up the *Necronomicon* and the long chant. Afterwards, I will present her as bride to Yog-Sothoth, a fitting end to the rainbow-hued meat that is the Antiquity Section."

"Act as if the task were done," said Chester.

As the Little Man strode off toward the road, Chester turned to Hutchins. "See ye to the details, and be quick."

"How?" Hutchins replied. "Jasper had the keener mind. I never pretended otherwise. I carted the sacrifices, infected Morgan, secured the children, while ye took credit for all. Will ye tell the Little Man that he just killed his most capable servant?"

Chester grew agitated and scornful, tentacles writhing beneath his jacket, creating a ripple effect. "Frightened, Malachi? The girl knows not formula, only drink. Watch ye and learn who is the most capable servant."

Hutchins was grateful for the dark as he fingered the butt of his pistol and thought of two things: how much he missed Jasper Frye, and how pleasing it would be to shoot Chester Sawyer in his vapid, chinless face.

Oct. 26

Mercy called Bongani from her car and said she'd be in late. Driving southwest from Arkham, she arrived in Newton mid-morning, parking on a residential street. Mercy knew the area well. Chestnut Hill was adjacent. The BC freshman dorms were proximate, as was the law school, and the Newton Campus Lacrosse/Soccer Complex. Mercy's freshman year, the pitch surrendered its grass for Astro Turf. On that turf she'd received her very first Division One red card after a referee caught her tripping a Florida State striker, then kneeing her in the back. Good times.

After knocking and ringing the doorbell of a house, Mercy strolled cautiously around the Mansard Victorian home, glancing up at the second story windows. Curtains closed, no movement. Bursting through a gate into a fenced backyard, Mercy paused at a cedar deck with a glass-topped patio table. On the table were an ashtray filled with filter cigarette butts, a quart bottle of red wine, and a half-filled goblet. Stepping onto the deck, Mercy prepared to call out, but froze upon hearing claws click on the sidewalk. Turning, Mercy observed a Rhodesian Ridgeback heading for her. No snarls or barks; the dog moved as quietly as a nuclear sub.

"Good boy, good puppy," said Mercy, then felt stupid. This dog was as serious as a blood clot in the lungs. She backed up. Behind her, a sliding glass door opened. Hands clapped twice. The dog trotted off into the yard. Mercy turned to face a balding wrinkled man in his late seventies wearing a cardigan sweater with elbow patches, khaki slacks and carpet slippers, his bloodshot blue eyes seemed somewhat oversized behind spectacles, staring at Mercy as if she were a football field away. With gin blossoms on his sagging facial skin, he frowned and said, "Aren't you supposed to be at Boston College?"

"I graduated. Then I got a Master's at Miskatonic. Now I'm actually chair of the Antiquity Section. It's a long story."

Louis Armitage stared at her until Mercy thought he'd frozen in place. At last, he indicated a chair. "Give me the short version."

Mercy rapidly brought him up to speed on events at the section since Deale's September visit. She left out the part about her and Erin selling formula. Louis Armitage listened, asked a few questions, sipped his wine, smoked. There were times Mercy thought him mentally removed, off on some reverie. But his detachment wasn't affectation or boredom, merely some personal spontaneous attribute.

Mercy finished up, "I told Armand Deale last week that I believed the world might end if we returned the book. I didn't really believe that myself until I said it. It still sounds strange."

Crossing his legs, he stubbed out a cigarette, lit another, exhaled, coughed, cleared his throat, "You know from reading the section journal that our role was never easy. But in the past there were verities we could count on: that our watch was seen as a noble task, and that good and evil were real and not political labels. But today we live in a degraded era. To glibly redefine a menace is easier than naming the threat and smashing it flat."

"I don't know what to do."

"Keep the *Necronomicon* safe. Because if you can't, then you'll have to face Obed Whateley and stop him with formula."

"He'll slice and dice me."

"That would be my guess."

"Feel free to build me up, Uncle Louis. Any tips?"

Louis tapped a cigarette filter on the glass top. "Only once did I visit Galen Rice. Not that he knew. But I couldn't face seeing him. In fact, I was glad when he finally died. He reminded me that there are worse things than death."

"Insanity?"

"Life with dread. Maybe it's better if we're all scrubbed from the earth."

Mercy closed the gate behind her and walked slowly back to the P.T. Cruiser.

Great-Uncle Louis was a fiery, stupendous, nine-story buzz kill.

Oct. 27

After some fun girl chat, Mercy entered the cage and returned with the Dee version of the *Necronomicon*. Audrey Klumm-Weebner smiled warmly, made a sad face at the smeared windows, then turned to examining the book. Mercy noticed her constantly checking her watch as if waiting for a bus. Back at her desk, Mercy leafed through the journal and reread a 1973 police interview with the surviving member of what-came-to-be called the Funwich Commune.

GOLDBERRY: I thought I was freaking out, having a bad trip. So I wriggled out of the orgy and ran back past the stone pillars and sat down in the tall grass with my head between my legs. But I sat on top of a whippoorwill and that was stone freaky. On the hill behind me I heard more shrieks and felt a freezing wind and the hill hissing and then the storm cut loose with a far out, sky-busting thunderclap that was so loud it hurt my ears and I started crying.
DETECTIVE DUNN: And your friend, Meadow?

GOLDBERRY: She screamed her guts out, 'Oh, Jesus God, no.' Stuff like that.

DETECTIVE DUNN: Go ahead.

GOLDBERRY : And then I blacked out. I woke up around dawn, lying in the grass. Up on the hill, everyone was gone except Meadow. She was never Meadow again after that. I mean, her eyes didn't line up right. And she had gorgeous brown eyes, but one would kind of look up, and the other would sort of drift off to one side like it wanted to roll out of her eye socket and explore stuff. Grim to the tenth power.

DETECTIVE DUNN: Why did you wait so long to leave Dunwich?

GOLDBERRY: I thought everything that happened on that hill was all part of the acid trip. Plus this Obed guy and his friends kept hanging out. They'd bring food and plenty of pot and this far out tea. I mean, it was tasty and spiked with something because you'd get real mellow and not do much of anything except rap and drink more tea.

DETECTIVE DUNN: What did Captain Cannibis and the others say about Thumper?

GOLDBERRY: That he probably split, or shacked up with a Dunwich chick or something. No one wanted to believe invisible things ate him. And I wanted them to be right. But they weren't.

DETECTIVE DUNN: If I recall, you said you were squatting in an abandoned farmhouse?

GOLDBERRY: Yeah, so, like I was saying, this Obed cat keeps dropping by. Mostly he'd talk to Meadow and say stuff like, 'Ye must eat more witch root.' or 'That which ye carry need be strong to serve they which walk the spaces between the spheres.' Everyone thought he was, you know, artistic or Taoist or something. But he knew she was pregnant.

DETECTIVE DUNN: Did you?

GOLDBERRY: Yeah, but I didn't want to deal with it. And with free pot and munchies and Dunwich tea, it *was pretty easy to let things slide. By New Year's Eve, Meadow's belly was swollen and she'd rock back and forth holding her tummy and saying, 'Baby's got him some tentacles.'*

DETECTIVE DUNN: What happened to your vehicles?

GOLDBERRY: Obed borrowed the mini bus, but never brought it back, which, I think, is how we got it in the first place. And the ice cream truck had engine parts missing. You know, for a while, we called our commune Funwich because it was, you know where we could ball and get high in a hassle-free space. And if you didn't remember Thumper, or look at Meadow's eyes, you could pretend everything was righteous.

DETECTIVE DUNN: You said the other commune members vanished?

GOLDBERRY: Sometimes a chick would leave to hitchhike into North Aylesbury and panhandle. But she'd never come back. Other times Obed would invite a few cats to a party and they'd, you know, poof.

DETECTIVE DUNN: What do you think happened?

GOLDBERRY: I think they went up the hill into Obed Land.

DETECTIVE DUNN: Can you describe the day you fled?

GOLDBERRY: Oh, man. There was this trippy snowstorm with the flakes blowing sideways. Obed and his Dunwich dudes hadn't been around for a while and we were hungry, and burning Zap Comix and a peace manifesto, and huddled together under a blanket, shivering big time. But then Obed showed up and wanted to take away Meadow. Captain Cannibis wouldn't let him. Anyway, he stopped the Dunwich dudes long enough for Meadow and I to squeeze out a window. Obed and his pals started yelling and chasing us. Meadow and I got separated in the storm. If that county snowplow hadn't picked me up, I'd have, you know, frozen to death to the tenth power.

There the interview ended, but the document included a typed note:

Here are some of the things you asked for:

"Goldberry" is Clarissa Hammond, a 19-year-old Yale dropout from Far Rockaway, New York.

Massachusetts State Police discovered a mutilated corpse in the abandoned house used by the Funwich Commune. It appeared to be the body of a male, completely inverted, turned inside out. Cause of death was listed as unknown, or possibly involving electricity.

"Meadow" was discovered to be Nancy Ann Czarnik, a 20 year-old Vassar dropout from Lake Forest, Illinois. An unknown motorist brought her to St. Mary's Hospital in Arkham. She died during an emergency caesarian procedure that also failed to save the life of her child. Reports indicated that the dead infant was very bizarre in appearance even for Dunwich — an abnormally large, chinless male with furry black legs and odd rounded feet like a circus elephant; piebald reptilian skin on the chest and back, yellow and black, and with a belt of tentacles around the waist that writhed and nipped at medical personal. Post-mortem, the body dissolved into a greenish-yellow liquid that soon evaporated. The child's condition was attributed to the mother's heavy drug use, or out-of-season fruit.

Hope this helps.

North Aylesbury Detective Sgt. Edward Dunn

"Up into Obed Land."

Mercy closed the journal. Another luscious chronicle of doom: innocent people die wretched deaths, Obed Whateley is involved, then escapes to repeat the cycle.

Lisa buzzed from downstairs and whispered, "I know this sounds crazy, but some SLUGs walked past the front door of the library carrying a long ladder."

"Maybe they got real jobs."

"They've been running around all morning."

"Thanks, Lisa. Keep up the updates. Yummy angel food cake is heading your way."

"Lemon icing."

"Tomorrow."

Mercy alerted Bongani, saying, "Can they get in here from the roof?"

"I think maybe not."

"Another raid?"

"Perhaps when Klumm-Weebner goes."

"When she bounces, I'll walk her down to the door. You stand ready on the landing. I'll bet they're going to try the roof."

Hanging up, Mercy glanced at the ceiling, listening for muffled thumps and bumps.

Nothing. She returned to reading.

Suddenly, breaking glass sounded from outside the Special Collections room in the corridor, followed by a loud whistle blast.

Mercy rushed into the corridor in time to see Bongani sprinting past the Coke machine, hands clutching pistol and nightstick. "Baba Morgan's office."

"I'll be right there."

Heart thudding, Mercy returned to Special Collections and swept up the book from in front of a surprised KW. "Sorry, Audrey, but there's an emergency."

Unlocking the special collections cage, Mercy laid the *Necronomicon* onto the floor inside the door, then relocked the cage. Fob and keys still clutched in her hand, she ran from the room.

Audrey scowled, slapped the desk in frustration, stood and smoothed her pants. She walked outside Special Collections to the guard

station. On the radio, a raspy man's voice thanked
God and a phantom trucker for saving his life
from a motorcycle gang. Audrey searched around
the guard station desk, at last locating a white
button.

She pressed and held the button.

Downstairs, a door opened and the pounding
of twelve feet sounded on the stairs. Six male
undergrads streaked upward, wearing tee-shirts
that said, #givebackthebook and
#istandwithdunwich and "IF YOU DON'T LIKE
MY NON-TRADITIONAL RELIGION F*** OFF."

At the same time, down the corridor, past the
melted drinking fountain, inside Morgan's office,
Bongani dueled a gutsy SLUG standing on a
ladder outside the smashed office window.
Fiberglass nightstick clacked against a crow bar.
Mercy shoved fob and keys into her pants pocket,
relieved that Joe B. was holding onto his nightstick
this time. She grabbed the desk phone to dial 9-1-
1. Jabbing with the nightstick, Joe B. forced the
SLUG to retreat back down the ladder rungs out of
sight.

Outside Morgan's office, crashes echoed in
the corridor, young male voices whooped and
roared, whistles blew.

Oh, crap. Mercy dropped the phone and
rushed into the hallway. Near the top of the stairs,
four SLUGs overturned the guard desk and
smashed the monitors. One crushed Bongani's
radio by leaping on it with both feet. Audrey
Klumm-Weebner and two other SLUGs
disappeared back into Special Collections.

Mercy exploded, "I'll kill that two-faced cow.
Joe, they're inside."

As Bongani darted from the office, Mercy
realized they'd have SLUGs behind them now,
pouring in the broken window. She slammed shut

Morgan's office door, feeling idiotic because there was still no door glass. Today was turning into sucky choice day.

Together, Mercy and Joe B. ran past the bent-over Coke machine as Mercy cried, "I'll protect the book. Do you what you can."

Bongani dashed ahead. To Mercy's surprise and delight, he collided with four SLUGs at the guard station like a bowling ball. Protestors flew, yipped in pain, swung fists, blew whistles in a wild melee that reminded Mercy of the parking lot of a Bruins game.

Into Special Collections, Mercy spotted Audrey Klumm-Weebner and a SLUG behind her desk, attacking the cage lock with a pry bar. Mercy decided to seal the cage door in their stupid SLUG faces. Focusing all her anger, excitement, and fear into the Chaldean words, Mercy flung out her arms. But before she could fully activate the Forge of Nin-Agal, a burly SLUG burst low from the cloakroom and tackled Mercy to the floor.

"Got her," he yelled a moment before Mercy spun around and cracked him in the cheek with her elbow. "Owww. Hey, Professor, you said she wouldn't fight."

"Barry, grab her arms," said Audrey to the bespectacled, woolly-headed SLUG with the pry bar. Dropping the tool, Barry Gristleman hurried over and knelt on Mercy's shoulders as the burly SLUG sat on her thrashing legs. Both students fought to contain the enraged woman as Audrey patted Mercy's pants pockets like a cop checking for heroin packets.

"Why are you so mean?" Audrey asked. "You hate this place. Seriously, you can't tell me you went through six years of higher education to protect a stolen book?"

"You're going to get people killed," said Mercy.

Audrey and her SLUGs laughed in derision.

Barry marveled, "A true believer. She won't hear a word we say."

"Drank the Kool-Aid," said Burly SLUG.

Yells and curses from the corridor, followed by more whistle blasts and running feet. Three more SLUGs arrived from the direction of Morgan's office as they zipped past Special Collections. Voices shouted in the hallway:

"He broke Dillon's wrist."

"Look out for that pepper spray."

"Oh, shit, it's all over my shirt."

"There's a drinking fountain down the hallway."

Audrey fished the keys from Mercy's pocket. "Sit on her until we finish up," she said to the burly SLUG. "Get the window, Barry."

As Audrey and Barry rushed off, Mercy arched her back as Burly SLUG leaned stiff-armed onto shoulders. He smirked, "Give it a rest, babe. You're not going anywhere."

Mercy channeled her frustration, humiliation, pique into the Hebrew formula; focusing her intention on Burly SLUGs hands. Using the Selective Inferno, she aimed to make the guy's hands temporarily super hot so she could wriggle free. Crying out the words, Mercy tensed, ready to escape.

But the results were unexpected.

Burly SLUG's arms burst into green flames from fingertips to shoulders.

Screaming, he hopped to his feet and fled in panic around Special Collections, flapping both limbs as if desiring immediate flight. Crashing into desks and chairs, knocking over green-shaded banker lamps, he finally lumbered into the

JP MAC

hallway to a chorus of spooked profanity and alarmed shouts.

On her feet, freaked out over Burly SLUG, Mercy saw the cage door open, keys dangling in the lock. Barry held a smeared window open as Audrey gripped the Dee *Necronomicon* in both hands. However they stood motionless like two ice sculptures, gaping as Burly SLUG and his flaming appendages ran back into Special Collections. Not waiting for Audrey and Barry to recover, Mercy charged.

Barreling into Audrey, Mercy ripped the book from her hands, knocking the professor backwards into the cage. Mercy felt herself slammed from behind as Barry leaped onto her back. As he attempted a chokehold, Mercy snapped forward at her waist, hoping to flip him. But all she accomplished was to drape the co-founder of SLUG across her back.

Snarling, Audrey returned to the scrap and seized the book. Like a rugby scrum, the three spun around the space between the window and the cage clutching, squeezing, gasping, cursing.

A deafening *POP!* from the hallway.

"Holy shit, someone's shot," said Barry, jumping free from the scrum.

Mercy kicked Audrey in the left calf, delighting in her pained scream. But in snatching free the book, she lost her balance. Barry stuck out a foot and tripped Mercy. Both hands pressing the book to her chest, Mercy fell, striking her head against an oak desk.

Stars and lights, then blackness.

CHAPTER 9

TO THE VICTORS GO THE SPOILED

October 29 article from the *Miskatonic Scholar:*

TOP COP DENOUNCES CAMPUS VIOLENCE
Cites Antiquity Section Attack on Students
by Quinn Bisque

"No one's getting bullied on my watch," said Zane Underkrammel. The forty-eight year old head of campus security is continuing his investigation into yesterday's wild incident inside the Antiquity Section. Located on the second floor of the Henry Armitage Library, the section was the scene yesterday of a peaceful protest that ended in a series of savage assaults that left several students hospitalized.

"Every campus Safe Space is absolutely filled today," said Professor Audrey Klumm-Weebner. "Students are hugging each other, watching kitten videos and otherwise attempting to cope with yesterday's unprovoked brutality and trauma." Present during the occurrence, Klumm-Weebner blames the turmoil on Antiquity Section Chairman Mercy O'Connor and a deranged security guard. "Several students entered the section to protest and explore," said Klumm-Weebner. "Isn't that what college is all

about? But instead they [Students Loyal to Underserved Groups] were beaten, set on fire and shot for no reason."

Students echoed Professor Klumm-Weebner's concerns.

"I've never been to the Antiquity Section," said sophomore journalism major Heather Oddis, "and I've never met anyone who works there. But I hear it's a weird place and all my friends say everyone up there is creepy. So maybe they shouldn't be allowed to attack students for no reason."

Antiquity Section Chair Mercy O'Connor declined to comment as she was hospitalized yesterday for fecal incontinence. Arkham Police detained security guard Joseph Bongani for discharging a firearm into the ceiling of an old library. According to Chief Underkrammel, Bongani has been terminated from the Miskatonic security force and may face further charges pending investigation.

University President Armand Deale this morning issued a measured plea for calm. "Let's allow the investigation to proceed at a comprehensive, unhurried pace. We shouldn't be hasty in our judgments, no matter how much evidence is on one side."

As the campus attempts to heal, Professor Klumm-Weebner offered a number of thoughtful insights. "They've [Antiquity Section] gone mad looking for madness in others. They've claimed to fight monsters, but become monsters themselves. Don't they know that an eye for an eye leaves everyone blind? Let us all strive to be one-hundred percent pro-eyes."

A misty late morning found Armand Deale triumphant. Seated on his office couch, Audrey, Leo Hameyes, and Carter Fong laughed and *mmmmmm'd*. On the floor, Angelo Silent Feather enjoyed a late breakfast of hot pond lilies and salted deer lips. In the center of the glass-topped desk rested the *Necronomicon*. Deale found he didn't like touching the book, or even being in its presence. But he could think of no rational reason for feeling that way, so he shut up and raised his latte in a toast, "to a bold plan by Audrey and Angelo."

Polite applause and grins.

Dolphin smile creasing her face, Audrey counter-toasted, "to Armand Deale: the definition of forceful leadership."

More enthusiastic applause and smiles.

Carter held up his smartphone: "I went live on Gabby Face during yesterday's protest. We got the fourth most tickles in history."

Phone call. Autumn Cryer. Deale held up a 'wait a sec' finger to his guests and answered. "Autumn, great article this morning in the *Scholar*. 'Fecal incontinence' was hilarious. I was laughing my butt off. . . . Mild concussion? Really? Oh, boo-hoo. . . . Yes, but keep it short. It'll be four faculty and administrators, plus Barry Gristleman and Honna Pegler. . . . Play up the students' activism and credit them for rescuing the book. (Deale winked at his guests.) . . . . Actually, Audrey dropped it out the window and Honna caught it in a blanket, but skip that. . . . Right. Carter Fong will be your media point man. He'll have lots of stills and footage when they return . . . Oh, and toss in something about 'a public conversation,' either starting one or needing one. People enjoy that phrase."

Deale wrapped up the call as Leo's pink tongue flicked out and licked coffee from his chin. He said, "Leland Janus must be excited to learn we have the book."

"Screw him," said Deale. "I know it's wrong and he's been trampled between the toes of the privileged, but Janus talks to me like I'm his idiot butler. And to answer your question, Leo, no he doesn't officially know. I'm not taking his calls. If you read today's *Scholar*, we mostly play up student injuries.'

Audrey rubbed her left calf. "You don't have to play them up. That bitch really kicked me hard."

Laughter and sympathetic sounds. Carter said, "How did Mercy O'Connor set Brandon's arms on fire?"

Uncomfortable silence. Deale touched thumb and forefinger to his chin. "Underkrammel said that's exactly what the cops asked. No one smelled or found gas, lighter fluid, propane tanks or any kind of accelerants; nothing electrical. O'Connor had no lighters or flares or matches. In fact, Brandon had her pinned to the floor."

"He left the hospital yesterday," said Angelo. "Second degree burns, blisters on his forearms, a bad sunburn, really." He paused to munch a deer lip. "Brandon told me, and I quote, 'O'Connor said a bunch of Jewish words, then every hair on my body stood up.'"

"Obviously static electricity," said Audrey.

Leo scratched the fine hair on his hands, "Did he mean Hebrew words?"

Hebrew words, fire; some other words, legs wrapped; Coke machine, drinking fountain, hair standing up, the abominable stare of Leland Janus. Deale felt as if he were plunged into a whirlpool, vertigo swelling inside him like a chia pet, engorging him with the disorientating fact that forces roamed Arkham beyond manipulation, bribery, threat, social media shame, legal action, mockery, humiliation, or brute force. Deale was coming to hate and fear such forces.

Rising to his feet, he said, "What matters is that we set a goal and achieved it. The book is returning home where it belongs."

Applause, power fists. Carter Fong glanced at his smartphone. "One of our SLUG kids posted a selfie he took right before he was cracked in the elbow with a night stick. You think someone would've told him that selfies make fighting harder."

Angelo's eyes laser beamed the younger man, "Are you implying that the stupid Indian exercised poor leadership? Sure, go ahead, finger-point at the Red Man; massacre his women and children, shoot his sacred buffalo from train windows."

Audrey interrupted, "Armand, are we still booked at the North Aylesbury Ramada?"

"That was the original plan, but in between caustic snark, Janus insisted everyone stay at Ye Great Old Inn. It'll be in today's travel email."

"Wicked," said Carter. "Right in the middle of town."

Deale added, "Janus felt it vital that everyone from Miskatonic be part of the ceremonies. Then he called me a 'moon-faced dung eater.'"

Leo Hameyes said, "His anger is justified, understandable in the face of hegemonic cis religious coercion."

"Annoying old clown," muttered Deale.

"And wasn't there a page we were supposed to copy?" asked Audrey.

Deale glanced outside and frowned. A black priest walked quickly across the quad from the direction of the library. Under the cleric's arm Deale noticed something rolled up like a yoga mat. Head down, the man passed from sight. Brow furrowed, Deale tried coaxing forward some priest recollection lost in the rough of his peripheral awareness. *Nada*. Turning back to his peers he said, "Yes. Page blah-blah from the blah *Necrooboe*. Find out while you're there and we'll mail it to Janus next week. I'm sick of his pestering."

Deale thought of the coin in his smart phone case. Did he really need a sack of gold from Janus? Sweet, but with the federal government backing student loans, Deale could jack up annual tuition into the troposphere. *Necrodisco* off campus, he could taste savory, tax-deductible donations rolling in like a cash tsunami.

Audrey leaned back in the couch and inclined her head toward the smeared windows of the Antiquity Section, "Any reason I can't begin some preliminary improvements?"

"Let's wait until it's officially closed. I need time to prepare the dinosaurs on the board, alumni association, etc. for the sad news that Miskatonic University has dropped Dark Age book wardening and entered the 21st Century. Professor Klumm-Weebner, consider the Antiquity Section your Winter Solstice present."

To Deale's delight, Audrey's eyes displayed irritation, impatience. *Play little games with me, huh?*

Carter set his phone on the couch arm. "If they fired the guard and O'Connor's in the hospital, who's over there now?"

Deale pondered the question, sipped his latte, and then said, "Who cares?"

As her parents left the room, Mercy sat up in bed. "Thanks for the clean clothes, Mom."

"I'll come get you tomorrow, sweetie. You rest up. And if you need anything at all, call us at once."

Her father added, "Don't let 'em stiff you on your paycheck. Your injuries are work-related."

At the door, she called out, "Daddy, please don't go protestor hunting with James, Clancy and Kevin. I'll be fine. Let me work this thing out."

"We'll wait. For now. You know, that Bongani guy sounds okay. Bring him over for dinner sometime. We'll have clams or cheese."

Waving 'bye,' her father's eyes sparkled. Mercy never ceased to marvel. James and Clancy had visited last night. Kevin had stopped in this morning before work. For all her family's emotionally chaotic Irish tribalism, they were there when you needed them. Unfortunately, there were also there when you didn't need them. Still, anyone messing with her had better be ready for advanced trouble.

Folding her arms across her breasts, she returned to a full afternoon slate of resentments and self-pity involving ways to humiliate Audrey Klumm-Weebner. Mercy wondered how she could have been suckered so completely. *Miserable little slut Judas.* She hadn't wanted to believe anything bad about a chick who loved *Mysterious Dunwich.* Conned the whole time. *Why did this happen to her?* Where was everybody else? Why was she the one left to guard the *Necronomicon? Thanks, world. Now you'll be horribly destroyed because you were too busy to help me.*

Father George arrived with Mercy's pentagram mat, returning her swipe card. Checking her watch, Mercy was shocked to see over an hour had passed in feeling sorry for herself and hating people who weren't there.

"Thanks, Father. Anyone on duty?"

"No one. But the cage was locked and I could find no keys. Also, someone swept up the wrecked and destroyed equipment, and placed a covering across the broken window in Conrad's office."

Mouth dry, Mercy pointed to the plastic water carafe on her nightstand. Father George poured her a glass and Mercy downed it in a gulp. "Did you see Lisa?"

"A nice woman, but very lonely. She holds you with talk like a snare. She said Armand Deale most certainly has the *Necronomicon*."

For a frantic moment, Mercy considered calling Uncle Louis, begging him to respond. But that would be a waste of what few moments she had left. Mercy felt tears welling up, hating herself for crying. "Well, that's the buzzer. We're officially screwed. I got the Earth dragged into another dimension. Not many can say that."

Handing her a tissue, Father George waited as Mercy dabbed at her eyes. "Why not call Michael Vitale in North Aylesbury and see if the book has reached Dunwich?"

"I'd be ashamed. How's Joe B.?"

"Better. He was held overnight. A lawyer, a former parishioner, told me that since Joseph was on private property, at work and defending against many attackers, the police probably won't charge for the gunshot. But they have kept his guns, which upsets him."

"Doomed. The whole planet. Thank you, me, for killing billions."

"Joseph was very worried about you."

"You're kidding? That's, I don't know, kind of sweet."

"Both of you fought with much passion. You did all you could."

"Appreciate it, Father, but we lost. You know, you don't seem too worried about our upcoming, sphincter-emptying annihilation."

Father George scratched the back of his neck, "The end is not here today. Also, the book could still be on the campus. I will ask around. Also, please give this to Joseph."

The priest handed Mercy an intricate, handmade bracelet with beads of blue and white and black. She recalled the day Joe B. had hidden them from her. "Very pretty."

Father George nodded, "I found it on the floor. It must've fallen from his pocket yesterday."

"Does he make jewelry on the side? I wouldn't be surprised. I didn't know he could fight until yesterday."

Glancing out the window, Father George watched a UPS panel truck ease into a space on Boundary Street. "Joseph will explain."

They spoke for a while longer, until the priest was called away for an emergency. Mercy gently touched the bandage around her head. Her head felt tender. Mercy called the library, gave Lisa the fast version of yesterday's events, then asked her to check on the whereabouts of the *Necronomicon*.

On her phone were messages from the swing and midnight shift guards. Returning their calls, Mercy learned that the swing shift guard had cleaned up the section and pocketed the key to the Special Collections cage. Good man. She arranged for the guards to split the day shift, promising them time and a half. Something as mundane as scheduling lifted Mercy's spirits. Maybe humanity still had a shot.

Two concerned text messages from Erin. Mercy prepared to delete them, still angry with her cousin for storming out at Club Swill. But should the world indeed end, Mercy didn't want to check out hating anyone—except Audrey Klumm-Weebner. Mercy texted Erin that she would call once her head cleared up.

Late afternoon and Bongani strolled in, a bandage across the bridge of his nose. Band-Aids and surgical tape crisscrossed his dark face and knuckles. Nice jacket, pressed slacks, clean shoes. She'd never seen him not in uniform. To her delight, Joe B. presented her a regular Dunkin Donuts coffee.

"You rock big time," she told him.

"It cost me not a penny. I had one coupon."

"Awesome fight yesterday."

"Yes, and very proper formula. The burning arms was very good."

"It's not what I meant to do."

Pulling up a chair, he sat beside her. Mercy handed him the bracelet, "From your uncle. So what's the story?"

"I will tell you soon."

"I've been getting that a lot. It must be a Zulu thing."

They replayed the raid, what each had thought and done and felt.

"Everything moved so very slow," he said, "and there were odd things. A SLUG man stopped in the middle to take a picture of himself. I struck him in the arm with my baton."

"Good thing you didn't break his phone. He'd be in intensive care. Listen, we need to alert the cute-sounding Officer Vitale."

"I have called Michael. He will get me a spare gun."

"Did he say anything about me?"

"Only that you must face Whateley."

"Like hell. Does Whateley have the book yet?"

Bongani reached over and borrowed Mercy's coffee, taking a sip. "Michael didn't know, but thought maybe not."

Lisa called back. Mercy learned that Deale had the book in his office that morning. Mercy thanked her, hung up and informed Bongani. Joe B. sat back, thought for a moment. "Today a guard friend called to be sorry for my firing."

"That's such bullshit."

"He said he must do guarding at the administration building."

"Sounds like he's employed and rubbing it in."

"He must be guarding tonight outside Armand Deale's office."

Despite knowing it was unladylike to gape, Mercy's did so anyway as the possibilities swarmed around her mind like midges. "Is this a good friend?"

"Pretty good."

"Will he let us check inside the office for the book?"

"He will be afraid of being fired."

"Listen, we pop over there tonight. Or better yet, I'll wait downstairs. You go up alone and see if this guy will let you check out Deale's office."

"And what of the *Necronomicon*?"

Mercy thought of various euphemisms, evasions, dodges, then blurted out, "It can't go to Dunwich, right? We know that."

"Yes."

"So, if the book is there, we find a way to steal it back. If your friend gets canned, I swear I'll make my Dad give him a job with the IBEW Local 153. By the way, Dad wants you to come over for dinner. Can you learn to do a fake Italian accent? Watch a couple of Marx Brothers movies, you'll pick it up."

After discussing various aspects of the coming night's expedition, Joe B. and Mercy left to pay a visit to Professor Morgan. On the floor above Mercy, he lay in bed and blinked, rigid as reinforced concrete and just as mobile. The doctors were still baffled. Mercy felt sad and angry. She desperately needed his advice.

Below on Boundary Street, a chinless face peered out the driver's side window of the UPS truck, staring at the hospital, then quarreling with someone inside the vehicle. Minutes later, the engine started up. Windshield wipers flipped back and forth as the panel truck slowly drove off.

Night brought more light rain to Arkham. Mercy and Joe B. made plans for later. Bongani split when Mercy's supper arrived, but she barely touched her meal, eating some vegetables and Jell-O, keeping it light in case the evening required formula. It didn't seem likely. Besides, Mercy lacked any knockout or invisible formula. No forget-we-were-ever-here stuff. If necessary, she could set Deale's office door on fire, or seal it shut, or protect against someone else's formula. The more Mercy reflected on what she'd learned, heard, or read in the journal, throwing formula was, for the most part, pretty brutal. Many incantations resulted in ghastly and fatal modifications to the human form. Very few formulae could be reversed. Recalling her brothers as teenagers, she thought of their maniacal, single-minded focus on ditching school, sneaking off places with girls, acquiring drugs and alcohol, obtaining money without working, avoiding the cops, lying to her father, basically doing whatever they wanted without responsibility. Then she imagined some deranged teenage loner stealing his mom's formula DVD and channeling hate, alienation, and social isolation into the Selective Inferno. What terror he might unleash would eclipse school shootings by many magnitudes. Let Erin bitch. Formula needed the lid screwed on tight.

A little after 10:00 p.m., Mercy greeted the night shift nurse, made sleepy noises and asked her to close the door as she left. After waiting a moment, Mercy rushed to the closet, pulling on a sweater and jeans. They slid on easily, a tribute to six weeks of consistent formula. As she laced up running shoes, Mercy considered her choices. Best scenario would be to snag the book, have Joe B. stash it, then return to the hospital. But something would probably go wrong. Such had been life's recent pattern. In which case, she'd need to bring her things.

Grabbing the plastic bag lining of an unused waste bin, Mercy stuffed yesterday's clothes and shoes inside. Wearing a charcoal gray insulated hooded jacket, she peeked out into the corridor, then shut the door behind her. Arms full of plastic bag, pentagram mat, and purse, Mercy stepped quickly down the corridor, into the elevators.

Outside the hospital, on the corner of West and Pickman Street, Mercy flipped up her hood against the sprinkles and realized she didn't know the make of Bongani's car. *Probably an F250 pick-up with a God, Guns, and Guts bumper sticker.* A UPS vehicle cruised past Mercy, traveling west on Pickman, brake lights flashing red as the panel truck stopped suddenly in the middle of the lane. Mercy failed to notice, her attention on a 2014 Mini Cooper angling toward the curb in front of her. She couldn't see the driver and tensed, but then a window rolled down and Mercy heard steel guitars and a woman singing about seducing her man in the restroom of Arby's.

"Unbelievable, Joe B. A black guy driving a Mini Cooper and listening to country and western music. You're like matter and anti-matter all rolled together. You're your own universe."

"Uncle George knows a dealer who leases it for me. Come now. We must go."

Shoveling her belongings into the back seat, Mercy opened the driver's side door and paused, leaning into the car. Neither she nor Bongani observed the UPS truck backing toward them as Mercy said, "You know what? Parking is a bitch around campus. We should park here and walk over."

With Mercy in the shotgun seat, Joe B. eased the car forward, then turned right into the hospital's underground lot. Stopping sharply, the UPS truck U-turned on Pickman. Now pointing east, the brown truck pulled into a bus stop across the street from St. Mary's, idling as drizzle collected on the windshield, forming a watery blur. When two figures emerged from the hospital parking lot, the truck followed them.

Mercy hurried to keep pace with Joe B.'s long steps as they crossed West Street and turned left, heading north past computer stores, copy services, sports bar O Beer Thirty, and fast food joints. They headed toward College Street. Red brick-rich Miskatonic University waited on the other side of the street. Traffic on West was light, and pedestrian traffic even lighter. Campus housing had been moved to Litch Street back in the late 80s and the old dormitories converted to classrooms. A plastic trash bag spilled out of an alley. Mercy stepped around cans and dirty paper towels, turning to Joe B. "So you go up first, and I'll wait downstairs."

Bongani slowed. "I should call to the man first."

An engine accelerated behind them traveling north on West Street.

"Call on your phone?"

"Yes."

"You think? What if he says 'don't come by'? Just go."

"I will call."

Headlights flared. Mercy yelped as a UPS truck jumped the curb with a crash. Joe grabbed her arm and jerked her back. Patrons emptied out of O Beer Thirty onto the sidewalk, smart phones at the ready as the truck's passenger side door slid open. Mercy felt hair on the back of her neck rise.

"Stay close to me," she cried. Throwing out her arms, Mercy quickly recited the Greek phrase, praying she could form Pirandello's Aegis before they were engulfed by pitiless, inhuman formula.

CHAPTER 10

ROAD TRIPS

October 30 article from the *Miskatonic Scholar:*

Diversity Delegation Departs for Dunwich
Justice Served as Sacred Book Recovered
By Quinn Bisque

A ringing victory for religious diversity will occur today as Miskatonic faculty and students are to set out at noon to return a sacred text to a marginalized people. Said junior Barry Gristleman, co-founder of Students Loyal to Underserved Groups, "We're hoping this is the end of non-healing." Added junior Honna Pegler, SLUG's co-founder, "By returning the Necronomicon we'll start a much-needed conversation on the effects of cultural marginalization and oppression, 'cause no one talks about those issues. Ever."

A six-member delegation of faculty, students and administrators has been invited to participate in holy ceremonies tonight and Halloween evening atop Sentinel Hill. Meanwhile, an investigation continues into the recent violence at the Antiquity Section that disrupted a peaceful protest. Said Chief Zane Underkrammel, "While it's important to follow the facts, the outcome doesn't look good for the Antiquity Section."

Lying across a double bed, Audrey soaked a cotton ball in bath oil. Dabbing her upper lip, she hoped the scent would cut the pungent

Dunwich tang, wafting into her motel room like a gas leak. Apprehensive, Audrey flipped through a guest journal, scanning the arcane comments:

"Here, one may discuss the Furnace of Nug without explanation."

"By this time tomorrow I shall be eaten alive. I feel like a kid before Christmas."

"When I think about you, I cry Ia! Shub Nigguruth and touch myself."

Disturbed by the odd writing, Audrey set aside the journal and switched on a closed circuit TV. Graphics invited the viewer to follow along in a chant to mighty Cthulhu, succeeded by an ad to visit sunken R'lyeh, courtesy of Dunwich Travel. Finally, guests were reminded to display protective charms before going to bed. The cycle closed with the image of a sinister, octopoid-faced monstrosity and the graphics, "See You In Your Dreams."

Flipping off the TV, Audrey roamed the room, considered doing yoga to calm herself, flipped through magazines left on a chair. These publications included the disturbing *Human Sacrifice Quarterly* and a copy of *Amped Up Awesome Old Ones*. The latter appeared to be a teen-oriented glossy with articles such as, "What To Wear When You Absolutely Know You're Going to Be Crushed," and "Ten Signs-Yog Sothoth Likes You."

Audrey peered out the curtains. More young chinless males loitered outside her room like migrant workers around a lumber yard. Between the ominous rounded hills and the rank smell, and a growing sense of paranoia, all the gruesome legends and esoteric rumors that her book had debunked arose in Audrey's imagination. Looming like a rogue wave, they threatened to smash over the prow of reason, swamping her mind with enough unfiltered terror to send her gibbering down the road to North Aylesbury.

Stupid. Relax. Get ready for the meeting.

Sitting at a small desk, Audrey prepared to sample the complimentary tea. Marveling at the cup, she recognized genuine bone china in a Shelley Rosebud pattern: English, Worcester, 18th century, very good condition. Why use nice antiques for guest service in a motel? Sipping the hot beverage, Audrey's taste buds detected hints of mint and chamomile plus something pleasingly exotic. Another few sips and her anxiety lessened. Even the stench of Dunwich didn't seem so appalling. Sitting quietly with her tea in a warm room felt simply perfect on a rainy day.

A quarter hour passed. With great reluctance to move or take action of any kind, Audrey finally roused herself and walked down to Angelo's room. In the parking lot, she watched raindrops splattering gently off the bulky frame of Miskatonic University's brand new, forest green Chevy Pangaea. With a roof covered in solar panels and a large turbine blade rising on a tower from the rear like a pinwheel—designed to spin above thirty miles an hour—the huge SUV was Armand Deale's pride, a symbol of tomorrow.

Squeezing past guests and more idle chinless men, Audrey entered Angelo's room. Her mood brightened upon seeing a very large teapot, spare cups, and saucers. Everyone was present, including Barry in his #thisiswhatdunwichlookslike T-shirt and Honna wearing her blonde hair in cornrows. All were seated or sprawled except Angelo, who attempted to sit cross-legged on a pillow. But he wobbled too much and finally stretched out his feet, back against the wall. All drank tea. Room on the bed was made for Audrey, who couldn't recall what they discussed, but felt the conversation was dazzling and clever with much laughter and *mmmmmmmm's*.

Was there a knock? Who opened the room door? Audrey wasn't sure, but chinless women moved among them. A floral garland was draped about Audrey's neck. They were plastic flowers of the sort often found in furniture store displays, coated in dust, with drops of some dark liquid on the petals. But they seemed wonderful, the gesture heartfelt and thoughtful.

"As headwoman of the Friends of Sentinel Hill Women's Auxiliary, I thank ye all most deeply for returning our most coveted book," said a chinless woman with a strange suction mark scar on her lower jaw and neck. "Rest ye all tonight, save for the young. Tonight is their night of honor."

"Sounds freaking awesome," said Honna. Barry giggled and waved.

"Wait ye all here for yer supper," said Suction Scar as the auxiliary filed out.

"Where is Mr. Janus?" called Angelo from the floor.

Suction Scar's face wrinkled in confusion. A whispered conversation took place in the doorway between auxiliary members and several men loitering outside the room. At last, Suction Scar faced the room. "He rests up for tonight, but thanks ye deeply for the book, so necessary to the Great Return. Tomorrow, he will accept from ye that which belongs to him."

"We look forward to joining in your ceremonies," said Angelo.

"Ye will. Ye all most certainly will," said Suction Scar. Closing the door, there was silence outside for a moment, followed by a burst of laughter.

"Mocking, sardonic," said Leo, fingering the plastic flowers around his neck with delicate hairy fingers. "No doubt directed at the Antiquity Section."

General agreement, more tea. Lying across the bed, Carter said, "I forgot to take any video for Gabby Face."

Laughter, *mmmmm's*, gentle jibes, more tea.

On the night table, Audrey noticed motel stationary. She smiled at the enigmatic logo: Ye Great Olde Inn—It's Not the Cold Waste of Kadath, But Ye Can See It From Here.

How the afternoon did fly. Slowly, the gray light faded in the room. Like a technician dialing up volume, whippoorwill cries swelled, growing louder, joined by bullfrogs from the nearby Miskatonic River. No one rose or turned on a light until the auxiliary women brought supper. Audrey enjoyed two helpings of a delicious stew, with fresh baked bread, and homemade pie for dessert. And, of course, more tea. At some point, a squad of chinless men ushered Honna Pegler and Barry Gristleman from the room. The undergrads seemed reluctant to leave the teapot, but promised to relate every detail of what they saw and experienced.

Fong said, "Watch for fat lightning from one of those flat-bottomed black formations."

"Anvil cloud," said Barry. "Sure, Professor Fong."

As the door shut behind the students, Audrey glanced at a wall sampler. Embroidered in pink and blue was the aphorism, "There's No Place Like the Plateau of Leng." Very homey.

Angelo said, "A tremendous honor to invite outsiders to a sacred ceremony. I think of my people and our millet venerations: the slightest disruption, no matter how innocent, and the ceremony is ruined. By the time you start over, ants have gotten into the millet."

Leo scratched behind an ear, "Generous people, though there are accents of furtiveness, mockery, and a sense that our movements are restricted."

"Oppression has made them suspicious," said Audrey. "Who can blame them, given the region's history of persecution and coercion?"

"I believe I'll coerce myself into another slice of pie," said Carter Fong to chuckles and *mmmmm's*. But he never got up to get it. No one got up for much of anything except reluctant trips to the bathroom, an unwanted distraction from lounging around and drinking tea.

At some point, Audrey found herself wrapped in a blanket, sitting outside surrounded by Angelo, Leo, and Carter. Nighttime found the covered motel porch lined with guests, like spectators grabbing early seats for a parade. Mixed among them were young Dunwich men, arms crossed, eyes on Audrey and her party.

"We're tailgating," said Carter, his tea now inside a small water glass. "Tail gating on Hallow Mass Eve. Look at the freaking fires."

Even in a drizzle, fires dotted the round hillsides. Someone pointed out Sentinel Hill to the southwest, with a great bonfire flaring even at this distance. Much nearer, off to their right, the hillside of Round Mountain erupted in a tremendous hissing and rumbling. Carter Fong flashed the mountain a thumbs up. Leo Hameyes pursed his lips thoughtfully, "Those sounds convey supreme arrogance coupled with a withering distain for all life on Earth. But my impressions are guesswork, since I've never heard anything remotely like them before."

"I'm honored no end to be a witness," said Angelo Silent Feather. Very unsteadily, Angelo stood, cleared his throat and cried out to the motel guests and watching Dunwich men, "Not to be a noodge, but please know that we respect your ceremonies and we look forward to seeing every aspect of your faith fulfilled."

A guest with suction marks on his arms was puzzled. "Know ye the nature of our creed?"

Angelo sat down heavily, "It is an ancient creed, my oppressed brothers and sisters. For that is what I consider you: ancient people like myself."

"Aye, ancient before the world and masters of all," said a female guest.

"My people too were once masters of the earth in days of old."

Suction Arms exclaimed, "Say ye that ye worship the old masters of earth?"

Angelo was emphatic, "Yes. And I desperately wish they would return."

A change came over the crowed. Their eyes glowed with crafty delight and once again Audrey and friends were the center of backpats and handshakes. *We're like rock stars*, thought Audrey, beaming her dolphin smile. *This is all very heady.*

Suction Arms grinned at the Miskatonic contingent, his absence of dental work crying out 'crystal meth.' "Ye seek the Return? We work for it without ceasing. We thought ye but simpletons from the college."

Audrey couldn't say why, but her previous anxieties begged to return. Though muted by the splendid tea, these anxieties seemed to have gone off to shower and change, and were now back ready to uproot her serenity. Leaning in to Angelo, she said, "I think they're talking about something different."

Angelo ignored her and projected his voice like an actor, "The day cannot come too soon when the wilderness is restored."

"Aye. They will scrape clean the earth."

"Policies that will undo man's environmental blasphemy."

"Ye say the truth. Man's works will crumble like a sparrow's nest beneath the feet of the Old Ones."

"Ia!" screamed a middle-aged woman in a homemade dress.

"You have been a voiceless invisible people, but that is about to change."

An old woman answered, "Aye, well said. Those from the Air, too, are invisible."

Angelo roared, "I want back the forest and the birds of the air and the fish of the sea."

Suction Arms cried out, "Crave the sea where Great Cthulhu lies dreaming in R'lyeh."

Carter Fong said, "Isn't that the city on the commercial?"

Audrey said, "I don't think they're talking about the same thing."

Leo cut in, "Trust Angelo. He's bonding with these people through his heritage. He reaches them on a level we could never attain."

"I want a world liberated from climate terror," said Angelo.

"There will be no climate once Man is replaced by those from Outside," responded Suction Arms. "And the earth scraped clean and drug to that dimension which has been called H'lgpah."

"H'lgpah," whispered the others.

Audrey vaguely recalled that the locals desired Earth scoured of all life and hauled into an alien dimension by terrible beings of indiscernible

JP Mac

power. Why wasn't that eschatology as charming and quaint here as it was back in Arkham?

Attention shifted to Sentinel Hill. Audrey thought she heard a faint terrified human scream, godforsaken and agonized, but at such a tortured pitch she could not identify gender.

"Those From the Air dine well," said Sucker Arms.

"Or some fool rolled too far out of the orgy onto sacred ground," added the middle-aged woman.

"Orgy?" said Carter Fong. "Now you're talking."

"Orgy of devotion, no doubt," said Leo. "To paraphrase Freud, sometimes a cigar is just a cigar."

The whippoorwills erupted in a daemonic cackling and shrieking, tripling their already deafening chants.

"Caught one, they did," said a gleeful old man.

Suddenly Sentinel Hill received a massive lightning strike, bursting in the darkness with blinding incandescence. Wide and malevolent, a bolt struck the hilltop like a death ray from a dark alien craft. Audrey felt hair on her arms and neck rise. Electromagnetism from the super lightning strike? But hadn't Armand mentioned the same sensation during formula?

"Holy Fujita," cried Carter. "Can you believe the freaking size of that? In the flash, I saw the clouds and they had a little indent in them."

"Ye be talking a beaver tail notch," said Sucker Arms. "That means inflow."

"I gotta see one of those whoppers up close," said Carter. "Oh, hey, and I gotta remember to take more video. They'd have loved that lightning on Gabby Face."

Audrey startled as another thunderous crack erupted from nearby Round Mountain, followed by a loud hissing noise. Two chinless, well-dressed teenage boys, appearing like upscale relatives home for the holidays, discussed the auditory phenomena.

"That last one sounded like Yog-Sothoth farting."

"You'd shit if you saw He Who Walks Between the Spaces."

"That's total bull. I'd be so cool he'd let me stay on earth after it's cleansed."

"You'd cry like a little bitch and go mad."

"No way. You'd be all loony lunatic with your underwear full of crap."

"Remember that much of what we're seeing is theatrical," said Leo Hameyes to his peers. "The light show and audio are designed to appropriate dominant cultural myths and fears as protective coloring."

A young woman's horrified squeal echoed from Sentinel Hill. Audrey abruptly felt small and insignificant, like a snail at the feet of a cruel booted thug. Adrenalin and trepidation flushed out most of the pleasant tea effects, leaving her buffeted by the stench of Dunwich, cringing at the machine-like piping of the whippoorwills.

In as casual a voice as she could muster, Audrey said, "Did anyone else discover a magazine in their room called *Human Sacrifice Quarterly*?"

Leo patted her arm soothingly, "I believe you were the first to link Dunwich ceremonial tropes to the theories of Paz Encanto. Or am I mistaken?"

"I did?" she said, distracted. "Oh, yes. The locals are certainly primitive Encantoites."

"Audrey put it best in her book," said Angelo. "It's all cultural judo. Discover what the dominant society fears, then display it as a way of creating a religious safe zone."

"Paz Encanto said it first, but KW said it best," said Carter, now drinking tea from a jelly jar.

Leo added, "Without your book to light the way, Audrey, we probably wouldn't even be here."

Audrey smiled weakly, whispered thanks and gazed at her peers. She observed the identical pleasant, sappy expression she'd worn herself a few minutes before.

When it came time to refill her tea, Audrey poured it out into the parking lot when no one was watching.

Dream shifting again, Mercy now traipsed alone through a twilight realm. She wore a summery floral cotton dress and thin sandals, heavy air filled with the scent of mowed grass. Fireflies floated past, winking intermittently as if saving energy. Behind lush green hedges, a bobwhite whistled a lonely cry as if shunned by other bobwhites. Mercy followed the gentle turns of a gravel road. Consisting of thick stones, the gravel made walking in sandals uneven and treacherous. In her hands, Mercy carried a chunk of Trinitrite. Within the greenish rock, a pair of eyes behind spectacles blinked up at her.

Mercy said, "What happened?"

"Not sure," said a young man's voice from the eyes. "Parity, then a slight edge, then a massive energy pulse ripping across the Hop Yard like an H-bomb. Set your defenses first."

"Will I survive?"

The eyes blinked, "It's not enough. You must win, or everyone loses, the good with the bad."

"How can I beat Whateley?"

"You already know."

"Tell me."
"Watch your step on the gravel."

A dulcimer twanged under a chorus about a man who wished he had a dollar for every dream drowned in a Nashville bar. Mercy opened her eyes, mouth arid, lips slightly cracked, a black landscape zipping past the rain-speckled passenger side window. But even the song couldn't drown out the ear-piercing shriek of whippoorwills. A dire stench filled the car.

Smart-ass chunk of Trinitrite.

A water bottle appeared. She accepted, drank, rolled the liquid around her mouth. "Let me guess, we're almost in Orlando, Florida."

"Beyond Dean's Corners, but not very much."

She had *been told, but what was it?* Mercy's recollection crashed into a roadblock, unable to maneuver around last night's abnormal encounter with the UPS truck.

"I haven't been much help today," she said, placing the water bottle back in a cup holder. Fingers probed the new bandages around her throat and shoulder. "Professor Morgan said once that formula was like a credit card. If that's true, I'm in default."

"To face danger, you used much will."

"Must be. I've been nappy all day."

"In addition to your new hurts."

"I'm still freaked out. What happened to the UPS driver?"

In the headlights, unnaturally large moths flung themselves at the vehicle and windshield. *In the rain?* From the roadside weeds, little red eyes followed the Mini Cooper's passage as the blacktop road descended into a marshy region. Bullfrogs added their brutish croaking to the bog chorale.

Mercy said, "I thought frogs used to hibernate."

"Things here are not as elsewhere."

"That's a good motto for the Dunwich Chamber of Commerce."

Bongani wrinkled his nose at the marsh stink, both hands on the wheel. "The driver ran when the police neared. But many from the bar took our photos. I heard some say we threw acid on Sawyer."

"That'll be all over Gabby Face. Crazy stuff. If old Chester wanted to kidnap me, why steal a UPS truck? That's some free-range stupidity. Oh, did I thank you for . . . you know . . . what you did?"

"Yes."

"Pretty ugly deed. Had you . . . you know . . . done something like that before?"

"No."

"Well, if you want to talk or anything, it's cool."

As the marsh smell worsened, Bongani closed the vents. It didn't help. Mercy said, "Strong, silent type?"

"Yes."

"Okay. Well, you were right to make flash cards. We'd be dead without them."

Bongani sat a little taller in his seat.

"And I really, really appreciate all the other high-end work you've done the last day or so, saving my big butt being one of them. Baba Morgan would've been proud."

Nodding, Bongani upped the wiper speed as the rain increased.

"So, Joe B., I still don't get it. Why did he throw formula at all? Send out the guy with the gun first, and we're both dead—or prisoners."

"To see if you could also throw formula."

"That makes sense. Whateley hasn't survived this long without knowing all the players. So you figure Chester was told to check my game?"

"Yes. But now the other man has returned to Dunwich and Obed Whateley knows you are trained. He will be ready."

Mercy said, "Great. Adios, surprise. What if we turn around right now and drive back to Arkham? Turn ourselves in?"

"We will be in jail when the world ends tomorrow night."

"Atlantic City? My treat."

"No."

"What if you drop me off at home so I can spend the last day squabbling with my family?"

"Then I will go on alone."

Mercy sniffled, felt tears forming, "Dunwich isn't going to leave us alone, are they?"

"No."

Water flew up in sheets from low spots in the blacktop. Mercy's last 24 hours had been a carousel of pain, fear, confusion and exhaustion. Father George had disinfected and bandaged Mercy, hidden her and Joe B. overnight in the rectory, given them money in the morning. Bongani arranged a hideout in the apartment of a guard friend. Mercy was still asleep when Michael Vitale came by with spare ammunition and the latest news. Later, in between bouts of REM sleep on a lumpy couch, Mercy learned the police wanted her and Joe B. for questioning. Big surprise. Throughout the day, Bongani kept things moving, efficiently propelling them to their fate, which would probably be some unutterable, horrid termination atop Sentinel Hill. For not the first time, Mercy bitterly wondered how she'd ended up saddled with Conrad Morgan's destiny.

Drawing a deep breath, she glanced at Joe B. He might be the last semi-friendly face she ever saw. "How is that you're an Italian guy who likes songs about pick-up trucks and ex-wives and drinking beer with bitter rodeo midgets?"

"Because many of them tell good stories."

"Yeah, right; shootings and divorce and drunken brawls and heartbroken cowboys."

Silence. Mercy wondered if he was going moody. She really didn't know Joe B. But finally he spoke, "Sometimes there is also hope. A woman is beaten by her husband. She prays to the Lord God Jesus. Then her husband becomes drunk and falls down many stairs and she must care for him. Another song tells of a man who is an outcast, but now the train is his home."

"Hope, huh?"

"Yes."

"Well, keep listening. We could use some."

Mercy drifted mentally back to the night of Oct. 29. When the passenger door of the truck flew open, she'd recognized Chester Sawyer from the flashcards.

He threw formula that Mercy barely blocked. Pressure from his will pushed in the bubble of her aegis, and Mercy felt herself forced back a step. From the words he'd shouted, Mercy knew they faced the Translucent Python and twisting torment.

From around the front of the vehicle stepped a man in a bomber jacket, racking the slide on a semi-automatic pistol. He could shoot into the shield, but if Mercy dropped the aegis to run, the formula would snare her.

Boxed.

Backing up toward the alley, shield enlarged to cover Joe B., her heel touched an olive jar from the spilled trash bag.

Mercy kicked the container at Sawyer.

And missed.

But the jar shattered against the truck, spraying Sawyer with glass.

Mercy felt his formula veer off, like the cessation of a strong wind. Without thinking, she charged. From shouts and curses, Mercy guessed Joe B. had sprung at the gunman.

Striking Sawyer several times in the face, Mercy tried keeping the hybrid occupied so he couldn't throw more formula. And while she'd caught him by surprise, Sawyer recovered quickly. His upper body strength was overwhelming. Grabbing both her wrists, he lifted Mercy so that her feet barely touched the ground. Meanwhile, something snake-like broke free from within Sawyer's clothing. Mercy screamed as a round mouth closed on her throat, alternately biting and sucking. Blood flowed along her neck, down across her breasts as Sawyer laughed, his breath smelling like old Odor Eaters.

"So the little witch knows a trick. Ye will learn more and howl for me to stop the lesson."

Another ropy thing snaked beneath her sweater. A mouth closed on her trapezius muscle. More blood squirted. Straining, wriggling, a frightening thought consumed Mercy: Sawyer wanted her captive.

She yelled in frustration. Sawyer stood on the truck's metal landing in a narrow space and drew Mercy up and into the vehicle. Mercy's attempts to escape were checked by the mouths chewing on her neck and shoulder. She tried wriggling back, but the tentacles stretched, remaining tightly clamped to her like mooring lines securing a skiff to the dock.

Sawyer tugged her back into the truck.

Mercy was deafened by the first round.

Struck in the chin, Sawyer's blood sprayed her face with a greenish-yellow fluid. The hybrid's grip on Mercy loosened as a second round struck him in the right shoulder. A third bullet impacted with his forehead. Lifeless, Sawyer fell backwards into the truck, half propped up by the driver's seat.

Despite a new 9mm eye, Chester's snake-like appendages held tight to Mercy. She fell into the truck, atop Sawyer's corpse. Mercy gripped and twisted the things eating her. Joe B. reached over her shoulder, pinching the "necks" of the snake-like things the way a naturalist seizes a cobra. Disentangling herself, Mercy crawled backwards from the cab.

As a crowd from the sports bar gathered, Chester Sawyer disintegrated, his clothes collapsing onto the metal floor. A greenish-yellow fluid steamed out of his trousers onto the curb, then away into the gutter.

Mercy opened her eyes. Something was up. The Mini Cooper was stopped, wipers flicking slowly, engine running, brights illuminating a dirt side road leading off the blacktop to the left.

"What's up?"

"This is the first road which turns to the left."

"Did I say I knew my way around Dunwich?"

"Yes."

"Then I've got a big mouth. That was ten years ago."

"Drive straight?"

"Sooner or later, we'll hit Dunwich. We need to hide out until we can work up a plan. So, okay, yeah, turn here."

Bongani pointed the Mini Cooper down a muddy road, the vehicle fishtailing at the bottom of the grade. On either side were barren trees and brush, packed with shrieking whippoorwills. Far ahead, Mercy spotted huge fires burning atop several hills.

"Party night."

"Hallow Mass Eve."

Setting the car in low gear, Bongani moved cautiously forward, jostling and rocking across a road creased with ruts of various lengths and depths. Off to the left, Mercy noticed boulders and rocks like giant popcorn scattered in the car's headlights. An eerie sensation gripped her like cold moist fingers around the back of her neck. She thought of a bong and laughter and masking her desire to be home again.

"That's the Devil's Hop Yard to our left. Up ahead and slightly south is Sentinel Hill. Dunwich village is off to the right, I think."

"Do we stop?"

"Hell no. Get us out of here. Keep going straight."

Jolting around and through deep, impressive, water-filled potholes, the Mini Cooper plunged deeper into the haunted countryside.

CHAPTER 11

SEEK AND YE SHALL FIND

"It is well-known that our culture has demonized words like 'human sacrifice.' Clearly, agents of reaction are waging a destructive propaganda campaign against a misunderstood aspect of an outcast religion, whose only crime is being 'different.'"
—*Professor Audrey Klumm-Weebner,*
from her book:
Old Ones, New Values—Fresh
Insights on the Population of
North-Central Massachusetts

Audrey felt silly. How real were last night's screams? She'd been keyed up from the excitement of the last several days. Showering, she thought fatigue and strong tea, not diabolical mayhem, had to be responsible for yesterday's crackpot suspicions. Of course, the smell hadn't abated. If anything, Dunwich stank even worse this morning. After applying makeup and dressing, Audrey prepared a makeshift sachet, soaking a handkerchief in perfume and preparing to feign a slight cold so as not to offend. Wearing her sienna Adventure 16 anorak, she stepped outside into a blue, crisp Halloween day.

Entering Angelo's room, Audrey caught lots of 'hey, KW,' 'hi,' 'how'd you sleep,' laughs and *mmmm's*. On a folding table, arranged buffet style, were hot porridge, tomato slices, toast, honey and jam. Of course, there was plenty of tea in a large pot and a new addition: fresh apple juice. Audrey sampled a glass. Quite delicious. She had a second glass. After breakfast, she had a third. What a really great day this was turning out to be. Glancing around the room, Audrey asked, "Did anyone call Barry and Honna?"

Angelo, Leo and Carter exchanged puzzled glances as if the idea were novel. "We thought they were, you know, humping," said Carter. "That's what I'd be doing with Honna."

"It's almost noon. Did anyone call their room?"

Leo sipped more tea, "Angelo, you called, didn't you? After all, you are their faculty advisor."

Angelo sat against the wall, bits of porridge on his chin. "Oh?"

Audrey reached for more apple juice, then, with great effort, stayed her hand. *Maybe I'll wait a little bit before I have more.* A bit unsteady, she rose and walked to the door.

"I'm going to check on our sleepy heads."

"Hurry or you'll miss Janus," said Leo. "He's stopping by for the book any minute. Or did that already happen? *Mmmmmmmmm.*"

The room door slammed open in Audrey's face as a man with a pockmarked face burst in, wearing a faded Levi jacket. Audrey retreated to keep from being bowled over. "Well, excuse me," she huffed. The man's denim jacket hung open, and Audrey felt disturbed at the sight of his #thisiswhatdunwichlookslike T-shirt dotted with dark stains. Hadn't Barry Gristleman been wearing one of those last night?

"Where did you get that fascinating shirt?" she asked.

"'Twas a Christmas gift last year."

Another Dunwich man entered. He unzipped his bomber jacket, placed hands on his hips, peering around like a cop on a drug raid, "Where hid ye the *Necronomicon*?"

"Under the night table on top of the 1979 phone books," said Leo. "Your suspicion is understandable."

"We recognize your pain," said Angelo. "My people and I have lived it."

Carter Fong smiled at Levi Jacket, "Hey, awesome T-shirt."

"'Twas a birthday gift."

Outside the room, a thick knot of Dunwichers parted to allow passage for a little, white-haired man. Stepping into the room, Audrey noted a price tag dangling from the sleeve of his expensive-looking Patagonia insulated flannel jacket. She was repelled by the little man's green eyes and their acute lack of human empathy and compassion. Disturbed, Audrey turned away as he smiled with a crocodile-like warmth. The Little Man said to Bomber Jacket, "Chide them not, Malachi. These are dear friends and allies, here to help us."

"You must be Mr. Janus," said Angelo. "I am Professor Angelo Silent Feather, Assistant Vice Chancellor—"

As Angelo recited his title, Malachi Hutchins retrieved the thick book from under the night table, examining front and back, then leafing through the *Necronomicon* as if searching for something. The Little Man ignored Angelo, turning to Audrey, "Spoke we before, girl?"

"No, but my name is Professor Audrey Klumm-Weebner, not 'Girl.' I've heard nothing but interesting things about you from my colleagues."

"Gilded words. Have ye a husband?"

"That's rather personal."

"No matter. Ye will tonight."

"I beg your pardon."

"Dee version only," called Malachi, gesturing to the book.

Janus ignored Audrey's outraged expression and addressed the Miskatonic contingent, "Cunning, ye are indeed. Did Deale suggest this little gambit to up his price?"

"We freely returned your sacred text," said Leo.

"Swiped by Miskatonic University," said Angelo.

"What price?" said Carter.

Leo added, "We ask no price other than a sincere and lasting friendship."

Janus peered at Hameyes, "Ye have hands like a rat. Very well, tell me where is the long chant from page 751 of the Wormius *Necronomicon*?"

Angelo closed his eyes and softly chanted in Algonquin. Leo busied himself reading the letterhead on the motel stationary. Carter slowly poured himself more tea. Janus faced Audrey. With the door open, the Dunwich reek was stronger than ever. She held handkerchief to nose.

"You'll have to pardon me. A cold. Change of weather. As I understood President Deale, he will mail you that material next week. I'm sorry, I meant Federal Express you the page or pages."

Whateley asked again slowly, "Where is the Latin version of the long chant on page 751?"

Audrey turned to Angelo, who suddenly needed to check inside his deerskin pouch. Leo discovered something fascinating on a sampler. Carter held up his barless smart phone as if reading text. *Men.*

Audrey said, "The book you now have is what President Deale gave us to return."

Janus grinned knowingly, nodding his head as if in on a joke. "Deale raised his price. More gold delivers the long chant?"

Audrey said, "Oh, no."

"Play me not like a child. Ye have the page in a secure spot. Upon payment, ye will tell us where to retrieve the chant?"

Audrey shook her head 'no.'

Janus continued, "We set a new price. I deliver half. Then one of ye depart from Dunwich to fetch the chant while three remain behind as surety."

Angelo spoke up, "I believe we are entitled to know the details of any side bargain you've struck with President Deale."

"Go harvest yer maize, squaw."

Angelo blinked, "I have maize?"

Audrey quickly said, "We thought you'd be pleased."

"Ye tit-witted, doltish woman," snapped Janus. "Deale sends lumbering sheep to cheat me. I will pluck every living nerve from his body like string from a loom. He denies the Great Return. The formula to release the Old Ones is nothing without the chant." Face coloring a deep purple, The Little Man bellowed, "Nothing, ye feckless slabs of horse flesh."

An electric silence filled the room. Outside, several of the men quietly drifted away. Seconds passed, then Carter Fong dropped his head and giggled, "Seriously, Dog, your insults are like pure awesome."

Audrey kept silent, unable to quiet a frightful premonition. The Little Man threw out his arms like a furious orchestra conductor and uttered words in a strange language. Malachi Hutchins and Levi Jacket, pupils wide as tennis balls, backed up to the door. Audrey felt hair on her neck rise. *Formula.*

In a rush, the words tumbled out, "Please, Sir, we followed the instructions from President Deale. We've returned a sacred book that a cruel society kept from you. We very much wish to participate in your ceremony tonight, if you'll graciously allow it."

Malachi whispered something to the Little Man about 'side effects' and 'bride of the Beyond-One' and ending the world on 'Walpurgis night.' The Little Man lowered his arms, drew a deep breath, recovered his composure. Then he smiled again, his face reminding Audrey of a documentary she'd once seen about yellow jackets.

"So much pressure upon me. So little competent help. Aye, ye will indeed be part of Hallow Mass atop Sentinel Hill. A most vital, unforgettable part. Tonight ye shall meet Yog-Sothoth. Now I must rest."

A moment later, the room door closed softy behind the Little Man and his companions. Audrey collapsed in her chair, feeling as if she'd just talked an F-5 tornado out of annihilating a trailer park.

"Maybe we should've brought his dumb old chant," said Carter.

"Maybe you should not have belittled his anger," said Leo. "Your laughter contained traces of superiority, amusement, condescension."

"What about your *mmmmming?*"

Leo scratched his hairy hands, "I have been *mmmming* a lot. I can't explain myself. I've been feeling giddy all morning. All silly billy. All yesterday too, for that matter."

"I'm also pleasantly light-headed," said Angelo. "As in my undergrad days."

Carter Fong added, "I always feel that way."

"I think the tea and the apple juice are drugged," said Audrey.

"Great," said Carter. "I can't wait to pop some OxyContin tonight."

Audrey's heartbeat finally slowed, "We need to check on Barry or Honna."

Carter mixed tea and apple juice in an empty water bottle and shook it up. "You said that before. They're probably humping."

"May I have everyone's attention?"

Leo slurped spilled tea from his saucer, "Are you going to tell a joke? *Mmmmmmmm*."

Six eyes gradually shifted to Audrey.

Audrey waited to ensure their attention, "A great deal—pardon the pun—is at play. Stay with me, as I'll backtrack a bit. Obviously, Armand made some side arrangement with Janus and didn't tell us. He also knew that Janus wanted a chant, but chose not to find it, despite my offering to help. Also, I suspect the tea and apple juice are drugged. Also, no matter how we politically position it, Janus is unstable and dangerous. We've returned the book. I think we need to collect Barry and Honna, pack up, and leave here immediately."

Said Carter. "I like it here."

Said Leo, "We need to be present at tonight's ceremony. Our reputations demand it."

Audrey replied, "Do we really want to find ourselves up a dark hillside, in a region the police deliberately underserve, without outside communications, surrounded by people who fanatically believe the world would be better off without human life?"

"Put it like that and anything sounds bad," said Angelo. "In your book, you said that close observation and contact with marginalized groups was necessary to dispel dominant culture propaganda. You know, I'm surprised I remembered any of that."

"Paz Encanto covered all this," said Leo, "in ways that escape me right now."

Audrey grew impatient. "Did you hear Janus? He threatened to pull out all of Deale's nerves. Do you really want to participate in a ceremony run by Leland Janus, who, by the way, is probably Obed Whateley?"

Carter Fong stretched out languidly, "Who is Whateley?"

Relaxed, beaming, Angelo said, "Not to be a noodge, Audrey, but you're overthinking all this. We'll be home tomorrow."

Through the window curtain, Audrey spotted someone peeking into the room with a leering Dunwich smile. "They may not let us leave."

"We're safe," said Leo as he refilled his tea, "There are Federal statutes prohibiting the unlawful confinement of an academic."

Angelo waved a dismissive hand, "There's no reason to harm us. It's not in their best interests."

"I've gotta see that freaky weather," said Carter, lifting the teakettle and drinking from the spout. "I owe it to everyone on Gabby Face."

Audrey chatted a bit more, and made sounds as if they'd convinced her to stay. Then she borrowed the keys to the Pangaea. A few moments later, she rapped on the door to Barry and Honna's room. To her surprise, a middle-aged woman, hair in rollers, smelling of corn syrup, answered, "Did ye bring the toilet paper, girl?"

"Where are the young people who occupied this room?"

"I care not. Now go back and fetch us more toilet paper. The thick kind."

The door closed abruptly in Audrey's face.

Back in her room, Audrey slowed her rapid breathing with yoga exercises, gathering in positive air, exhaling negativity and fear. Picking up the phone, Audrey called the motel operator, who informed her that two young people in a certain room had either checked out this morning, or the room had always been rented to a woman in curlers. He couldn't remember which. In addition, telephone lines were "a-flutter" and no calls could be placed outside Dunwich, but ice in a bucket was available.

Still in her jacket, Audrey fell on the bed, making a high-pitched keening sound. She had run out of runway in which to land the Bullshit Yourself plane. Levi Jacket was wearing Barry's shirt from yesterday, which meant Barry and Honna were being held somewhere. For psychological reasons, Audrey elected not to marry the students' absence to last night's screams. There was no way to phone, text, or post a plea for help. Audrey considered alerting Angelo and the others, but they were cocooned in the cozy bliss of Dunwich tea. For all his devious bullshit, Deale had been right about formula, which meant Obed Whateley was a vile terror.

Rising from the bed, Audrey decided to decamp and send back help. Purse over a shoulder, composing her most alluring dolphin smile, she drew in a deep breath, exhaled, then strolled outside into the rapidly darkening afternoon. Thunder rippled above as gray clouds overwrote the blue sky. Approaching the Pangaea, she spotted Levi Jacket jogging up quickly, followed by another man.

"What have ye need of?"

"I'm running an errand for Obed Whateley."

"Ye lie."

Audrey sighed, "I know you're familiar with page 751 of the Olaus Wormius version of the *Necronomicon*."

"Aye, the long chant."

"Would Obed Whateley be mad if you stopped me from getting it?"

"Wait ye here." Levi Jacket turned to the man behind him, who dashed off toward the office.

Audrey played the cognitive dissonance card, unlocking the vehicle with her clicker, then hopping up into the driver's seat, saying, "No problem. You're in charge. I won't move. I'll stick around until you check things out."

Locking the door, Audrey fired up the Pangea. With a loud electric hum like a crackling power line, the Pangea backed out into the parking lot. Levi Jacket shouted and tugged on the door. Five men rushed forward from the porch and chased the vehicle. Two more men, one in a yellow rain coat, leaped into a battered, mud-caked Yukon SUV and drove after Audrey.

Rocking and jolting as fast as she could along the deep potholes, past Osborn's Store, Audrey approached the intersection. When arriving yesterday, they'd whipped right to reach the motel, so she'd whip left and head back. In Dean's Corners, Audrey would call the State Police and send them to retrieve others. Then she'd verbally rip the head off Armand Deale. Deale and his male pride. Because he got called a few names, Audrey and the rest wound up in a highly perilous, unstable situation.

With a screech, the muddy Yukon sliced inside Audrey's turn, cutting her off from the blacktop road. With running men arriving at the Pangaea, Audrey hummed off at an angle, down a dirt byway leading into the Dunwich backcountry. Tires squealing on the wet pavement, the Yukon sped off along the blacktop road leading to Dean's Corners.

Glancing in the rear view mirror, Audrey saw the running men fall away as she sped up. Atop the Pangea, the turbine spun. But Audrey soon slowed to a crawl in order to cross a rickety single-lane bridge. The five running men gained as Audrey tensed, negotiating the heavy vehicle across a narrow roadway with fast water visible beneath, rushing to the sea.

Headlights shone from behind. A pick-up sped toward her from Dunwich.

Rain spotted the windshield as Audrey cleared the bridge and accelerated, weaving around water-filled potholes of unknown depth, humming past forlorn farmhouses with barking dogs to the left, and the storm-gorged Miskatonic River to the right. Behind, the pick-up paused at the bridge, while two men continued a dogged pursuit along the dirt road. Three men slipped across country, disappearing from sight.

Ahead and to her right rose one of those hideous round hills. It seemed to vomit out latent menace, as well as an especially repulsive regional stink. Something about the stone ring atop the hill made Audrey feel alone, adrift, atomized, a random mote floating amongst billions of specks, a cosmic mistake, squatting on someone else's planet, slated to be erased of all life at the pleasure of the original owners.

Crazy. Don't think that.

Placing the sachet over face and mouth, Audrey despised Dunwich, wished she'd never written about it. She'd pull her book from circulation. Then she'd have an affair with Carter Fong. But first Audrey would tell him she was sexually involved with Armand Deale, and Carter couldn't tell a soul. That would guarantee Fong would blab all over Gabby Face and Chat Puss. The whispering and laughter would eat Mr. Proud Deale alive.

Rain fell in sheets and Audrey eased off the accelerator. Even with wipers on full blast, the windshield looked like an aquarium. Leaning forward, headlights on, she spotted what appeared to be a T-intersection to her left. Further ahead, she could see another precarious bridge. One was enough. Audrey spun the wheel left. Besides, this new road might connect with the blacktop leading to Dean's Corners.

Bucking and thumping, the Pangea seemed more like a carnival attraction than a vehicle. A low wheel clearance guaranteed few bounces and scrapes would be avoided. A mile, then two, Audrey drove as the thoroughfare gently curved east. To her right, she glimpsed a bleak, rocky area with huge boulders, as appealing and vibrant as the surface of Mercury, then a small forest of bare tree, branches waving in the wind. *Where did this stinking road lead?* The rain eased a bit and Audrey thought she spotted an intersection ahead atop a small hill. If it were blacktop beyond, she could turn right and zip to Dean's Corners, free of Dunwich forever.

Dropping the heavy Pangea into low, Audrey crept up the grade. Almost to the top, something horizontal suddenly blocked her access.

Go. Move, whatever you are.

Another five yards and she recognized the muddy Yukon. A man in a yellow raincoat leaped from the passenger side holding a pump-action shotgun.

Throwing the Pangea into reverse, Audrey rolled down the hill. She didn't bother with a three-point turn, continuing on backwards, bouncing and jolting. As the rain eased, Audrey peered out the driver's side window and spotted three figures dashing toward her across a field.

Ahead, the Yukon wobbled down the hill in pursuit.

Pickup truck headlights from behind flared in her rear view mirror.

Feeling like a squirrel in a wire snare, Audrey stopped, frozen. Seconds passed. Teeth grinding, she swung the wheel right and drove off-road. Down a small embankment, then up. Fifteen yards into a field, Audrey discovered another drawback to the Pangea's low clearance: the front axle hung up on a rock.

The Yukon arrived on the road behind, followed moments later by the pickup truck.

Grabbing her purse, Audrey threw open the door and fled into a field of weeds and ankle-high dead leaves. Like papier-mâché, leaves plastered her ankles and calves. Behind, she heard vehicle doors open and slam, men shouting. One voice cried, "Harm her not, Asa. She is prized." That triggered a jet of adrenaline, giving Audrey the speed to put distance between herself and the Dunwichers.

Into a copse, naked branches dripping rain, she slowed to catch her breath. Risking a look behind, Audrey saw no one in direct pursuit, but figures angled off to the left and right of the leafy field. Voices called back and forth, muted in the heavy damp air. On the ground before her, human ribs and a headless spinal cord stuck up from a large conglomerate of tissue, the mass covered in a fuzzy mold. Audrey gagged. Grimacing, wiping moisture from her face, she jogged out of the copse, almost stepping on a second set of ribs. *Corpse in a copse. Aren't I funny?* Audrey intended to angle left, hoping to intersect the blacktop road. Once there, she could watch for Dunwichers, possibly hitch a ride into Dean's Corners. Be flexible; have lots of options.

Wet hair plastered her face and neck. Audrey noticed the sinister rock field off to her right. Despite the fear, Audrey halted, sucking in air. *Yoga and Pilates don't do spit for your cardio.*

Walking quickly through brown knee-high grass, Audrey almost tripped over a young woman's body. Torso, legs and arms were wrapped tightly around the corpse like twisty bread. Audrey felt ill. *How do you even do something like that outside a carnival?* Passing the corpse, she caught a glimpse of facial features frozen in triumphant rictus. Audrey was fascinated and repelled, unsure why a woman whose body had been braided felt the need to die grinning.

Formula. Like what happened to Deale.

Men's voices, drawing even in the vegetation to her left.

Audrey sprinted straight, careful of her footing on the uneven, mushy soil. About a quarter mile ahead stretched a line of brush and barren trees. Cover. A spot to rest. Audrey focused on trotting along and not falling, purse banging against her hip. The rain increased. Behind her, she thought she heard the river roaring. *Good. Keep angling to the left.*

Entering brush and trees, Audrey flipped her bag around so it hung down her back. *Screw the second floor of the library-Deale-Miskatonic-Massachusetts.* Audrey would focus her life and passion on bettering the environment in California or Hawaii or New Zealand.

Deciding to stay in the trees for a time, Audrey wished she'd grabbed a bottle of water for her dry throat. She scanned the ground for a stick to scrape the mud and leaves off her shoes. Something partially covered in leaves near a thick broken branch caught her eye. *Oh, god, not another corpse.* A man appeared to have died crawling into a large dark sack. A bag? A balloon? Audrey wasn't certain. However, the leathery sack-like shape quickly assumed a familiar form. She winced at beetles crawling into nostrils and across rubbery lips, and scuttling into big empty eye sockets. It took a moment, but Audrey realized she was staring at a giant human head.

Her hands failed to block the entire scream.

Men's voice called out from behind.

This place is more lethal than Chicago. I need to reach the road.

Audrey bolted from the trees, stumbled and fell, lost her purse, lurched upright and fled in panic.

Fright and disgust propelled her along at a good pace. But mud clumped around her feet and ankles. Audrey felt as if she were running in bowling balls. She knew her pursuers were closing in, heard their yelling, then their running, then their breath. A staff or walking stick was thrust between her legs and Audrey sprawled into the mud and leaves. Men seized her. Someone used wire to secure her wrists and ankles behind her back.

"Let me go you stupid, idiot hillbillies. You backcountry, inbred, banjo-strumming, tree-dwelling morons. You'll spend the rest of your lives in court. I'll sue you so badly you'll have to divorce your sisters."

Audrey struggled, cursed, bucked, bit as she was carted off like a roll of carpet, back across the field, through the stand of trees, then the brown grass, through the copse, into the thick leaves, approaching the stranded Chevy Pangea, axel hung up on a rock.

"I have money. Retirement fund, 401(k), you can have it all. I'll pay the withdrawal penalty."

They passed the Pangea, door wide open, engine still humming.

"Take me out of Dunwich and I'll do whatever you like. Fun things."

The chinless men hauled her to the road.

"I'll be missed. You'll be locked up like on MSNBC. Convicts will use you."

One of them said, "Better buggered by a felon than cursed by the Little Man."

Ahead the Yukon waited, back door yawning wide like the mouth of a shark.

Audrey shrieked into the rain, a common autumn sound in old Dunwich, before a strip of duct tape silenced her wailing cries.

CHAPTER 12

DOUBLE DATE WITH DESTINY

"Allegedly primitive cultures link the release of sexual energy with magical ceremonies. To them it's a booster rocket, like adding gasoline to a blaze. Our failure to recognize the orgy as a religious expression is narrow-minded neo-Puritanism."
— Miskatonic University Professor Angelo Silent Feather, Associate Vice Chancellor for Contemporary Oppression Modalities, from an article in New Oppression Review *entitled: "Not To Be a Noodge."*

Despite rain drumming on the roof, Mercy heard vehicles to the north and east of their position. She and Bongani paused and changed dressings, reapplying Band-Aids and surgical tape. Joe B. rested a hand on the butt of the 9mm as Mercy wondered if one of Whateley's search parties had finally located them. Men yelled back and forth, then nothing, then more yelling, then quiet, then a short despairing scream for help. In time, vehicles started again, engines fading in the distance. By and by, the only sounds were rain and a far-off dog barking in monotony as if filling a quota.

Mercy said, "Sounds like someone got grabbed. I still think we're too close to Sentinel Hill."

"Here we're safer."

"That's a relative term in festive Dunwich. Listen, nothing personal, but we should review tonight's plan. Check me if I'm wrong: sneak up the hill, wait for the big Hallow Mass kick-off, then I crank up my formula and seal the dimensional opening, locking out the Old Ones?"

"Yes."

"I personally feel it sucks camel pies. Won't Whateley have extra guards now that we're expected?"

"We will fight them."

"I believe you. I saw you pop Chester Sawyer and his performing tentacles. And thanks for doing it, if I didn't say that enough times. But if Morgan's journal is only a little bit true, than Whateley can summon all kinds of nasty, diabolical critters. These aren't junior college Tokoloshe. And we're not even talking Old Ones. You need pro level formula to check that shit. Plus he'll probably have followers galore. How many rounds do you have?"

Joe B. patted his pocket. "I borrowed from Michael. Two of the magazines. Twenty-eight bullets."

Mercy touched the bandages around her neck. Snug, but not tight. Joe B. had done a good job. "So we've got the 9mm you took off the Dunwich guy, twenty-eight rounds and three formulae, one of which, the Selective Inferno, I stink at."

"But in the library fight you set the one's arms on fire."

"I was trying for his hands."

Bongani paused, collected the soiled dressings and stuffed them in a trash bag. Mercy thought he'd lost interest in the conversation when he said, "What plan would you make?"

"Something better than charging the hill like the Marines. You know, this is Morgan's fantasy fight. This is his freaking wet dream." Searching in her purse for a small brush, she lowered the visor mirror and angrily tugged at her snarled hair. "I should be home right now, getting ready for a party, celebrating the fact that I've dropped a size and a half. But Morgan slips on a bar of soap charging out of the locker room, knocks himself out, and here we are. I never really thought it would get to this point. I thought something would happen and the whole thing would get called off, or someone would step in and say 'I've got it from here, Merse.' But no. Now I'll never get married, or have kids, or find out what I'm supposed to be in life, except Old One chow."

A soft rattle and click. Bongani held out the bracelet of colored beads. Mercy set the brush down and accepted the jewelry. She marveled at the beads' intricacy, modeled the bracelet against her wrist.

"Gorgeous," she said. "Part of your anger therapy? Just kidding."

"They are for engagement in KwaZululand. A young woman in love makes them. The colors tell a story when together. The blue and white means faithful. If black is next to them, it means the marriage. A girl who loves a man will make the beads and give them to a sister or girl relative. She will then give them to the man. He can then read all that is in the loving girl's heart without her feeling unhappy."

"How very corny, sexist, and incredibly romantic. But you guys do it backwards. My friend Brianne started planning her wedding in middle school. The only thing missing was the name of a husband." Mercy gently ran a forefinger across the beads. "What was her name?"

"It is difficult to say everything. To begin, there was Londiwe. Her name means kept safe. Protected."

"I'm seeing blue, white and black. I hope you said 'yes.'"

"I wore the beads on the wrist to show all that I had accepted. Then I met with the father to make a bride price."

"You bought your future wife?"

"Not so much. It is tradition. Before once, I would pay cows. But now money is good too."

A sudden thought struck Mercy like 90 mph fastball. Her mouth opened and she covered it with her hands. "Oh, my God. Joe, I'm so terribly sorry. I know what's coming next."

Bongani frowned, puzzled. "How do you know I?"

"Something Morgan said awhile ago; your anger that one time when I asked about your fiancée. It all clicks. You left for Durban and your village was raided by the cult."

"Many villages were raided by the cult."

"It's okay, I know what's coming next. Londiwe was captured and sacrificed to Cthulhu."

"Londiwe went to Oslo."

"Ever since, you've devoted your life to vengeance, to battling the Old One cult."

"I am in Durban when the non-governmental Europe people come to my village to put in a new well. But they had much money and paid too much for ones to cook, and ones to fix things, and ones to drive them around in Land Rovers."

"Your Uncle George brought you to the Commonwealth to help fight the Dunwich cult."

"Londiwe cooked for a Norway man called Aksel Thorsen. He told her about Oslo and Narvik and the many free benefits one is given there."

"That's why you always wanted me to practice formula. So we'd be ready for this day."

"Londiwe goes to Oslo with Thorsen. She now lives from the Norway government and never again must cut firewood, or step on a cobra, or see a dog eaten by ants."

"Then what the hell is your point?"

Bongani added an empty Diet Coke can to the trash. Mercy shook her head. *Guys. Spotless cars but their apartments looked like refugee camps.*

"I explain too badly. The bracelet is not from Londiwe. It is from her sister, Sizani who gave me Londiwe's bracelet. But I did not know how to say I loved Sizani more. There is no bracelet for that."

"What does 'Sizani' mean?"

"To help someone, to be quick with opportunity."

"I'll say."

"She waits in Natal. I study to be an American, and to be a police man. Then I will bring her here. But I want you to know that even with trouble in life, you can still be married."

Mercy handed back the bracelet and gently touched his shoulder, "You're a sweetheart, Joe B. Seriously, thanks, Dude. But you've been engaged twice. I can't even find a guy who thinks I'm worth dinner and a movie."

Less than half a mile from the hill's base, the Mini Cooper sat parked at the end of a brush-choked road. As the rain diminished to a mist, Mercy slipped from the vehicle. Throwing up her hood, she wandered the weed-choked ruins of wooden outbuildings, aimlessly kicking at things. Holes blotched the ground everywhere as if someone had set out to create a moonscape. Mercy walked toward the ruins of an ancient house, engulfed in weeds and deadfall, roof collapsed, one side burst open. Here the Dunwich pungency was intense, rotten floor covered in a malodorous, sticky, tar-like substance. Bird and rat skeletons testified to its adhesive power. *This place needs a profile in* Dumps of New England. *("Unpleasant little country hideaway, needs monster-proofing.")*

Something about the spot called to mind Morgan's journal. But Mercy let the thought evaporate, dwelling on Sentinel Hill. To the southwest, its slope rose covered in strange, graying-yellow grass, top ringed by stone pillars like jagged teeth. Henry Armitage had marched up there in the daytime with Warren Rice and Francis Morgan, friendly locals in support, and a plan with a decent chance of success. Julian Rice had entered Dunwich with two formula-trained companions, state cops, and friendly locals. (Now all that remained were his spooky green glasses.) Louis Armitage had arrived for battle with future insane guy Galen Rice. But Great Uncle Louis had had mad formula skills, plus the university, the state government, and the cops all backing him. *We haven't got a prayer tonight.*

Saying the word 'prayer' made Mercy consider beseeching God, an uneven path for her on the best of days. She elected to give it a shot. *Dear God, I admit my prayers been shallow in the past. Like that time in high school when I prayed that Kirsten Patel would have a wardrobe malfunction at the junior prom and she broke a heel and fell on her butt in the middle of the dance floor. That was not a worthy prayer, though I laughed a lot then. Please get Joe B. and me through the night alive. He's a decent, good-hearted guy—okay dresser, but he drives a car that's too small for him. Nevertheless, Thy will, not mine, be done. Amen.*

Mercy stopped strolling; brow wrinkled, she glanced over her shoulder at the ruined house as if her name had been whispered. *Whoa, the Whateley place?* Here the 1928 horror escaped. From its moldy outbuildings, authorities had transferred Wizard Whateley's grimoires, including the Dee *Necronomicon*, to Henry Armitage. Around these grounds, Grandpa Tom and Julian Rice had battled Sirac Bishop and teenage Obed Whateley. *If departed ancestors do watch you, they must be pulling up lawn chairs right about now.*

As to the sea of holes, hadn't people said old Whateley paid for cattle with gold coins of ancient vintage? This lot must be Treasure Hunt City.

Back in the car, Mercy ate lemon yogurt and strawberries, with a carton of orange juice. She really craved more protein. Bacon. Tri-tip buried in fried onions and mushrooms, with thin cut French Fries garnished with cilantro and a mug of Budweiser. But something said the lighter the meal, the better the formula. Joe B. munched on a turkey sandwich, but ate it outside the car. Mercy said he didn't need to, but he went anyway. Sweet.

After lunch, in the waning hours of a sprinkly afternoon, Mercy and Bongani practiced. Mercy recited the Greek activating phrases for Pirandello's Aegis. Bongani rushed to lay down the pentagram mat on the run, drawing his pistol and jumping into the protective circle at the same time Mercy finished the last syllable. But it was tough finding hole-free ground. Mercy always checked herself, never saying all the words and thus activating the formula. She was saving every cent on her formula credit card.

Later, while Joe B. cleaned the 9mm, she ran through the Selective Inferno and the Forge of Nin-Agal. Then she worked on the Aegis once more. Greek-Hebrew-Chaldean. Mercy repeated the phrases over and again, whispering them, saying them out loud until they flowed like water down a stainless steel chute, rapid, precise, syllables pronounced with perfect enunciation.

At dusk, the whippoorwills struck up the band. Back in the car, as Bongani ran the heater, Mercy winced at the racket outside. She hadn't seen a single one while walking around the area, and now it seemed there was a loud chittering bird behind every blade of grass. *Early birds. Early birds get the soul. Dunwich standup. What would that even be like?— 'I just flew in, and boy are my colossal bat wings tired.'*

Over the shrieking, they heard the vehicles.

One-two-three from the north. Not fast, but steady, one behind the other like a caravan of football boosters convoying to an away game. Cars, trucks, and a yellow school bus passed by the turnoff to the Whateley ruins, heading south. There was no need to guess their destination.

"It is not all dark yet," said Bongani.

"Hallow Mass," said Mercy, "maybe the last one. Everyone wants to be early and grab a seat."

"We cannot climb the front way with all of them. And the back way is very much steeper."

"I read something in the journal by Warren Rice. Back in the Depression, some workers built hiking trails up the rear of Sentinel Hill. They disappeared—duh—but maybe there's still some switchbacks. At least enough of a trail to get us going."

"They will have more guards there."

"Probably, but let's get there first."

Several minutes passed. Mercy covered the bandage around her neck with a scarf. Bongani hesitated, then tapped his watch, "Tonight is happening quick. We must be away."

Mercy's mouth went dry. Her voice cracked as she said, "Give me a sec."

Bongani bowed his head as if wrapping up matters with the Divine. Mercy removed her earrings and necklace, placing them into her purse. From her key ring, she detached a little halogen flashlight and stuck it in her coat pocket, then dropped her key ring into a zippered side pocket before placing her purse on the floor mat.

Outside, they stood beside the Mini Cooper. The rain had stopped. Bongani held the rolled up Tetragrammaton Pentagram mat over one shoulder like a roofer hauling tarpaper, then placed the pistol in a jacket pocket. Mercy smelled the WD-40.

"Wow," she said. "This is it. I always thought that was a stupid thing they said in movies. But is this really it."

"We will go up now. We will stop them tonight."

Mercy forced a smile, "You Italian guys sure got team spirit. I like that."

Moving discreetly into the tall weeds, they noted more headlights, driving toward Sentinel Hill, rising above them on the other side of the road. In the growing gloom, Bongani led them south into wet grass and stunted brush. Mercy blundered into a half-dug hole and twisted her right ankle.

"Damn, Joe B., that hurts."

"Can you still walk?"

"Yeah. We O'Connors eat pain every day with gluten-free doughnuts."

Whipped by branches, they crept through the vegetation, stopping at a bend in the dirt road. From there, they waited to dart across, then down and around to the back of Sentinel Hill. With the road in plain sight, Mercy noticed northbound vehicles from the direction of Worcester. Cars, SUVs and pickups parked on the shoulder like attendees at a rock concert. Vehicle doors clunked shut as people exited, calling to one another with rising excitement.

"Ia!"

"Ia right back to you."

Mercy and Bongani waited for a break, then crossed the muddy track. Sentinel Hill towered above, clouds forming, black as obsidian. A low rumbling peal of thunder echoed, like an opera diva clearing her throat before curtain time. Cultists of all ages and races walked past Mercy and Bongani, heading in the opposite direction toward the front of the hill, casting suspicious looks their way.

Mercy whispered, "We're moving against traffic."

"Yes."

Bongani hailed a man staring at them, "Ia."

"Ia."

Mercy joined in, "Praise Cthulhu."

"Don't say that," whispered Bongani.

"Why not?"

"They do not say such words. Say 'Ia.'"

"What does it mean?"

"I know not, but they say it all the time."

"Ia. Happy Ia."

"Don't say 'happy.'"

"You're all freaking over me tonight."

To avoid any more foot traffic encounters, Joe B. moved away from the road, down a short steep grade, hopping over a water-filled ditch. Mercy shortened her steps to slow momentum, jumped the same ditch and yelped. Joe B. checked on her, but Mercy lied, saying the pain was manageable—which was true if she didn't walk. They advanced deeper into wet brush and weeds. To their left, the road curved south and away from Sentinel Hill. They wrestled their way through wild brambles.

Mercy felt discomfort kicking up a mark, but bit her tongue. She wanted a cold ice pack, a warm room, and the volleyball scene from *Top Gun*.

Bongani stopped, crouched, whispered, "Guards will appear soon."

"You see any?"

"Not yet."

Butterflies aloft in her stomach, whippoorwills piping from every direction, she advanced cautiously, eyes scanning the murky, fading light for sentries. Joe B. spotted something, motioning for Mercy to wait as he crept ahead on reconnaissance. A great hissing erupted from Sentinel Hill, as if some massive serpent disputed their presence. A rumbling deep in the earth commenced, grew in power and intensity, blending with the hissing, overpowering, dominating, shaking the hill, spewing out a malignant odor that made the normal Dunwich fetor smell like rose potpourri.

Where's Joe B.? Once more, the thought of bailing out nudged Mercy like a relative demanding the return of a twenty. She imagined herself dying in horrid ways, or blowing all her mental fuses at the sight of things better left unseen, soiling herself in sublime witlessness until squashed by an Old One. Bushes shook and Mercy tensed.

"Here, here, come now," said Joe B.

Following him as the hill hissed, Mercy swiveled her head, checking for sentries. All around the wan light dissipated in a slow transition from gray to black, dusk to nightfall. After a minute or so, Bongani stopped and used the rolled up pentagram mat to gesture to some brush.

Mercy squinted, "Whatever you're showing me, I'm missing big time."

Joe B. walked into the brush for about eight steps, then turned and loped up a slight grade for about three steps, then walked another eight steps.

"Get out of town on a Honda. It's a switchback."

"Much weeds and grass, but it goes up, maybe far, maybe to the top."

Mercy dropped onto her rump, breathing heavily. Even with perfectly tended switchbacks, she doubted her ankle could manage the trip. Then what? God was paying her back for Kirsten Patel.

Mercy looked up at Bongani, "You're pissed off, aren't you? Because of the ankle?"

"We must go to the top at once."

"We're on a mission to get killed. Shouldn't we, at least, enjoy the view?"

"No."

Mercy gritted her teeth, extended a hand. Joe B. pulled Mercy to her feet. Hobbling along, she followed Bongani up the next switchback, then another, then a third. Maybe it wouldn't be so bad. Then Joe B. halted, peered around.

"I cannot find the rest."

"We can't be out of switchbacks. We just started."

A short search revealed nothing but dripping wet brush and thorns. Mercy cursed. There was nothing to do but scramble up the slope, grabbing at roots and bunches of grayish-yellow grass. The whippoorwills blasted in their ears, masking all sound save for the loudest of the hill eruptions. Sometimes they would find traces of the old hiking trail. But decades of rain, snow, and erosion had obliterated much of what was once cleared. Neither of them peered down at the long drop below. Or above at the ominous ring of stone obelisks, slowly growing closer. All focus was on the next handhold.

Pausing for a breather, Mercy observed a hazy gibbous moon, cold and indifferent to her agony and toil. To take her mind off the ankle, Mercy remembered something from a contemporary poetry class about the writings of Dac Encanto. Cousin to the famous social scientist, poet Dac nursed a pathological hatred for the moon, a leitmotif critics called "lunar hatred," or, in German, *Mondblindheit* or "moon blindness." For stuff like that she was 40k in debt. Mercy stared out across the Dunwich countryside at other hilltops, bonfires flaring atop them like distant pilot lights. Far below, the dirt road was no longer visible, swallowed by a fog, rolling in quietly like lymphoma.

Trying not to whimper in pain, Mercy resumed the climb. Sharp branches slashed at her cheeks, hands and fingers lacerated and bleeding. After several minutes, she grabbed at the back of Bongani's jacket and tugged. Thunder rumbled from the velvety black cloud, blocking out the stars above Sentinel Hill.

"Ankle's swollen, Joe B., worse every time I put pressure on it."

"We'll rest now."

For a time, they stood precariously on the hillside. Stationary, Mercy could feel the chill, see her breath. She couldn't shake a feeling of shame, as if she were getting ready to quit. On her swollen right ankle, Mercy's shoe felt like a vise. Her fear of death buried the needle with thoughts of perishing hard, gruesome—Dunwich style. Her butterflies were now condor-sized. Was her injury a good excuse to quit? (*'I really wanted to save the world, but I twisted my ankle. Crazy bad luck. Enjoy your new dimension.'*) Bending over, Mercy threw up from anxiety and tension, then dry heaved and spat, trembling as the whippoorwills around her slowed their chant. The birds sounded very Dunwich: derisive, heavy with giddy scorn.

Lips close to her ear, Bongani said, "'There is no hillside without a grave.'"

"Is that a Zulu real estate slogan? Over here, you'd have trouble moving property with that one."

"It means Death waits for us all, and so could be anywhere."

"So why press on, old chap? Aren't you scared wet?"

"Yes, but I pray to the Lord God Jesus, because even a termite may hurt an elephant."

"Wow, you are like the Zulu Aristotle."

For a moment, their mission seemed to hang by a cat hair. Mercy sensed that if she started back down right that instant, Joe B. wouldn't stop her. He might even follow. Around them the whippoorwills continued to be an audio nuisance, while firelight danced off the pillars above, and the first faint chants arose, interspersed with generous *Ias*.

Bongani chose that moment to bend at the waist, gesturing to his back. "I'll take it from here . . . Merse."

Mercy stared for a moment, unsure of his meaning, then laughed, "Well, if you put it that way, I might go a bit more."

Mercy hopped on his back, then wedged the pentagram mat between her chest and Bongani's upper body. Arms under and around his shoulders, she clung tightly as Joe B. exhaled, then advanced up the slope. A minute passed. Another. The stone ring appeared closer now, a fiery glow shimmering off the pillars.

A cold wind rustled through the scrub.

As they neared the crest, the chanting grew wilder, more frenetic.

A terrified man's scream sounded like a coyote yipping.

A woman moaned in fright.

More chants, shouts, bellows, wild cries of ecstasy, wonder, astonishment.

A man pleaded to be left alone, followed by a horrible hoarse laugh, growing louder and louder, cut off neatly as if a switch were flipped.

Butterflies as large as Cessnas. Mercy focused on a stone pillar, shadows flickering, growing larger, more distinct. Her breathing sped up. She was almost hyperventilating.

Over the crest, onto the hill and level ground.

Joe B. rested against a stone pillar, breath pluming in the cold.

Mercy climbed down, standing on her good ankle. "I guess this is my stop."

Her eyes swelled in shock as she beheld Hallow Mass.

CHAPTER 13

DINING AL FRESCO

"Yog-Sothoth is the gate."
—*Abdul Al Hazard,* The Necronomicon
(Latin Version)

*"Maybe cyclones rage because children
are hungry? Hey, how come we don't study
stuff like that?"*
—*Professor Carter Fong, from his book:*
Weather Thou Goest:
Critical Weather Studies and the New
Atmospheric Paradigm

Audrey watched naked men and women milling around the hill. Some bore creepy circular, suction-like wounds, laced with scar tissue, ranging from the size of a drink coaster to the circumference of a dinner plate. A number of people appeared in furry pants with round, elephantine feet, and animated, ropy objects wriggling below multi-colored torsos. That morning, Audrey would've stated without question that such deformities were the result of pollution and trans fats. But her outlook had since matured.

Stripped of clothing, shivering in the cold, Audrey's arms and legs remained bound. She was upright between two naked chinless men whom she'd dubbed Left Arm and Right Arm. A few yards away, several box spring mattresses were being tested by a naked Carter Fong, who bounced on them like a newlywed evaluating beds.

"May I have some water, please," she asked.

Left Arm said, "Ye won't die of thirst."

Right Arm said, "Aye, true and well said."

In front of the growing bonfire stood the stone altar.

My wedding bed, thought Audrey, recalling Whateley's remark from the motel room.

Angelo Silent Feather emerged from the shadows near the back of the hill. He said something to Carter that amused the younger man, then strolled toward Audrey. He wore Bass Weejuns, a deerskin bag, and nothing else. Weaving across the rocks, Angelo's long, silver and gray hair fluttered unbound in the wind. His thin legs and hairy potbelly made Audrey glad they had remained only colleagues.

"Janus has asked me to join the ceremony," he said proudly. His eyes were red, pupils dilated. Clearly, Professor Silent Feather had enjoyed his afternoon tea.

"I thought Whateley marginalized you."

"Janus was very apologetic."

"Who is Janus?" asked Right Arm.

Left Arm said, "'Tis a name the Little Man used."

Audrey said to Angelo, "Did you catch any of that?"

But Angelo flashed a sloppy smile, "In fact, Leland said my ceremonial role was once reserved for Armand Deale. But my heritage makes me perfect for the part, which, I admit, is kind of vague."

"Doesn't one of those heads in the bone pile near the altar have a few blonde corn rows? Sort of like Honna used to wear?"

"Will you stop, please. The whole way up the hill you did nothing but cry and whine that everything is real, we're all doomed, yadda-yadda. At first, I thought you were being ironic, getting into the spirit of things. But seriously, you're embarrassing us. If word of your intellectual backsliding leaks, it could torpedo your credibility in the Post-Structural Hierarchies community."

Audrey erupted in bitter laugh. "You might've noticed me trying to run earlier. You might've noticed me fighting and screaming when they sliced off my clothes with a box cutter and hauled me up this hill. You might even notice now that I'm being held by the arms so I don't escape."

Angelo waved a hand as if brushing at fruit flies, "All metaspiritual symbolism. Not to be a noodge, but you wrote the book on this."

"Charming little fiction, wasn't it? But I've become more enlightened over the past few hours. Now I believe without question they're shabby, abominable, hick devil-worshippers."

"Audrey, you'll be symbolically sacrificed, then released. End of story."

"No, *you're* going to be sacrificed. *I'm* the bride of Yog-Sothoth. See me blushing?"

Angelo exhaled loudly. "You sure know how to piss on a mood. Let's discuss this back in Arkham."

"Ye won't see Arkham no more, Indian," said Left Arm. He and his pal chuckled.

Angelo scowled, "One more disempowering crack and you're going to face Federal hate crime charges."

"And ye shall face the Lurker at the Threshold," said Right Arm.

"Spawn of Azathoth," said Left Arm, then added, "And no one will help ye, Buck."

"Bait the Indian. Sure."

"Won't be us that baits ye, red scoundrel," said Right Arm. "Those From the Air have their own sport."

Angelo sputtered, head swiveling from Left Arm to Right Arm, huffing, chest rising and falling, glaring, grimacing, leaning forward, raising his chin—basically suggesting he was owed an abject apology. But his mood shifted and he chuckled behind a big wide smile.

"You two are certainly in character for tonight."

Audrey said, "Run, Angelo. That's the smartest thing you can do."

"I thought I'd be colder without any clothes." With a wave 'bye,' Angelo stumbled over to talk with Carter.

Away to the right, Audrey caught sight of Leo groping among the stone pillars. He appeared to be the only one on Sentinel Hill who was completely dressed. Audrey envied him the warmth of his garments. From his erratic actions, Doctor Leo Hameyes had enjoyed even more tea this afternoon than Angelo. "*Mmmmmmmmm*, theater. All theater," he said. "Silly billy."

"Leo, please get out of here right now. Take Angelo and Carter."

He hid behind a pillar, his arm waving at Audrey.

Minutes passed. Audrey shivered from the cold. Seconds seemed unnaturally long, but time itself felt sped up like film of a flower opening to the sun, then closing in seconds as a day passed. The stinking whippoorwills chirped like a digital recording left on loop, the monotonous shrieking punching into her brain.

Carter Fong wobbled up, "Hey, KW. Hey, guys, how you doing?"

"Dandy and squat," said Left Arm. "And ye?"

"When's this orgy get rolling?"

"When the energy is needed most," said Right Arm. "But ye have a right way to ye. Enjoy now, before the Lurker is summoned."

Left Arm smiled, "Try pleasuring a woman while being eaten screaming by the Son of the Nameless Mist."

Right Arm laughed, "Be a trick, and fair one at that."

Carter waved off what he assumed was a compliment. "I'm a guy with guy needs, you know?"

Said Left Arm, "Many needs will be filled tonight."

Audrey watched Carter staring up at the black roiling cloud. He asked, "Hey, I'm signed out for the Pangea. What happened to it?"

"Stuck on a rock when I tried running."

"Why would you even do that? This place is sick. I just took my OxyContin. Hey, you were really pumping out some major league yells."

"I'm remarkably calm now. I think it's numbness. Perhaps shock."

"Leo loved your yelling. He said it added to the ambience. Angelo was kinda bitchy. I think he thought you were upstaging the ceremony."

"He knows my thoughts now," said Audrey.

"We were talking to Janus down at the bottom of the hill. He's got some rough edges, but he's an interesting guy. Got his own way of looking at stuff."

Audrey could feel the bonfire heat on the other side of the altar, perhaps fifteen yards away. She recited, "'To market, to market to buy a fat hog/Home again, home again, jiggety-jog.'"

"Is that rap?"

"No, Carter, an old nursery rhyme. My mom taught it to me when I was little."

"I like rap music. I wish they'd brought speakers up here."

"I fancy WBGO and Jazz Night in America," said Left Arm.

Said Right Arm, "Aye, Christian McBride is a middling host, but played a cracker jack bass in his day."

Carter pointed out a deep jagged gash across the hill, over a dozen yards long. "That's where the Boston TV crew vaporized in 1986. Analyzing the film, the experts said it was a lightning bolt eight feet across. Awesome."

Audrey sighed a deep, mournful exhale, "Dunwich is more naturally lethal than Australia. I really wish I could redo the last six weeks."

"Hey, then what?" Carter returned to the mattresses where he chatted up a reclining, chinless woman of around forty.

Audrey's guards straightened up and tightened their grip on her biceps. She heard "oooo's" and "ahhhh's." Minus clothes and bomber jacket, Malachi Hutchins walked through the crowd sporting his snakeskin torso and holding up a thick book, moving with stern purpose like Moses raising the Ten Commandments. Audrey guessed the *Necronomicon* had arrived. Her respiration increased. *Almost show time.*

A fat chinless man stepped into the inner ring wielding a shiny rapier. By the flickering light of the bonfire, he used the sword to draw a large circle in the dirt, round as a pitcher's mound, perhaps ten feet from the altar. Inside the circle, the fat man drew various cryptic signs and symbols. Audrey couldn't see much, but thought a few resembled images from the Zodiac. Finishing up, the fat man stuck the sword point first into the ground within the circle, then scampered off as if trespassing in a backyard full of leopards. Malachi passed by him with the book, stepping into the circle, his back to the altar. He flipped through the *Necronomicon* to a certain page. With the book open in both arms, Malachi waited, a dutiful acolyte, a human lectern, legs trembling from cold or fright.

A rolling peal of thunder cracked overhead, echoing across the valleys and glens of Dunwich. For a brief moment, even the whippoorwills lowered their volume as if acknowledging superior might. A moment later, they returned to their relentless piping.

Audrey wasn't sure when he arrived, but Obed Whateley faced her, his wrinkled, naked body covered by a dreadful collection of scars, slashes, zigzag Frankenstein stitches, and odd suction wounds. Whateley's eyes reminded Audrey of an owl preparing to swallow a plump young gopher. She gulped in fright.

"Ye have heart and spirit," he said. "And yer flight caused an idiot to disturb my most needed afternoon rest."

Audrey said, "There's no way I can change tonight, is there?"

"No. But I admire yer craftiness. Ye should see the steam wits I'm forced to deal with. Not a Chester Sawyer among them."

"Please let me go."

"Prepare for yer spouse, Umr-at-Tawil."

In a little voice, Audrey said, "Does it matter that my divorce isn't final?"

But Whateley was already crossing to the large circle. Drawing the rapier, he faced Malachi and the open book. For several long moments, Whateley paused like an orchestra conductor an instant before dropping the baton. Then in quick succession, the Little Man used the sword to cut horizontal slashes across the inside of his forearms. Arms and sword skyward, blood streaming past his elbows, dripping like a faucet, Whateley bellowed in a voice of amazing power:

"Ai ai g'fh!

Moans, gasps, cries of passion. Audrey supposed the green flag had been dropped and the orgy was underway.

She felt the hair on her arms and neck rise up. *Oh god, formula.* Thunder roared and sheet lightning flashed above the hilltop like an unearthly photo op.

Whateley cried out again, more indecipherable, vowel-challenged gibberish.

The cult—at least those not orgying—answered in unison, "Ia!"

Arms bloody, Whateley jammed the rapier into the earth. He read out a passage from the *Necronomicon* in a loud commanding voice, again throwing out his arms, blood drops flying. The crowd responded, their voices louder, agitated, feral.

Audrey's heart pounded in fifth gear. She sensed things oozing into the space around the altar, flitting in like moths through a rip in a screen window. Audrey sensed these invisible entities drifting about, flying above Whateley's circle in erratic airborne ellipses, weaving through the bonfire on their travels, inhuman and famished.

To her left, the moaning, groaning orgy continued unabated, a writhing mass of aroused humans squirming together like earthworms in a can. Audrey guessed Whateley was channeling the uncorked sexual energy as an auxiliary stream to the rest of his diabolical crap.

With a red streaked, outstretched arm, Whateley gestured to Angelo.

"Step forward, Mohawk."

Angelo remained the model of stoned self-assuredness as he said, "I am Nipmuc. Does the ceremony require a native person from another nation?"

"Ye will do."

Like an actor making his entrance, Angelo strode forward to the altar, stopped, looked around, uncertain. He said to Whateley, "Here?"

"There."

"May I speak?"

"You may attempt as much."

Left and Right Arm watched, eyes glittering with gruesome prescience.

"My brothers and sisters," improvised Angelo, projecting his voice. "We are here to honor a new earth."

But his remarks were cut short after his left leg was torn away at the hip.

Audrey's lips moved, but no sound emerged.

Angelo's lungs emptied out in a high-pitched series of coyote-like yips.

As a child might eat a gingerbread man, invisible things devoured Angelo Silent Feather limb by limb: right arm to the elbow, left arm to the shoulder, left leg to the knee, remainder of the right arm, balance of the left leg, swarming over the professor like bees onto pancake syrup.

Snap-snap-snap-snap-snap.

Blood, fingers, toes, a scarp of hairy stomach rained to the ground. Finally, Angelo's head and neck were taken, silencing the yips. His deerskin pouch fell to the dirt, along with a clot of gray and black hair.

His limbless pot-bellied trunk was snapped up last.

"Ia! Ia!"

Left and Right Arm kept a fainting Audrey upright.

"An offering in advance of service," cried out Whateley to the sky. "I compel you by Azathoth and the Shambling Fright and the gibbering madness that is Magrist to seal this inner circle against all intruders. Know that I summon the Opener of the Way, the Eater of Souls, the Terror at the Portal. Touch not those I mark as mine."

From the air, a soft ageless, genderless voice answered almost in a whistle, "We heed . . . for a time."

Whateley directed the rapier toward Audrey. She felt a damp warmth down her legs as she wet herself. Left and Right Arms nervously guided her to the altar, lifting her up onto her back atop the chilly stone. Audrey wasn't sure how the two men did it so quickly, but her arms and legs were freed, retied to the altar ropes. Splayed in an x-shape, surrounded by bones, some of them child-sized, facing up toward the black cloud, Audrey unleashed a loud, mournful groan as her guards hurried away.

Sword in hand, Whateley read once more from the *Necronomicon*. He cried out formula above the frenetic orgy and the whippoorwills and the powerful thunder peals, and the whimpering Audrey, whose head turned rapidly back and forth as if a side profile would save her. Whateley's voice was tremendous, dominant, the booming declarations of an unamplified man determined that everyone in a football stadium hear his words.

"Yog-Sothoth knows the gate."

"Yog-Sothoth is the gate."

"Yog-Sothoth is the key and guardian of the gate."

Around a panicked Audrey, the atmosphere grew charged, pulsing with fantastic energy, like the annihilating might of a nuclear weapon at the moment of chain reaction. Cultists lowered their heads and the orgy slowed, then stopped as all eyes focused on a spot in space beneath the black thundercloud.

Whateley continued, "Past, present, future, all are one in Yog-Sothoth. He knows where the Old Ones broke through of old, and where They shall break through again."

Audrey felt as if the air were about to rip apart. Lifting her head, she could see Whateley's head encased in an eerie aural light like a halo. From the rapier tip and his outstretched hand, ectoplasm flowed in sinuous, blurry white, undulating streams. A wind blew down upon Audrey like a frigid downdraft from outer space. Below the black cloud, the sky rippled and shimmered in the manner of heat waves rising from the summer asphalt.

From somewhere behind her, Audrey heard Leo's frightened yell. "Stop it. I don't want to. Carter, Carter, help me."

"He knows where They have trod earth's fields, and where They still tread them, and why no one can behold Them as They tread."

Yells and shouts. Audrey turned her head to see Leo stumbling along. For a brief moment, it appeared he might flee the hill. But a Dunwicher jammed a long staff between his knees, tripping the Chief of Campus Diversity Enforcement. Naked chinless men fell upon Leo Hameyes.

Thunder cracked like the splitting of a continent.

Audrey forgot the struggles of Leo, blinking rapidly, eyes skyward. Like kelp bulbs bobbing on the tide, iridescent globes floated down from the shimmering air above the altar. Varying in number and size, the globes evoked contradictory impressions. They seemed familiar and impossibly alien, peaceful and yet representing something heinous and macabre, like a four-color advertising brochure for Dachau. Confused, her body trembling from the cold and terror, Audrey focused on the changing colors, so many, some very subtle, others quite unidentifiable.

I'm dreaming, but a subtle one, where you think you're asleep, but then you wake up and have a yummy bowl of Kashi with low-fat milk and green tea.

Bawling like a calf, Leo Hameyes was shoved sprawling into the dirt near the altar. Jumping up, staring at the descending globes, he lost balance, spun around and fell again. Left and Right Arm erupted into sardonic laughter joined by the other cultists.

Carter's voice rang out, "Hey, Leo. What are you doing out there?"

In a high-pitched voice, near cracking, Dr. Hameyes said, "Theater-sham-mummery. All designed to fool and trick. There's nothing but nothing."

Wisps, tendrils lazily unspooled from the globes, falling like rain seen at a distance. Audrey imagined party decorations dropped from a ceiling. As if blown on a breeze they wafted past her. Leo began *mmmmmming*.

"Mmmmmm. What are these? Mmmmm. Ha. Mmmmm. Hahaha. It's a trick. Silly billy. Hahahahaha. Very good. Excellent special effects."

"Ia! Ia!" screamed the crowd.

This is strange. Audrey watched an upside down Leo rising into the air, a tendril wrapped around his ankle yanking him up. Keys and change fell from his pockets. But the most surreal aspect was his clear laughter.

"Ah hahhahaha. Heeheeheehee. A trick, you see? Ohhohohohoha."

Ascending higher, voice growing hoarse, his laughs morphed into a horrid set of seal barks. A moment and he vanished, engulfed by festive globes. His laugh continued briefly, then stopped, followed by a soft rain as liquid mixed with small particles of something soft and damps sprinkled upon Audrey, drawing forth many *Ias* and triumphant, vowelless shouts.

Lower, closer, wisps and tendrils withdrew as the jouncing globes neared Audrey. Now she couldn't turn away from the colors even if she'd wanted. Ranging the length of her body, a large globe the size of an exercise ball hovered above her belly. Audrey couldn't be certain, but she sensed herself no longer present, shivering atop stone. She felt warm, toasty, on the edge of hot. Before her in the distance stretched a spiral galaxy, a clot of stars, brilliant white, streaked with blues and oranges, encased in a stygian blackness. *Am I dead? Is this eternity?*

Her tummy gripped with a queasy sensation, as if she'd crested the top of a steep rollercoaster and now barreled down into the first turn. A sense of vast distances beyond time and space filled her consciousness. Audrey felt light years zipping past in nanoseconds while she navigated through blackness toward the star mass as if thought, movement, destination were united. With a delicious thrill, she entered the star mass, immersed in the surrounding light. For a time, Audrey felt herself a universal being, transcendent, immortal. A scintillating creature.

Tilting face forward, plunging; Audrey's ecstasy shriveled into doubt, foreboding, the mordant knowledge of a jumper who realizes impact is a breath away. Stars and light faded.

Audrey's cosmic belly flop accelerated toward a dot racing up to meet her.

Dot expanded, assumed form, crystalized into a gigantic vacuous human face, chin slick with drool, eyes molten with scorching alien lust.

In a small mercy, Audrey's mind selected that moment to snap.

CHAPTER 14

MORGAN'S WITCH

October 31 blurbs from the *North Aylesbury Transcript* online edition:

Halloween Hijinx Hosted by Bailbondsmen
The Association of South Aylesbury Licensed Bailbondsmen will host their 34th Annual Children's Costume Party, beginning at 5 P.M. in the parking lot of Nick's Kwick Bond.

Local Cop Keeps Solo Watch

In his Jeep Ranger, off-duty North Aylesbury patrolman Michael Vitale has once again volunteered to patrol Highway 29 outside Dunwich, monitoring the strange, often dangerous, seasonal festivities. Two years ago, decorated army veteran Vitale rescued a teenage boy from Newton, the only survivor of a group that thought it would be fun to visit Sentinel Hill and "prank the weirdos."

A vast Hadron Collider of formula seemed to marinate the hill. Every hair on Mercy's body felt vertical. Standing against a pillar next to her, staring at the multicolored globes above the altar, Bongani's jaw gaped, blood draining from his cheeks. He gulped and made the Sign of the Cross.

"We need to figure out where to set up," she said, hopping on one leg, clutching Bongani's arm.

A rock clacked off the pillar.

Bongani said, "Elsewhere."

Furious chinless people rushed around the hill toward them from both sides.

Bongani fired his pistol. Using both hands, he shot high right, then left, spooking the charging cultists, who scattered behind pillars. Mercy recognized the danger of attackers skulking below the hill and creeping up on them.

"We're gonna charge, Joe B. How's that for a plan?"

Carrying the pentagram mat, Mercy limped forward into the hill's inner ring. But after only a dozen steps, her spine froze at the threat of imminent rending death. Dropping the mat in the dirt near a jagged fissure, she and Joe B. squeezed onto the small plastic surface. Mercy rattled off the Greek phrase, activating the aegis. Crowded against Joe B., she perceived Those From the Air circling the mat. Keeping weight off her bad ankle, back against Bongani, she imagined a bubble like in *The Incredibles* protected them. Unseen entities tested her defense like wind buffeting the outside of a tent.

A voice whispered, "Let us in, little mage. We know much."

"Back off, invisible ass-clown."

Pressure to lower the aegis increased from multiple wills. Mercy felt beset as if cornered by relentless vitamin salesmen eager to overcome all objections. But the pentagram seemed to lend her will and imagination a boost.

Another rock flew past.

A woman's voice sounded from the gloom, "The Lurker will crush ye like lice."

More shouting, frantic calls. In the uneven illumination of the hill—bonfire, torches, lightning flashes—Mercy spotted naked reinforcements running toward them on the edges of the hill, close to the stone pillars.

"You take the congregation, Joe B., I'll take the weird stuff."

"Yes."

Confident she could hold back Those From the Air, Mercy's eyes turned toward the fearsome thing hovering above the altar, where a motionless woman was spread out on the surface. Beautiful iridescent globes seemed plump with gargantuan power and menace, making her feel like krill drifting toward the mouth of a blue whale. Should the Old One lash out in her direction, Mercy sensed her own shield would be as useless as a kitchen sponge in stopping a seventy-foot wave.

In addition, the globes emanated a stench transcending all previous Dunwich foulness. They battered Mercy's senses like poo-scented tear gas. Eyes watering, nose sniffling, she battled the effects, as well as the suffocating terror of being forty yards from a freaking Old One.

Beyond the globes and altar, Mercy spotted a little naked man throwing formula, partially blocked from view by a second, taller man with a snake-like back. She guessed the little guy was Obed Whateley. Sword in hand, arms outstretched, Whaley must be shielding his followers from the Old One, as well as Those From the Air. Mercy was awed. Whateley's mastery of formula soared beyond formidable. *He's holding a black American Express Centurion Card, while I've got a maxed out Shell gas card.*

Snake Back spoke with Whateley, then hustled away. Neither the Old One nor Those From the Air bothered him. *Protected.* Passing a crowd huddled on mattresses, Snake Back rifled through a pile of clothes, looking for something.

From the dark, another rock whooshed past Mercy's head, thudding into the dirt.

Ka-pop!

The gunshot deafened her left ear. An ejected 9mm round burned her cheek.

"Hey, wow. I got a lot on my plate, Joe B."

"Sorry, Merce."

She smiled. Bongani had used her nickname twice in one night.

A man's voice called out of the dark, "Ye will die puling like kittens in a trash compactor."

Bongani yelled back, "You will die from a bullet for the rocks."

Another Dunwicher hollered, but his words were lost in a rippling peal of thunder as a yard-wide lightning bolt struck near the altar. Mercy gasped, blinking away a field of white dots.

More Old Ones arriving at Gate 10. It's the end.

A rock struck Mercy in the back, beneath the right shoulder blade, dropping inside the pentagram.

"Ahh, shit."

Ka-powpow.

A man cried out in pain.

Between the aggressive stench, a ringing ear, her vision being disrupted, knee-weakening jitters, and the throbbing pain in her ankle, Mercy almost lost the aegis. Ravenous pressure increased. Those From the Air darted close like lions around a weary buffalo.

Use the fear. Use everything.

Mercy accepted the confusion, fright, disorientation, funneling the emotions into her imagination and will. In her mind, she envisioned once more the force field from *The Incredibles,* strengthening the energy bubble around her and Joe B. For good measure, Mercy pictured a second force layer atop the first, thick as a curb.

Powpowpow.

Like a bee, something zinged overhead. Mercy saw Snake Back running at them in a crouch, firing a revolver.

Joe B. ripped off several rounds.

Kapowpowpow.

Glancing at Whateley, Mercy yelped as the Little Man pointed his sword directly at her.

Throwing formula. I'm not gonna like this.

Something struck her aegis with the force of a wrecking ball.

Around the hill sounded wild shots-whippoorwills-thunder-crackling bonfire-stinking whippoorwills. But Mercy didn't notice. Every last tatter of her concentration focused on stopping Whateley's formula from battering her aegis. Ruthless and hostile as a truncheon across the forehead, the force seemed intent on crumpling the shield and ramming her and Joe B. off the pentagram and onto the menu of Those From the Air.

Despite the cold air, sweat drenched Mercy. Hair and forehead were salty, sweat drops dripped onto her nose, and she felt her camisole plastered to her spine. Mercy's uninjured left leg trembled. She sunk at the knees, fear and panic eroding her concentration. Sensing weakness, Those From the Air nibbled at her will.

"Release the aegis and rest, woman."

"We'll not touch you."

Mercy's shield felt more and more like a damp napkin. Anxiety blossomed, and her time for maintaining the aegis could be measured in seconds. Bongani's left arm reached back and gripped Mercy's shoulder, holding tight.

Positive physical contact fed her focus, but it wasn't enough. In desperation, Mercy shifted full weight onto her sprained right ankle. Unaware of her own screams, Mercy used the pain to channel her will. In her imagination, the shield thickened, glowed, grew rounder.

Mercy sensed Those From the Air withdrawing.

Whateley's hostile formula flowed around the aegis, like tap water on a snow globe.

The attack abruptly ceased.

Mercy eased the pressure off her injured right foot. Sapped of energy, breathing fast from ankle pain, she felt too drained to try anything other than maintaining the shield.

"You held," said Bongani. He sounded proud of her.

"Barely," whispered Mercy. "No wonder Uncle Louis passed on a round two."

Bones crunched and dropped onto the ground. Several yards away, Snake Back sprawled lifelessly, providing eats for the invisible beings.

Mercy said, "Good shooting. Nice that Those From the Air are socially responsible, keeping the environment tidy."

"He was the man I took the gun from Thursday night."

Mercy nodded, "Dude's had a rough last few days."

More vitriolic death threats floated out from behind the stone pillars. Bongani held his 9mm at the ready, but didn't fire. Mercy wondered about the rest of the invaders. Every second without another Old One was gold. *Maybe formula is more like a battery. I was really wasted all day Friday. And here's Whateley throwing major formula, probably for the second night in a row.*

"Someone is upon the altar."

"I know. A woman. There's nothing we can do now. I'm hanging on by my cracked and chipped fingernails."

Finished munching Snake Back, Those From the Air returned, hovering around the pentagram, drifting away, always returning, pressing, whispering, cajoling Mercy to rest her mind. It was having an effect. She made herself focus on the altar.

What's with that stinky Old One?

More activity near Whateley. A young man trembled in the chill wind, glancing apprehensively at the colored globes as Whateley issued him orders. The Little Man inclined his chin toward Mercy and Joe B. Pausing to put on running shoes, hands in the air like a prisoner, the young man walked around the hill toward the pentagram.

"Don't shoot this one, Joe B. He's got mail."

Stopping ten yards away, cold and terrified, the young man looked familiar. Mercy said nothing, waiting in the flickering light.

"Please don't shoot me. I have a message."

"Say it."

"I've been without social media for almost two days. I have no idea what's trending. I'm very disoriented."

"That's your message?"

"He wants to know if you're Morgan's witch. But I'm not sure what that means."

Mercy said, "I remember you. Carter Fong. You like snarky little tweets and Gabby Face put-downs."

"Please help me. I think terrible things have happened, but I'm really stoned."

"Put your arms down, Fong. Whateley already knows who we are. He sent people to stop us."

A rumble from the tar black cloud.

Fong said, "I'm scared of those invisible eatey things."

"Yeah. Without Whateley's formula, you'd be cheese Doritos."

"I thought his name was Leland Janus. But Audrey knew he was Obed Whateley."

"Klumm-Weebner? Where is she?"

"Altar, but she hasn't moved in awhile. Leo and Angelo died really horribly. I think. It's a bit muddy."

Mercy recalled a journal passage regarding the Funwich Commune and what happened to a certain woman stretched out on that altar. ('Yog Soda.') It depressed her.

"Other than an introduction, what does Whateley want?"

"For you to stop shooting and something about not throwing formula. He said he'll let you go and I can leave too. He said you're spoiling the ceremony."

Mercy frowned, "If he's ending the world, who cares?"

"He's not. Or he can't. Another page, or a part of something that he needed never showed up. Hey, Whateley was real pissed. Can we leave now?"

Mercy smiled, heard Bongani chuckle, then together they laughed.

"Joe B., the old earth will keep spinning after all."

"You can eat hamburgers."

"I'll do a hell of lot more than that."

A flash of sheet lightning brightened the hill like a floodlight. Mercy spied movement above the altar. Noxious malignant globes bobbed, swirled in colors of sunflower, metallic silver, azure, aquamarine. First one, then several clumped together like pearls on a string, separating, recombining, fusing in an intricate sequence of alien movements. *Yog-Sothoth. How big was it?*

Mercy sensed that while the globes were visible, they were only partially present, an overlay from another dimension. Whateley might summon, propitiate, and protect his followers from Yog-Sothoth, but he did not control. A solitary globe drifted upward like a balloon. *Leaving?*

Fong said, "I have to find my clothes first. Don't bounce without me."

"Wait a second, Fong."

"I'm freezing."

"Shut up."

Bongani asked, "What is wrong?"

"Give me a second, Joe. Fong, what about the eatey things?"

"Whateley will protect us."

Mercy's mind raced: drop the aegis. Let Whateley screen them. Leave alive and with honor, sanity still intact—more or less. For whatever reason, it was over. Or could be. Mercy wanted to burst out singing, sob in relief, kiss Joe B.

Thoughts pecked at her mind like ravens.

"And the *Necronomicon*?"

"Whateley didn't say."

"And Klumm-Weebner up on the altar?"

This drew amused catcalls from the hidden cultists.

"Ye must arrange matters with her husband."

"Aye," cried a woman, "petition the Eater of Souls."

Called out another woman, "Will ye nip the bride of the Faceless One?"

Bongani silenced catcalls from behind the pillars by firing twice in the air.

Above the altar, a second globe sailed upward. The thing seemed in transit.

Fong said, "He didn't say anything about Audrey."

Hisses and groans from the hill. The ground shook in a violent spasm.

Bongani whispered, "We can tell the police. They will find her."

An ageless sexless voice whispered, "You have won. Depart as victors."

Mercy snarled, "Close your unseen yap."

From the gloom, a man's voice called, "Are ye to stand there all night like living firewood? Get ye gone from sacred ground."

Mercy yelled, "Has everyone commented yet? Do I have all opinions?"

Fong walked back toward Whateley. Mercy called out, "Where are you going?"

"To accept. Don't leave without me. I'll be right back."

"Put it in park and give us a moment."

Mercy said, "Joe B., what do you think? If I drop the aegis and we leave the pentagram, do you trust Whateley to protect us from our invisible chums?"

"Cannot the shield move with us?"

"I don't know. I'm afraid to try in case it can't."

Bongani said nothing as the thunder boomed and the Old One stank, and the hilltop hissed and rumbled in the crisp night air.

At last, he replied, "Whateley is a liar."

Mercy sagged. A little hope is a deadly thing. She'd really wanted it to be over. For a moment she hesitated, then Mercy's voice rose above the whippoorwills, "Fong, tell Whateley we fight it out. And tell him I'm not Morgan's witch. I'm the Chair of the Antiquity Section of Miskatonic University."

Fong threw up his arms, voice rising several octaves, "Hey, that's nuts, insane. This place is beyond crazy. I can't hang here any more, even though the tea is really good."

"We're throwing formula, dude. Stand clear."

With a terrified screech, Carter Fong bolted toward the stone pillars.

As if dumped from a cargo aircraft, ozone permeated the atmosphere.

A spectacular flash lit Sentinel Hill—the pop of a moon-sized strobe light.

Almost to the edge of the hill, a colossal fat lightning bolt halted Fong's frenzied flight, eleven feet wide, snaking from the onyx cloud like the Wrath of Jehovah. Mercy clamped her eyes tight, convinced she was blinded. Sentinel Hill seemed paralyzed, other aspects of nature overwhelmed by the apocalyptic illumination. The chill wind died out. Whippoorwills and bullfrogs stopped their freakish canticle. Hissing and groaning from the ground ceased. For several long moments, the only noise came from wood popping and snapping in the bonfire. Above the hill, the black thunder cloud rumbled once, short and sharp, almost a belch.

Oh, God in Heaven, did Whately pull a Sirac Bishop and vaporize us all?

Grabbing Bongani's arm for reassurance, Mercy waited, head lowered, for her vision to clear. When at last she peered around, a deep smoldering fissure occupied the space where Fong had last been seen.

I guess he's off the hill.

A chill wind stung Mercy's face.

Whippoorwills and bullfrogs resumed their mantra.

The hill hissed and shook.

Above the altar, two more globes rose.

"Ye stink."

A rock struck Bongani in the calf.

"Oww."

Ka-pop.

A woman ululated.

Bongani said, "We can not leave Klumm-Weebner or the book."

"I know. It's all-in or bust. But he's overloaded, Joe. I mean, Whateley's focused on the Old One, and protecting his cult, and fighting us. His battery must be low. I think he was buying time just now so we wouldn't clash while he's super strained."

"Then we may win?"

"Maybe. But I think we've only got a small window until the Old One splits. Keeping that bad boy chilled must take most of Whateley's concentration. Once it's out of here, I think he'll have enough left in the tank to flatten us."

"Can you use the fire one?"

"Selective Inferno is not my best. Listen, turn around and shoot Whateley."

"Oh?"

"Best things in life are the simple things."

Bongani shifted about, took aim and cracked off three rounds.

Kapopppoppop.

No flashes or indications of any kind that the rounds had struck home, plus no defensive reactions from Whately.

"Are you sure you were on target?"

"Yes."

"Shit, then he's got a first class shield. The Bulwark of Zom or a Royal Encasement. Whateley's protected from both physical attack and formula."

Only two globes remained above the altar, bobbing at a leisurely pace like a man walking past a Little League game, mildly interested in the outcome. Mercy felt dog piled by fear and exhaustion. She wanted to hide. *What do I do? I need an information download fast.*

The sentences returned to her mind in exact order:

'Precision is vital.'

'The greater the formula the more unbending the concentration.'

'A small distraction can unravel all.'

The last one was right on the mark. And if Whateley wasn't throwing great formula tonight, there was no such thing. As to precision? Well, that would reveal itself. Mercy felt her strength ebbing.

"Joe B., we've gotta run fast and wild like dope-addled monkeys."

In a few terse sentences, she explained her plan. Bongani smiled. "I will do as you ask, Baba O'Connor."

"You sweet-talking Zulu."

"To be certain, that is a greeting for a younger to an older man. But this is America and words can be new here."

"I accept. Now put a fresh magazine in that boom stick, get on your half, and wait for the whistle."

Clicks, chinks as Joe B. swapped magazines. Mercy experienced a pleasant glow, then a dark pessimism.

Wow. 'Baba.' Let's see if I've got the energy left to earn it.

CHAPTER 15

ALL SAINT'S DAY

November 1 blurb from the *Arkham Advertiser* online edition:

Deale Disses Parent Allegations
by Holt Manatee

In comments on the university's web site, Miskatonic President Armand Deale belittled claims that he initiated the protests that resulted in violence and the closure of the campus Antiquity Section. "Oh, sure, what's next?" wrote Deale, "I'm responsible for 9/11? The invasion of Iraq? McDonald's serving breakfast 24 hours?"

Families of students injured in last week's campus brawl have made a number of allegations against President Deale. Several parents have claimed Students Loyal to Underserved Groups was created by Professor Angelo Silent Feather, a staunch Deale ally, at the behest of Deale, to circumvent the Board of Trustees. "Silent Feather answered to Deale, and Deale wanted the section gone," said Manny OnKloster, father of Wimble OnKloster, a Microaggresions Studies major who suffered a broken collarbone while attacking a security guard. OnKloster continued, "In fact, Deale had already promised the Antiquity Section space to his girlfriend."

Deale is said to be romantically linked to Post-Structural Hierarchies Professor Audrey Klumm-Weebner, author of the popular text book Old Ones,

New Values—Fresh Insights on the Population of North-Central Massachusetts. *Deale has denied any sexual relationship with Klumm-Weebner. Professor Klumm-Weebner was unavailable for comment as she is spending the weekend inside Dunwich returning a book and attending what has been termed a "diversity seminar."*

Taking its own sweet time, Yog-Sothoth was decamping Sentinel Hill. As another globe meandered upward, Mercy felt a diminishing in the cold, hateful, cyclopean energy emanating from above the altar. Higher ascended the globe, rising toward a warped, shimmering spot in the sky below the thundercloud.

"Ia! Ia!" screamed several exultant voices from the shadows.

Another rock flew past.

"Joe, pump some lead at the rock throwers, keep 'em ducking. I'll need you locked on target when I throw."

"Yes."

Slow fire, measured. Ka-pow. Ka-pow.

Mercy remembered her *Beauty and the Beast* coloring book. She recalled sprawling across her bed as a little girl, using crayons to carefully color within the lines of Belle's dress. She would hold that image in her imagination: an orange crayon. Make that a fiery orange crayon. Mercy would use it to try and burn a hole in the warlock's shield.

The stench was noticeably less. Mercy needed to hustle buns with this formula or she'd face a greatly empowered Obed Whateley.

"Ready?"

"Yes. I will shoot as you say."

Those From the Air lurked, swooped, chewed at her resolve like attic rats gnawing on electrical wire. Mercy blocked them out as best she could, focusing on immediate thaumaturgical chores. Trusting her instincts, she selected the amount of will necessary to hold the aegis. *('Set your defense first.')* Every other scrap of will and imagination would be fuel for her concentration and the maneuvering of the fiery crayon. Mercy glanced at Bongani, face a quilt of bandages and surgical tape, grimly facing Whateley, pistol at the ready. Beyond the altar, Whateley's bloody arms remained outstretched, head tilted up toward the last globe.

Mercy grappled with a fatigue that seemed to penetrate to her DNA. All charge was rapidly draining from her battery. Her torso wobbled, her neck felt heavy as a marble counter top, her ankle throbbed and ached.

A voice from the air whispered, "So weary now. Rest your eyes."

Mercy replied, "I wish I knew enough formula to kill you. Rest on that."

Imagining the fiery crayon pointing a foot above Whateley's head, Mercy inhaled deeply before shouting the Chaldean phrase that activated the Forge of Nin-Agal. Across the hill, an orange spot popped into view a foot above Whateley's head, sparking like a welding torch. Mercy felt as if she were shoving a shopping cart full of cinder blocks as she mentally pressed the orange crayon in and down, imagining it drawing a laser-like line, cutting a gap in Whateley's protective shield. Progress was good. Her orange line seared downward past the warlock's head, burning a vertical path in his aegis.

Obed Whateley's head snapped around in alarm.

What counter formula he used Mercy couldn't say, but moving her blazing crayon suddenly felt like encountering reverse polarity on a magnet.

The amount of vitality necessary to force the crayon down and slice open the shield seemed to have doubled, then tripled. *Amazing. How deep are this mook's reserves?*

Bongani asked, "Shoot now?"

Mercy croaked, "Naw."

Time passed with excruciating torpor, breath to breath. If the orange crayon burned at all it was in a minute increments, followed by her maximum concentration with zero results, followed by Whateley's intense pushback to erase the fraction she'd gained. Mercy felt she was attempting to sear a gap in a titanium wall using a scented candle. She desperately wanted to release the formula and quit, only hanging on instant by instant. Fatigue dulled her thinking, and Mercy almost dropped her own aegis in order to access more will. Only a mental voice screaming "Don't" saved her and Bongani from being torn into Bolognese.

It's a sealing spell, not for cracking shields. If I let go, I'll die, but I can't last. I've killed Joe B. and he trusted me to make the right call.

Millimeter by millimeter, her fiery orange crayon was pushed back up, nullifying the gains. Sweat poured off Mercy's forehead, skied into the hollow of her back, rolled into her eyes. Joe B.'s face showed concern; he glanced often at Mercy, still standing by for a command to fire she'd probably never issue. *Maybe he can shoot me. I'll take that over being ripped apart like buffalo wings.* Sensing weakness and collapse, Those From the Air swarmed tight against her aegis, agitated with bloodlust.

Something happened above the altar.

Like fire hoses unraveling, wisps and tendrils of energy extended out of the last globe. Like the tentacles of a giant squid, they floated above

Whateley's shield and toward the mattresses. In a burst of speed, they plunged into the cultists.

Screams of horror and fear. Two terrified male voices bellowed in fright, crying for 'help.' They were joined by an ululating female cry of ecstasy. Wisps and tendrils retreated, carrying three wriggling figures up above the altar toward the remaining globe.

He's weakened. He can't protect his own followers anymore. Mercy found she once again could force the fiery orange crayon downward.

At the same time, Those From the Air broke off their psychic assault on Mercy and departed.

From behind her pentagram, Mercy heard agonized cries from the stone pillars. A fat, chinless man frantically hopped past the pentagram on his right leg, his left limb ending in a blood-pumping stump below the knee. Waving his arms wildly as if swarmed by locusts, he was lacerated and devoured by Those From the Air. Blood splattered Mercy and Bongani like water from a sprinkler head.

Mercy felt the moisture, but concentrated on tearing open Whateley's defense. With unexpected ease, her fiery orange crayon pushed down past the warlock's chest, frying open a five-foot vertical slit in Whateley's aegis.

Voice hoarse, Mercy said, "Shoot now."

Ka-powpowpowpowpowpowpow.

Hot ejects struck Mercy on the head and cheek, but she didn't notice as Bongani ripped off half a magazine at the Little Man. At least one round penetrated through the hole in his shield as the warlock spun around, dropping from sight. Mercy released the fiery crayon and almost lurched over onto her face.

Above the altar, the last globe of Yog-Sothoth vanished, hauling along its trio of writhing road snacks. Stink level on the hill immediately shrank to merely unpleasant, and the ominous sense of utter, crushing doom lifted entirely. A tremendous thunder outburst detonated above, peal after peal, like Baal's church bells, finally fading out, the last echoes rippling across Dunwich. As the onyx cloud shredded, breaking apart, a starry night sky shone through.

Hisses and groans from the hill and a long tremor. A chill wind swept the ground, drying Mercy's sweat and leaving her shivering like an epileptic. Light flickered weakly as the last bonfire wood disintegrated into guttering flame. Other than a few torches near the mattresses, Sentinel Hill was lit by star and moon.

Mercy wasn't certain, but it seemed Those From the Air had also withdrawn. Maybe they didn't like being summoned. Maybe they preferred free-range humans. Perhaps it was just another trap. She hated them. Whatever else had departed, it wasn't the whippoorwills. In the yellowish-gray grass around the hill, they continued shrieking in defiant, raucous unison.

Mercy rubbed a sleeve across her forehead, "I've got that fat guy's blood all over my face."

Bongani stood quietly, head cocked.

"That's a pretty wicked thing to say and you don't respond?"

"There. Do you hear?"

"Over the birds?"

"Listen, listen."

Weary beyond exhaustion, still maintaining the aegis, Mercy caught the faint sound of engines at the base of the hill. Firing up, ebbing away into the distance. Some of the cultists must be bailing out. A soft click as Bongani engaged the safety and lowered his weapon. Too gassed to care, Mercy poked a finger outside the pentagram. Then a hand. Then an arm. Then she waved the arm as if signaling someone across a parking lot.

Mercy said, "I'm liking the results."

Bongani extended a leg outside the pentagram. As if doing the hokey-pokey, he shook it all around, then waited several moments before answering, "Yes."

Mercy released the aegis.

"Dude, did you bring any water?"

Before Joe B. could answer, she sank to her knees, tried to stand, then folded up like a marionette.

A gray landscape covered in ash. Some rock outcroppings in the distance. A silence so profound, it rang out as unnatural. Mercy wore a neat work outfit. Her right ankle was perfectly healed. She wore sandals and could see her toes. Nice nail color; it matched her top. Arms loose, fingers interlaced, Mercy watched the fat chinless man hop past her, unafraid but forlorn. No longer in a hurry, he bounded along as if enroute to a destination where arrival time didn't matter. Was he one-legged? She supposed not. But certainly not two-legged. You couldn't say that anymore. Was it proper to say one and a half legged? And was he armed? That was funny. Was the one-legged man armed? Most certainly not. Then who was shooting?

Eyes glued shut with grit, Mercy sat up on the plastic pentagram. She threw aside the coat covering her, spat on her fingers and rubbed her eyes. Whippoorwills wailed as if enchanted by bird-centric entertainment. With some difficulty, Mercy stood up, weight on her left foot. Voices, curses, Dunwichers; near the altar, an altercation.

Adrenaline refreshed Mercy as she fast-clumped toward the melee. Drawing nearer, she spotted two chinless bodies crumpled in the dirt.

Beside the altar, the pair of half-dressed male cultists whom Audrey had named Left Arm and Right Arm swung shin bones and thigh bones at a prostrate form. With muffled *thunks*, they impacted the head.

"Think ye a hard man, now?"

"Die, ye vile baboon."

A motionless Joe B. lay sprawled in the dirt, absorbing their brutality.

Mercy gasped, certain the Dunwichers had murdered him. She flung out her arms as ectoplasm streamed from her fingers like rays, and a violet luminous aura surrounded her head. A terrifying, enraged being, Mercy bellowed out the Hebrew words, activating the Selective Inferno. The Dunwich duo looked up in alarm, dropped their bloody bones and fled. But there was no flight from Mercy's formula.

Emerald flames consumed their every centimeter as if they'd been soaking for a week in gasoline. Screaming in pain, swatting at themselves, Left Arm and Right Arm spun, leapt, twisted as if performing a dance routine at the Academy Awards. Running and stumbling in torment and panic, one man toppled to the ground and rolled back and forth, trying to extinguish the blaze. But these green fires were fed by Mercy's fury and she had a surplus. Pupils melted, fat crackled like butter in a hot pan. In seconds, Left and Right Arm were consumed like blazing toilet paper, embers linking up with those of the dying bonfire, glowing chards drifting away on the breeze.

Mercy's apoplexy continued unabated, stoked by weeks of pressure and anxiety, days of violence, pain, soul-tearing fear, and now grief.

"You can't leave us alone, can you?" she hollered. "Can't ever park your 24/7 evil bullshit.

Warren Rice nailed it. Dunwich should be blown up, razed to bedrock, soaked in chlorine, then paved over and used for county fairs. You people are savages."

Eyes hard as life, Mercy roared out to the Dunwich countryside.

"You want my full attention, you've got it. I'll study formula, astounding skull-popping shit. And you'll live in terror that I'll lay it on you. By the time I'm finished, you'll kidnap yourselves, sacrifice your own kids, throw formula at each other because otherwise the Antiquity Section will smoke out your chinless hybrid asses. And if you ever attempt to end the world again, I will drown your smelly, tart-filled land in a lake of green fire. I swear to God, try me."

As the rage expired, Mercy exhaled, nerves tingling around a heart that felt hollow and brittle. Smoke drifted past from the last of the bonfire. Gray light spread across the hillside in a languid, unhurried pace as if employed by the Federal government. But dawn had no effect on the whippoorwills. Shriek-shriek-shriek. Mercy had heard that Dunwichers sometimes beat them with bats or shot them with pellet guns. She was beginning to understand why.

From her pocket, Mercy removed the little halogen flashlight. Near the altar, she found the 9mm, carefully lowered the hammer, clicked on the safety and placed the weapon in her coat pocket. Several expended casings lay visible in the dirt. Of the Dunwich quartet that had jumped Bongani, Mercy guessed Joe had popped the first two she'd passed before the other pair brained him with bones. Illuminating his face, she noted blood seeping from Joe B.'s scalp, down his face, covering old bandages with fresh gore.

"I'm so sorry, Joe. You were there for me at every step. And the one time you needed me, I screwed up. You were right, dear friend. I should've practiced more."

Eyes shut, he seemed neither at peace nor distraught. This was in sharp contrast to Conrad Morgan in the hospital, eyes wide open and unmoving, but somehow giving the impression he could see you. Mercy wanted to weep, but there wasn't anything left in her tear locker.

Trickling liquid?

Looking toward the altar, Mercy spotted water dribbling from the stone surface, forming a little pool near a deerskin pouch lying at the altar's base.

Standing, Mercy directed the flashlight beam onto Audrey Klumm-Weebner. The Post-Structural Hierarchies professor lay covered in coats, a windbreaker beneath her head. However, her ankles and wrists were still trussed. Illuminating Audrey's face revealed the reason: her eyes were the big, trusting orbs of a child. Her auburn hair was now colored a dramatic albino white. Untethered, Audrey might wander off, fall, injure herself like any two-year old.

"How are you?" whispered Mercy.

"Jig. Jiggetty jog. Jigjigjigjigjigjig."

Near Audrey's head, a plastic water bottle lay tipped over, liquid draining down one of several gutters. Joe B. must've covered her up, found some water, and was probably ministering to Audrey when the Dunwichers attacked. Mercy picked up the bottle and drained it.

Gray daylight increased as Mercy crossed over to examine Whateley's pentagram. As expected, it was an Eliphas Levi special. Powerful symbols. You could throw some hefty formula from here and Whateley had indeed done so. She

276

was relieved to see the *Necronomicon* open in the dirt, grateful some cultist hadn't scuttled off with it to Dunwich. They'd never find the lousy thing again. Blood stains inside the pentagram trailed across the dirt toward the stone pillars. Joe had hit the warlock at least once.

So typical. Whateley escapes. '56, '91, now. Unbelievable.

Mercy paused, recalling something about bloodstains she'd heard on a televised crime show. How long would blood flow after you died? Could blood seep if there weren't a beating heart pumping it?

She needed to check.

Mercy knelt by Bongani. Her hands sought his neck. Kneading the skin, she found the carotid artery and pushed in.

A faint pulse.

Her heart sped up. *Dear God, he's still alive.* For a moment, Mercy panicked, *Cell phone no good. What do I do? There's no one around.* What action could she take? Rummaging in Bongani's clothes, Mercy snagged the keys to the Mini Cooper.

"Hang in there, Joe B. I need you to be strong for a little more."

To Audrey she said, "I'll be back very soon, Okay?"

"J. JJ. Jog."

Cursing her ankle, she hopped over and collected the *Necronomicon*. After all they been through, Mercy wasn't about to leave this malevolent cookbook lying around.

Dig deep. Find more.

Battling pain and tiredness, Mercy hopped, hobbled, limped past the mattresses still permeated with the smell of sex, around clumps of abandoned clothes, mostly shoes, coats and jackets, to the stone pillars, then down a winding path through the grass. Despite daylight, the whippoorwills would not shut up. Mercy considered a massive application of the Selective Inferno, but feared there were too many birds and not enough charge left in her formula battery. In future, an anti-whippoorwill formula might be worth exploring.

Descending was awkward, agonizing. She traveled downward ten minutes, pausing frequently. On one such break, a few yards off to the side of the trail, she spotted the head of a little old man. Eyes shut. Motionless. Seemingly dead. Setting down the book, Mercy drew the pistol, flicked off the safety, drew back the hammer and aimed at the skull. Just to be sure. But there weren't enough rounds to afford a miss. Into the grass, she limped toward the head, discovering a skinny, scarred old man in an expensive, bloody Patagonia insulated jacket with a price tag dangling from the sleeve. Mercy noticed his chest rose and fell, sometimes rapidly as he hyperventilated. In the surrounding grass, the whippoorwills chanted in time with the old man's breathing, fast or slow, always mirroring his cadence.

Mercy was caught off-guard when cold green eyes opened, "What used ye against my Royal Encasement?"

"Forge of Nin-Agal."

"Sealing formula? Yer ignorance would fill an ocean."

"Fire warms and burns. What did you throw against me the first time?"

"Plow of Ajax. Had I not been over-occupied ye would have tumbled like piglets into the jaws of Those From the Air."

"I believe you."

He hyperventilated once more to throw off the whippoorwills. But the birds recovered quickly. "So who are ye? Before he could tell me, that Chinaman married the lightning."

Mercy kept the pistol trained on him. "You're kidding. You sent Chester Sawyer to test my formula. Your other man escaped. Didn't he tell you what happened?"

"I am ill-served by steam wits. Ye must be the O'Connor woman.

"Yeah. Seriously, you didn't have search parties looking for us the last few days."

"To what end? I thought ye a wine cork without nerve. Yet ye challenged me with your child's formula. Now I perish, flabbergasted."

"It's about time."

"Have ye a radio? I crave a final hearing of *Morning Edition*, mayhap with Cokie Roberts as guest."

"I only have two hands."

"Then two favors I ask: ye will reap a most kingly reward."

Whateley's breath slowed, forcing the whippoorwills to lengthen their chant. But they were equal to the job, quickly aligning with his breath.

Mercy said, "Let me guess: save you and you'll teach me dark, fantastic formula that'll make me powerful beyond my wildest imagination."

Whateley snorted, "Ye think with your titties. I prefer seeing ye awash in your own drool, like that girl upon the altar. But time speeds and I must choose with precision."

"You're pretty nasty for a dying scum asking favors."

"'Tis my way. Look ye here, when I signal by dropping my chin, shoot me in the head."

Mercy's finger extended along the trigger guard. "I thought you wanted something difficult. What's the other favor?"

"Shoot Armand Deale."

"That may be on the house. What's in it for me?"

"A great cache of gold coins, a fortune to last four lifetimes. What say ye to a pact?"

Whateley hyperventilated again, but the chanting whippoorwills rode his breath like master surfers upon a breaking wave. Mercy paused. Shooting Whateley and being paid for it was the essence of doing well by doing good. No more debt. The money could be used to help the homeless, acquire more grimoires, level up her wardrobe. Noting Mercy's hesitation, Whateley smiled like a piranha hearing a funny story about dumb cattle wading a river.

"Go to the clerk at Ye Great Olde Inn. Read him the verse from the *Necronomicon* at the top of page 664. He will direct ye to your gold."

Far below, Mercy observed a lone vehicle— SUV? Jeep?— speeding south toward Sentinel Hill.

"I can't shoot Deale. It's not how I roll."

"Then me, quickly. These cursed birds are on the mark today."

"Page 664?"

"Aye, aye, top of the page.

"Same payment as if I drilled Deale?"

"Aye, yes. I fade at speed."

Mercy took careful aim at Whateley's head.

The warlock grinned in feverish triumph. Holding his breath for several moments, expelling it quickly, he threw off the whippoorwills.

Then dropped his chin.

Mercy drew up the trigger slack and squeezed …

JP Mac

… Ka-powpowpow …

… rounds struck into the grass alongside Whateley.

The slide locked back.

"Oh, fruitcakes, those were my last rounds. I guess I was thinking with my titties."

"Ye treacherous, humpbacked slattern."

Whateley sighed deeply, terminally, as the whippoorwills reacquired the rhythm of his breath. Gazing up at Mercy with wasp eyes, he grinned slyly and said, "'That is not dead which can eternal lie . . . '"

Mercy said, "Maybe. But it's not you. You gonna die or what?"

Obed Whateley spat out, "Stupid gabby-woman." Then he toppled over dead.

Whippoorwills erupted in a cackling gale, a daemonic pandemonium so piercing Mercy covered her ears. From the yellow-gray grass, from Cold Springs Glen, from Round Mountain, from the Devil's Hopyard, from the length and breadth of Dunwich, an enormous avian host rose into the early morning sky. Birds filled the heavens, their victorious cries deafening, ascending in a tremendous body higher and higher until they filled the sky like a brown storm front. At last, the whippoorwills wheeled south in an immense cloud of gibbering, chittering jubilation.

Weight on one leg, watching the bird legion glide over the horizon, Mercy marveled at the sight. And for the first time in many hours, the only sound was the wind.

Gazing down at Whateley's corpse, Mercy muttered, "Dude, you sure knew how to get in the last word."

CHAPTER 16

INGNIS AURUM PROBAT

Dec. 17 article from the *Arkham Advertiser*, online version:

No Charges Sought
For Antiquity Head
by Holt Manatee

In a day of victories for Mercy O'Connor, Arkham DA Sandra Giffoon declined to prosecute her for leaving the scene of a crime. O'Connor had been wanted for questioning in relation to the October 29th incident outside popular sports bar O Beer Thirty. University Antiquity Section Chairman O'Connor, along with former Miskatonic guard Joseph Bongani, were attacked on a West Street sidewalk by two men driving a stolen UPS truck. According to smartphone videos sent to police, one of the assailants pulled a gun on the pair. Bongani wrestled the weapon away, then used it to shoot an unidentified man who was strangling O'Connor with rubber tubes. Authorities have discounted initial reports that one attacker dissolved into a liquid. Giffoon stated, "It's safe to say that a lot of alcohol was consumed that night. To the best of our knowledge, both assailants escaped and are still being sought by police."

O'Connor triumphed again over in Worcester County as a Grand Jury in Athol heard closed-door testimony regarding mysterious events in Dunwich last Halloween. One of three survivors of a Sentinel Hill religious service that turned deadly, O'Connor was the only one capable of testifying. Aforementioned Joseph Bongani was beaten about the head with blunt instruments and lapsed into a coma, from which he has yet to recover. Another survivor, Miskatonic Professor Audrey Klumm-Weebner, remains confined after suffering severe shock.

Northwestern District Attorney Ruether E. Lynx refused to comment on the many missing persons resulting from the bizarre ceremony. "A Federal investigation is underway," said Lynx, "and I have no wish to compromise their work by hasty disclosures." DA Lynx did confirm that no charges of any kind would be sought against O'Connor, and commended her actions. O'Connor stated she was pleased with the day's legal outcomes, adding, "I can only say that the Antiquity Section will be back in business very soon, and conducting original scholarship."

In addition, Lynx stated that North Aylesbury Police Officer Michael Vitale volunteered testimony regarding his discovery of the body of Obed Whateley. A notorious local man wanted for numerous felonies spanning over forty years, Whateley died the morning of November 1 from two gunshot wounds. A subsequent Massachusetts State Patrol investigation was unable to uncover any suspects. Insiders related that Lynx's investigation is examining unspecified ties between Whateley and Miskatonic University President Armand Deale; Deale was also called before the Grand Jury. But despite three Miskatonic Professors disappearing in the Halloween incident, Deale pled the Fifth Amendment under advice of legal counsel.

In addition to possible criminal charges, the beleaguered Deale continues to draw fire from the Miskatonic Board of Trustees for serious violations of university policy. President Deale referred all media

questions to Miskatonic attorney Gleason Fundament,
who stated that Deale was "the victim of a witch hunt."

Lisa erupted in delight upon opening her Christmas present: a hundred dollar gift card for Cake Planet. The women hugged, and Mercy left the library. She crossed the quad, boots crunching in the snow, face lean, coat and clothes hanging loosely on her thin frame. All around Mercy, students laughed loudly, hurled snowballs, and belly slid on the ice, engaging in public mirth such as hadn't been seen on campus in some time.

Mercy thought the new Antiquity Section day guard seemed pretty sharp: former Air Force Security Police, not too savvy on Dunwich, but ready to learn. And cute, with a boyish flip of blonde hair Mercy found alluring. The new curator for the Joseph Bongani Special Collections, however, was another matter. She was a Morgan relative: smart and funny, with her own retro style, fantastic with the section's new presence on Gabby Face, and yet the chick would need serious library sciences schooling.

Mercy's smartphone rang. Erin.

"Hey, Merse, the most astounding, neo-happy news."

Mercy smiled, "'Neo-happy.' That's very serious glee."

"Listen, hear me out, don't cut me off. I heard from my old money guy . . . "

". . . Erin . . . "

"Seriously, after I apologized 87 times for walking out and leaving you alone in Club Swill with an Emerson guy, you owe me one more listen."

"I paid you back all the money you lost on the video shoot. Besides, you already know the answer."

"I'm telling you anyway. So Money Guy's hearing about all your court cases last week, and the whole amazing freaky Halloween thing and a dead felon and a live university president and black magic ceremonies and fat lightning and he flipped. He's been on the phone to Hollywood. There could be, and I'm not saying there is, but there could be a special, one-hour remake of *Mysterious Dunwich*. I'm also not saying they've signed Christopher Walken, but his people have been contacted."

Mercy used her new friendly-but-official, voice. "Please tell Mr. Money that in keeping with longstanding Antiquity Section policies, we decline to cooperate in any media aired for the purpose of sensationalizing this section's scholarship."

"Who said that? Conrad Morgan?"

"Me. I just made it up. Cool, huh?"

"But the section has social media pages."

"True, but we're charmingly opaque."

Erin snarled in mock anger, "Why do you hate making money?"

Mercy walked off the campus onto College Street, breath pluming in the wintery air.

"I don't. You've seen my new apartment. I'm styling."

Erin said, "I still don't get it. If you didn't shoot Whately, how did you end up with all the reward money?"

"I didn't. But Michael shaded his report. And those lawyers from the Isaac Levinson Foundation are scary sharp. Of course, I had to kick some cash over to the Mass State Patrol, park half for Joe B., and give a taste to Mike Vitale. But I got a pretty big chunk. And the Levinson lawyers said they'd help me with taxes. By using the same loopholes as members of Congress, I'll be able to keep most of my cut."

Erin's voice rose in a singsong tease, "So it's 'Mike' now? Tell me juicy details. Divorced? Living with his Mom? Lots of cats?"

"Stop. You'll meet him Christmas. He's very nice, and believes in making a girl feel like something other than a depository. Definitely not your type."

Mercy crossed West Street, turning south toward St. Mary's.

Erin squawked, "I like being wined and dined, just not at Sizzler."

"Mostly you like being wined. Everything else is negotiable."

"Sometimes. Speaking of which, you want to meet tonight for swank cocktails?"

"Can't. I'm heading over to see Joe B., then I'm meeting Morgan in Boston."

"Really, Merse, what's happened to you? You never go clubbing or party or even drinking at lunch for a few hours. And Addison saw you Christmas shopping in Kingsport right after Thanksgiving and said you'd lost at least three dress sizes. Why do I have to learn that from Addison?"

"Well, I don't drink very much anymore. And my eating habits have changed. Diminished, really. Let's meet for coffee tomorrow."

"Irish coffee? That's the old Merse."

"Dunkin Donuts."

"See what I mean? You're weird."

"Don't use that word until you've walked a mile in my pumps."

Beeps, clicks and hisses.

Somewhere on a hospital bed within a thicket of medical equipment rested Joseph Bongani. Mercy finally detected him behind the ventilator that kept him breathing, the Foley catheter draining his bladder, the IV lines feeding him, arterial linesare tubes maintaining blood pressure, a nasogastric tube, and a clamp-like pulse oximeteris measuring oxygen in the blood stream.

On his wrist was a bracelet of handmade beads in colors of blue, white and black.

Over his ears were Bose headphones, plugged into a Sirius XM Home Satellite Radio that rested on a night table, next to a statue of the Blessed Virgin Mary and a plastic water carafe. Flowing into the mind of Joseph Bongani were songs of old dogs and small towns in summer and big cities in winter, of loves lost, but never forgotten, of whiskey, divorce and brawls, big rigs and shotguns, Jesus and forgiveness; of family shame and family valor. And every now and then, a song of hope.

Under the light of a desk lamp, appearing to be under interrogation in an old movie, Father George sat reading his Breviary. He offered Mercy his seat and they spoke of little things: the weather, family, holiday shopping, Miskatonic basketball, and the War Scholars' second place finish in the Middleton Holiday Invitational.

"Doctors say nothing new about Joseph, except that he lives on."

Mercy noticed an envelope addressed in female handwriting, sticking out from under the radio. "He gets mail here now?"

"From his fiancée, Sizani. I want him to read it when he awakens."

"What if she dumped him for Norway?"

"If so, and I see Joseph's disappointment, then it will mean he has returned to be disappointed."

"You're a glass half full kind of guy, Father. Listen, I'm pretty sure I'll get more grant money by March, so I'm putting you and Mike Vitale on the payroll as consultants. Or spies. Anyway, we need more residents working for us in Dunwich, North Aylesbury, and Dean's Corners. Julian Rice was an intelligence ace in the war, and we can do the same. Better."

Father George clasped his Brievery with both hands, "There are good people in the region, but they are very scared. Obed Whateley has many children and relatives. The Whateleys are, as a rule, wily and dangerous. And vindictive."

"So I've been hearing."

"I am pleased to help you in any way, Mercy."

"You have any more nephews like this one?"

"From all I've heard, none with the heart of Joseph."

Mercy teared up, lowering her head and rummaging through her bag, "He carried me on his back in all kinds of ways."

Father George placed an arm around her shoulder, holding her for time. "Talk to him now. He will be pleased."

They said 'good-byes,' and Mercy removed the headphones. Joe B.'s bruises and cuts were long healed, his face placid under the masks and tubes, youthful as if he dreamed of kicking a soccer ball across the veldt. Mercy remembered him as he'd been on the hill: scared and pale, but resolute, with a spine of carbon steel.

"Joe B., it's Merse. My brother James said I should watch *Rocky II* because they have a great scene where Rocky talks to his wife when she's in a coma. He reads her Westerns and meatpacking union by-laws. Then one day, her eyes open and she tells him to ditch the stupid, center crease fedora and chase a chicken. I'm not sure why. In fact, I'm not even sure James has the right movie. But if you want me to chase a chicken, forget it. I don't take orders from a pushy guy in a coma."

Devices beeped and clicked and whirred in a medical symphony. Across the room, a narrow vertical window showed a portion of snowy Boundary Street four stories below and a block away.

"So I hired this new guard today, former military, squared away. I'm making him study your old flash cards, minus the players we knocked out of the game. But I couldn't help but wonder: when formula's thrown, with cultists charging and Old Ones knocking on the old dimensional door, will the new guy man up and be a Zulu badass? Mike Vitale said the cult hates our guts. The Whateley clan's looking for big-time payback. So whenever you're done screwing around, milking everyone's sympathy, just know you've officially been rehired. Better bring a new radio, but don't play any of that mandolin and banjo crap."

Carts rattled past in the hallway, pushed by Filipino nurses in pastel uniforms. A muted PA system informed Doctor Segall that he had a phone call. Replacing Bongani's headphones, Mercy sat quietly for a time, holding Joe B.'s right hand to her cheek.

Two floors below Mercy, Audrey Klumm-Weebner dragged a chair over to a sink. Above the sink was a stainless steel mirror. Wearing a sleeveless gown, with her white hair secured in a bun, Audrey filled the sink. Next she lowered her right bicep with the dolphin tattoo into the water. Then she splashed her arm around the basin, making the tattoo break the surface like a Sea World attraction.

"Fishie-fishie-fishie."

Through a glass window, Armand Deale peered into the room, watching the former professor of Post-Structural Hierarchies. Next to Deale stood a sad-faced, balding, pear-shaped man in a dark suit.

"Every night, Gleas?"

"For about twenty minutes until they whack her with evening meds."

"I guess another fruit basket wouldn't help."

Gleason Fundament shook his head, "They don't seem to make an impression. Have you tried speaking to her yet?"

Deale rubbed a finger against his chin, "Most of the time she's on enough atavin to knock out a caribou. But no. She had a brilliant mind, wicked sense of humor. I couldn't."

"Not to pile on, but you know Autumn Cryer lawyered up."

"Delightful."

"Those Levinson barracuda deposed her for one of the twelve million lawsuits barreling your way. I heard she sang like Celine Dion in Vegas. You should've told me about Whateley."

"Everybody knows what I should've done. You, the media, the Northwestern DA, the Board."

Fundament adjusted the strap of his laptop case. "The only one not suing is Leo Hameyes' widow. She came in the other day to sign some paperwork, wearing a dress that was way too short. Humming, singing. She asked me out for a drink."

"Fishie-fishie-fishie-fishie."

Audrey paused in her manic splashings to peer through the glass, cocking her head to one side like a dog, chin awash in drool. But there was no recognition, only the delighted grin of a happy madwoman.

The attorney chose his next words carefully. "Any thought about the baby?"

"How's that?"

"I did some checking on her condition. Audrey is pregnant."

"Son-of-a-bitch."

"First trimester. You guys were intimate, right?"

"Well, it's complicated."

"Big fetus, from what they say. Unusual size. I guess one thing at a time."

Fundament departed to prepare Deale's legally-tortured, indefensible defense. Deale remained at the window, watching Audrey jump her tattoo over a bar of soap.

"FISHIE!"

All those cuddly little moments. All those breathy promises. All those obtuse, red-hot academic phrases. Here I was actually feeling bad over what happened, and all the time she was playing me.

Furious, Deale kicked the locked door. "Psycho. Feckless lying, treacherous bitch. I'm glad you're nuts. I hope you die nuts."

Deale sensed, then saw, the middle-aged Filipino nurse, holding a tray of plastic pill cups, watching him with surprise and disgust.

"It's a lover's communication."

"You are the one sick."

Deale watched the nurse storm off, then moved quickly toward the elevator. When a car arrived, he swung inside and stabbed the button for the lobby. Only when the car resumed descending, did Deale note the only other occupant was Mercy O'Connor.

Mercy said, "Visiting Audrey? I hope she's better."

"Not really. And the guard?"

"My close friend Joseph Bongani remains in a coma."

"I seem to recall he was a pretty violent guy."

"Are you referring to the incident when a university president sent sock puppets to do his heavy lifting?"

A ping as the door opened and a husky, blue-scrubbed Filipino orderly pushed an empty wheelchair into the car, then right back out a floor later. Alone once more, Deale glared, "You should be giddy. The Dark Ages won."

"I thought reality won out over wishful thinking."

"I've never heard reason referred to as 'wishful thinking.'"

"I've never seen dogma mistaken for logic with such passion."

In the lobby, Deale flippantly waved 'bye' to Mercy, "Enjoy your little moment, because you're on the wrong side of history. Happy Holidays."

"Merry Christmas."

Deale stormed off toward the parking garage, patting his pockets. He couldn't seem to locate his parking stub.

With the lights of Beacon Hill shining behind them, they watched the skaters on Frog Pond: dads and moms holding hands of little kids, high school girls clinging to each other giggling as they skated in a clump, teenage boys blazing around the rink as fast as they could. Strings of Italian lights glittered from leafless branches as a light snow dusted Boston Commons. Mercy sipped from a cup of coffee, feeling the heat through her mittens, hazel eyes relaxed, but wary, scanning the passing crowd for the 'Dunwich look.' She said, "Are you running again?"

Morgan adjusted his coat collar, "I walk a treadmill now, but no running for another month. Even though I snapped out of it the day after Hallow Mass, I'm still pretty weak. The doctors have no clue. But Dunwichers know strains and varieties of poison that would shame the Borgias."

"Must be a trippy reversal for you, visiting Joe."

Morgan said, "He fell fighting long odds in a desperate scrap. I thought I wanted that once, but the morning my condition changed for the better, I thanked God I was still alive and would see my family again. Perhaps Joseph was better suited for the battle. I don't know. But I read him the soccer news."

"He's the best hire you ever made."

"Next to you."

Mercy laughed, "You don't have to butter me up because I'm in charge. Sure you won't change your mind?"

"Someone with practical experience should lead the section. I'll be content to serve in an advisory capacity, like Great Grandpa Francis. Oh, and thanks for letting me keep my old office."

"It would take a decade to backhaul the junk out of there. But you'll be happy to know a new pane of pebbled glass finally arrived. I'll have them paint 'Chairman Emeritus.'"

"And 'Ignis Aurum Probat.'"

Mercy saw a five-year-old girl fall, then awkwardly clamber back to her feet.

"'Fire Tests Gold.'"

Morgan paused, bent over and touched the ground. "My hamstrings still feel tight all the time. The full quote is from the Roman philosopher Seneca: *ignis aurum probat, miseria fortes homines*.

'As gold is tempered by fire, so strong men are tempered by suffering.' It's a perfect quote for another age."

"There might be a spot for it today. Hey, back in September, why did you mention Joe B. and his fiancée? I thought maybe Old One goons snatched her. But his first honey fell in love with Scandinavia, so he got another."

Morgan chuckled, "If you were ever going to team up, I figured talking might be a good start."

"Well, Mr. Crafty Psychologist, did you also notify the Isaac Levinson Foundation?"

Morgan ran ahead a little ways, sliding along a patch of ice. "I haven't done that in a few years. Actually, your Uncle Louis alerted them after you left his house. I almost had a heart attack when he called around Thanksgiving and told me. I think you shamed him. Consider making him a consultant. He could be ready to get back in the game."

Mercy finished her coffee and dropped the cup into a trash bin.

"I'll call him. You know the Levinson Foundation sent me a letter, congratulating me on my legal triumphs, etc., etc. It was signed 'Goldberry.' Is that who I think it is?"

"'Fire tests gold'—and Goldberry. After her Funwich days, Clarissa Hammond became an actress in New York, and married a stockbroker named Isaac Levinson. After a long stage career and an impressive number of children and grandchildren, she assumed control of their foundation when Isaac died. Goldberry's passion was always restraining Dunwich and seeing Obed Whateley brought to justice. You've done both, to her immense delight. Make sure you thank her personally."

"I will. But I still can't get over feeling I screwed something up. And the way I killed those Dunwichers. If there'd been more around, I'd have torched every one. I can't stop replaying it all."

Morgan waved to a middle-age woman and two teenage boys on the other side of the rink. He gripped Mercy by the shoulders. "Two alone against the best of Dunwich and their followers and their demons. And you're here to tell the story. So figure out what you need to learn and get ready: they're not returning in twenty years. Dunwich is super pissed, and they'll be coming hard soon. You need to gear up and rally others for what's ahead."

The loss of Joe gnawed at her like a mouse on crank, but she smiled and hugged the older man. There'd be plenty of help next time around.

"Merry Christmas, Baba Morgan."

"Merry Christmas, Baba O'Connor."

Conrad Morgan walked quickly to meet his family.

Mercy turned away, her mind on a formula that would nail Those From the Air like bug spray. She thought of Mike Vitale and how he was driving all the way from North Aylesbury to be with her for Christmas. That was an encouraging sign. Mercy felt a little thrill. She couldn't wait to show him off to Erin and her family.

Crossing the Commons, Mercy passed two shivering homeless guys trying to ignite a fire in a trash bin.

"Can't get it started?"

"Matches are wet. You got a lighter?"

"Stand back."

Mercy thrust out her arms and muttered a Hebrew phrase. The trash bin contents burst into a green flame. The astonished homeless men rushed forward to warm themselves. As Mercy strolled off, one yelled, "How'd you do that?"

Mercy called back, "It's something I picked up in college."

CAST OF CHARACTERS

MISKATONIC UNIVERSITY
University President Armand Deale
Professor of Post-Structural Hierarchies Audrey Klumm-Weebner
Professor Angelo Silent Feather, Associate Vice Chancellor for Contemporary Oppression Modalities
Chief of Campus Diversity Enforcement Dr. Leo Hameyes
Professor Carter Fong, Chairman of Critical Weather Studies

Now

Miskatonic Antiquity Section
Chairman Professor Conrad Morgan
Special Collections Curator Mercy O'Connor
Security Guard Joseph Bongani

Dunwich
Obed Whateley
Jasper Frye
Chester Sawyer
Malachi Hutchins

1991 Horror

Miskatonic Antiquity Section
Louis Armitage
Galen Rice

Dunwich
Obed Whateley

1956 Horror

Miskatonic Antiquity Section
Julian Rice
Thomas Armitage
Francis Morgan

Dunwich
Sirac Bishop
Obed Whateley

1928 Horror

Miskatonic Antiquity Section
Henry Armitage
Warren Rice
Francis Morgan

Dunwich
Wilbur Whateley

1972 – 73 Funwich Commune

Miskatonic Antiquity Section
Clarissa "Goldberry" Hammand
North Aylesbury Police Sgt. Edward Dunn

Dunwich
Obed Whateley

Supporting Characters
Erin Douchette
The O'Connor Family
North Aylesbury Police Sgt. Michael Vitale

Miskatonic
Librarian Lisa Tice
Campus Security Chief Zane Underkrammel
University Legal Counsel Gleason Fundament
Students Loyal to Underserved Groups activists
Honna Pegler and Barry Gristleman
Head of Environmental Services Barney Reznicek
Vice President for Public Affairs and University
Relations Autumn Cryer

Acknowledgments

Thanks once again to Copy Write Editorial for proofreading and managing production on both the ebook and softcover versions. A salute to artist D.C. Richter for her excellent ebook and print cover. A nod to photo ace Dan Hoffman for his back cover impression of me. Also, hats off to the beta readers, including Ken Segall and Armando Torres Puerto, for their keen observations. Any remaining errors are my very own. Of course, I'm grateful to H.P. Lovecraft for his short story "The Dunwich Horror," which provided the foundation for this book. Finally, a big thanks to my generous mother-in-law, Sharon Goodwin, for helping to bridge some very troubled waters.

About the Author

An Emmy Award-winning TV animation writer, JP Mac (as John P. McCann) has worked on shows such as *Animaniacs, Freakazoid!, Pinky and the Brain*, and *7D*. Mac was a student of T. Coraghessan Boyle's at the University of Southern California, and his short fiction has appeared in print as well as online in venues such as *The Best of Every Day Fiction* and *The Cthulhu Mythos Mega Pack*. He is currently working on a sci fi novel about a giant monster, unpleasant aliens, and a man caught between them as he tries to drive his aunt to Walmart.

Contact JP Mac

Facebook: JP Mac
https://www.facebook.com/JP-Mac-
255185854620255/?ref=br_rs

Twitter: @jpmac5

Write Enough! (The author's blog):
http://writeenough.blogspot.com/

Goodreads: JP Mac
https://www.goodreads.com/author/show/7535
682.JP_Mac